JUST ONE DAY

Just One Day

Carol M. Creasey

UNITED WRITERS
Cornwall

UNITED WRITERS PUBLICATIONS LTD
Ailsa, Castle Gate, Penzance, Cornwall.
www.unitedwriters.co.uk

British Library Cataloguing in Publication Data:
A catalogue record for this book is
available from the British Library.

ISBN 9781852002121

Printed and bound in Great Britain by
United Writers Publications Ltd.,
Cornwall.

I dedicate this to
my dear friend Emma Davis
from Walrus and Oyster and
thank her for all her
support since 2019.

Chapter One

1961

"There's something I want to tell you, Ellen."

Jeremy had been dreading this moment. Would she be angry with him or upset? For the past year he had truly believed he was in love with Ellen; such a beautiful and bubbly girl, with her bright blue expressive eyes and curly blonde hair. But his teenage infatuation had run its course, and he had met dark, exotic Simone, a French girl whose family had moved to England. It had started off as just a friendship, as he was helping her to speak English, but yesterday he had asked her to be his girlfriend, and because he didn't want to hurt Ellen any more than he had to, it was time to come clean.

Ellen had her own worries to contend with, and today she had planned to tell Jeremy her news. But something in his tone of voice worried her; there was something wrong. After a year together, she felt she knew him very well. She had fallen for him as soon as she met him. Who could resist his dark brown eyes that softened when he spoke to her, his dark brown hair which he carefully applied Brylcreem to every morning, and his smile. He was the most handsome boy she had ever met, but what she most loved about him was that he was sensitive and kind. Every time he walked her home from school she felt so proud that he was her boyfriend. She knew she was the envy of all her friends.

Her mother had not been pleased to find out that her sixteen year old daughter had a boyfriend. Vera Payne had made no secret of the fact that she believed a boyfriend at sixteen was bad news, and told Ellen she was far too young. She had also been warned about 'Boys getting her into trouble' and how, if it happened to Ellen, her father would be so angry that both of her parents would throw her out of the house and disown her, because their shame about her sin would be too much to bear.

In the beginning their romance had been nothing more than a few kisses after Jeremy had walked her home from school, but just recently it became more passionate, and in spite of all the warnings her mother had given her, Ellen knew she wanted Jeremy to make love to her. It had happened just a couple of times, when Jeremy had invited her back to his empty house and his mother had been out.

She had arrived home an hour later than usual. She felt flushed, but very complete. Her mother's eyes seemed to bore into her, and it was almost as if she knew what had happened; but Ellen felt no guilt, she just didn't understand why having a loving relationship made you into a bad person or a sinner. She knew she loved Jeremy with all her heart; he was the love of her life. But regretfully she knew her parents would not understand, so it had to be kept a secret.

She had never been close to her father. He went off early to work and arrived back at tea time. The family sat in silence whilst eating, and Norman was usually buried behind a newspaper whilst Vera scurried around, making sure his dinner was on the table as soon as he sat down. Norman was a man to be feared when he was in a temper. Sometimes he went to the pub, and after a few pints inside him he came home, and was aggressive. Ellen's older brother Tom had been on the receiving end of a beating once when a neighbour had come round to complain Tom had been scrumping apples. Ellen and her mother had hidden in the back room, and tried not to listen to her brother's cries of pain whilst his father unleashed his temper on him. Tom was now no longer living at home. He had joined the army, and they didn't see much of him.

Ellen was now seventeen and due to leave school very shortly. She had been interviewed by the careers' officer, and with some good advice and help, she now had a job at a local insurance company, ready to start in August. Jeremy was a year older, and having just completed two years in the sixth form, he was keen to go to university and study medicine if his A level grades were good enough.

After noticing her periods had stopped, Ellen realised she must be pregnant, and now she had become very afraid. She knew her parents would not stand by her. In fact, if her father found out about Jeremy, he might attack him. Although Vera had known her daughter had a boyfriend, Ellen had never disclosed his name. There was no way she would let him be a target for her father's wrath.

She smiled nervously at him, wondering what he would say. He hadn't walked home from school with her for a couple of days. Exams were done now, and he just had to wait for his results, so he didn't go in every day. In her very wildest dreams she had imagined that, when he knew about her pregnancy, they could elope and get married. But coming down to earth she realised, even if that were true, he would still go off to university and she would be left alone.

Jeremy stopped and put his arms around her. There was so much he liked about Ellen, and he knew she was going to be hurt by his words, so he still held her close when he spoke the words that broke her heart.

"Ellen, I am so fond of you. A year together, but I think we have become too serious, too young. I think we should cool it for a while."

Ellen stiffened inside his arms, pushing him away, and staring him straight in the face. Jeremy blushed. He had been about to remind her he would be off to university in September, rather than implicating Simone.

Although her heart felt as though it had been shattered into tiny pieces, she was determined to keep her dignity. She wasn't going to scream and shout at him; what was the point if he didn't love her any more?

"So who is it, then? You have moved onto someone else, I take it."

If her voice sounded sarcastic, it was because she was being realistic. Jeremy would always have someone, as he was just too good looking not to. And as hurt as she was, she knew she still loved him, because he wasn't vain or selfish; he was a decent person, and she had thought they were so good together.

"Well, I have been helping Simone with her English, and we have grown fond of each other."

9

Ellen felt a stab of jealousy coursing through her insides. Of course it was Simone, she should have realised. Ever since she had joined the school, Simone had been floating around him, gushing at him in her broken English, which everyone thought so charming. Maybe that is why Simone had become friendly with her; just so she could steal her boyfriend! Right now she felt like she could strangle Simone. But all this passion inside her was futile, and she knew it. If he wanted to be with Simone and not her, then they were done, and there was no use trying to fight for him.

Her rage subsided as quickly as it had come, and she felt the tears in her eyes. If only he would be nasty to her, it would make this parting so much easier; but he didn't, he cradled her in his arms whilst she could do nothing to stop the tears from flowing. They stood there until she had stopped crying, and he then wiped her tears away with a tissue.

"Ellen, can we stay in touch? I still care for you, and Simone likes you too."

She couldn't believe she was hearing this. He wanted to stay in touch, and she would have to put up with him parading his new girlfriend in front of her, because they both liked her! Oh, what trouble she could cause by doing that! Every week she would be getting bigger, carrying his baby; they wouldn't be so cosy if that happened. But she couldn't bring herself to tell him. It would be the ultimate humiliation. She wanted him to love her, and he didn't. She did not want his pity. She composed herself, thankful that he could not see the turmoil that had taken control of her body.

"I think you should take yourself off to university and forget about me. Our teenage romance is over. We don't need to stay in touch."

His face crumpled with disappointment; but amidst her pain, she felt anger towards him. He wanted to have his cake and eat it too. Well she was not hanging around to see him with Simone. Who knows, now that she had broken them up, sultry Simone might quickly go off him. She didn't particularly seem the faithful type, and because it made Ellen feel better to think it, she remembered Simone was not perfect, and her legs in a mini skirt were bulky, whereas Ellen prided herself on having good legs.

Having said her piece, she walked away from him, determined not to look back whilst Jeremy stared after her. Something in her demeanour had made him feel as if he might be making a mistake. After a year together, it had seemed cruel to cut her right out of his life, but he knew he had hurt her, and fully understood that she wanted to move on.

Jeremy glanced at his watch. He was meeting Simone in a few minutes. He had promised her he would end it with Ellen today, so now they could be a couple without feeling guilty about it. He shook away a lingering doubt inside him. No way could he be with two women at the same time. He had done the right thing, and Ellen would soon forget him.

Chapter Two

As Ellen walked home, she realised how much her life was falling apart. Not only was she pregnant, but also she was alone. Jeremy didn't know, and she didn't want him to, but when her parents found out she would be homeless. She would only be able to work for a short time after her bump showed, and when her baby was born, she would have no one to care for it. She touched her stomach gently; this was all she had left of Jeremy now, and it did feel like precious cargo, but what on earth was she going to do?

She used her key to let herself in the front door, but to her surprise sounds could be heard from the kitchen. Her mother was in, and she hadn't been prepared for this, so she quickly wiped her face, hoping her tears would go unnoticed.

Vera looked up as the door opened. Noting Ellen's flushed cheeks, and wondering what was going on, she asked, "You look very hot, what is wrong?"

"Nothing." It felt too raw for Ellen to share the pain of her breakup.

But Vera persisted. Something about Ellen was different. She was being cagey, and trying to avoid her by heading towards her bedroom. "I can tell you are hiding something, Ellen. What is it?"

"If you must know, I've split with my boyfriend. That will please you, I know," Ellen said defiantly. But she avoided meeting her mother's intent gaze.

In spite of her tough exterior, Vera did feel sorry for her daughter.

She was always slightly in fear of Norman. With a drink inside him he became bad tempered, so she had spent most of her marriage keeping on the right side of him, and keeping the peace. If Ellen had lost her boyfriend, it was probably a good thing, meaning Norman had one less thing to get bad tempered about.

"Well, you know your dad and I both think you are too young. You are just about to start work." She tried to sound comforting.

Something inside Ellen snapped. Nothing in her home life made her feel secure. Her father was a bully, and her mother was his whipping boy; he treated her like a servant. She couldn't ever imagine a time when they had been close. Her relationship with Jeremy had been nothing like that, it had been real love. Her words came tumbling out, and she made no effort to stop them.

"I will never regret the last year. He made me so happy. But now he is with someone else, and I have to accept that. . ." her lip trembled, ". . .I think I am pregnant, but he must never know, and you and dad won't want me around, I know that. I have brought disgrace on you, according to you, but all I did was fall in love."

Fear rushed through Vera. It was history repeating itself, except that her irate father had insisted that Norman married her. But it hadn't worked out, he had always resented Tom, and even when his daughter had been born, it hadn't made them closer as a couple. Vera stayed with him because she really had no other choice. She had no independence, so became a home maker, a wife, and a mother, but with no income of her own coming in. She knew Norman's reaction to their daughter's pregnancy would be absolute fury, with no compassion whatsoever. There was no way that Ellen could stay.

But she couldn't help remembering how she had felt when she was in the same position. Only seventeen, with parents who never showed their emotions unless they were angry. She was not a hard woman, and she did love her children, but Norman seemed to think that showing feelings was a weakness, so she had got used to hiding how she felt. Even though she was angry with Ellen, she also felt very sorry for her too. She was only just about to leave school, and her boyfriend had dumped her.

"So even if you told him, he wouldn't want to get married?" she asked, hopefully.

"I don't want a shotgun marriage. It wouldn't work, and anyway he no longer loves me, he has another girlfriend," she said sadly. Ellen had expected her mother to be full of rage, and shouting at her, but she could sense her compassion. In fact, it made her feel even more guilty for letting her parents down.

"Mum, I am so sorry. I wish I had known we were going to split up."

"That is the trouble with men; once they get what they want they lose interest and find someone else," Vera said, with a touch of bitterness, remembering back to her own pregnancy. Her father had gone round to Norman's house and threatened him with a beating if "He didn't do right by her." So Norman had to settle down and become a married man at an age when he would have preferred to play the field.

Seeing Ellen so upset moved Vera. Norman wasn't there to see her wrap her arms around her daughter. Ellen was carrying her grandchild and she could not ignore that.

"Ellen, say nothing about this to your father, for your sake and for mine. I will try and find a solution for you, but, of course, it will involve leaving home."

This was not the sort of reaction Ellen had expected from her mother. She had expected anger and tears, but there were none. Her mum was not as uncaring as she sometimes seemed. But she knew her dad was a different story.

"I won't say anything to him; and mum, thanks for being so understanding."

Vera's voice became stern: "It doesn't mean that I am not angry and disappointed in you."

"I know."

"How far gone do you think you are?"

"Possibly two or three months."

"OK, we'll have to get you to a doctor, but not our family one, and then we can take it from there. You must not breathe a word of this to anyone, and just carry on normally. Have you had any sickness in the morning?"

"Yes."

"Well, thank goodness your father goes out early in the morning, so he won't hear you."

14

Ellen swallowed nervously. It was going to be a secret that would be hard to keep. She knew she wanted to keep her baby afterwards, but where would she live? How could her mother possibly fix this mess?

Vera's mind had gone into overdrive. Ellen would have to go to a mother and baby home. She knew they weren't the nicest of places; Ellen would not be welcomed with open arms, in fact, the staff were quite tough towards the young girls that they regarded as 'fallen women'. Then she would have to give her baby up for adoption. But there were so many hurdles to overcome. How could she explain Ellen's absence to her father in the next few months? As soon as she started 'showing' she would have to go away.

"Ellen, we are going on the bus to the hospital. We are not known there, and we need to make sure that you are pregnant."

Ellen glanced at the clock, startled, it was five o'clock. "What now?"

"Yes, right now!" said Vera firmly.

"We might not be back before Dad comes in, and he will wonder what is wrong," pointed out Ellen.

"I don't want to take you out of school tomorrow. I will tell your dad you have had stomach pains, so they checked your appendix."

"If you are sure," said Ellen.

Vera was not sure of anything any more, but she had to know for sure if Ellen was pregnant. She wrote a note to put on the table for when Norman came home. His dinner was a casserole, cooking very slowly in the oven, so all he had to do was put it on his plate. This was the first time in her married life that she wasn't there to bring it to him at the table, but the knowledge of Ellen's possible pregnancy had totally taken over, and she had to know for sure.

Dr Meredith left Ellen to dress herself behind the curtain, and sat back in his chair opposite Vera. He could feel her eyes boring into him, but he bent his head and made notes on the pad in front of him. He didn't know this lady or her daughter, but he guessed why they had come so far away from their local surgery, and chosen to wait in the hospital until a booth was free.

15

He waited until Ellen had dressed herself, and beckoned her to come and sit on the seat next to her mother. She sat down with her head bowed.

"Ellen, you are not sure about the date of your last period, but judging by the size of your stomach, I would say you are about fourteen weeks pregnant."

Ellen lifted her head and looked at him. She saw no judgement in his eyes, but only concern.

"I am supposed to be starting a job in August," she said, gulping.

"That is three months away. You won't be able to work. Your baby will be due soon after that."

"I know," she said miserably.

He turned towards Vera, knowing this was going to be a very difficult situation. She was such a young girl, with her whole life ahead of her, but at least her mother had come with her.

"Mrs Payne, I am sure Ellen is grateful for your support. Will Ellen and her baby be able to live with you after it's born?"

Fear ran through Vera at his words. This doctor had no idea of the situation. Of course that wouldn't happen. There was no way Norman would want to be ostracised by judgemental neighbours. "No, my husband has no idea about this. We just wanted confirmation of Ellen's pregnancy."

Ellen looked at the doctor. He had a kind face, and she saw concern in his eyes. To her he looked old, but his age was probably no more than fifty; his hair was grey, and he wore glasses. He took them off and cleared his throat, before polishing them with a tissue and putting them back on.

"Ellen, is there going to be any support from the baby's father? Does he know?"

"She doesn't want him to know because they broke up," said Vera quickly.

Dr Meredith could sense just how tense they both were. He knew there were other patients in cubicles waiting to see him, but this girl with her sad eyes, and her nervous and jumpy mother, had touched his heart, so he would have to put them in the picture and then move on to his next patient.

He addressed them both. "If it's not possible for Ellen to have her

16

baby and live at home, then there is a mother and baby home in Wrexham. I hear it has quite a good reputation. The staff there will help Ellen to find adoptive parents for her baby."

Ellen looked at him in horror. There was no way she wanted to go in a mother and baby unit, and she had absolutely no intention of giving up her baby. It was her last link with Jeremy; their baby was conceived in love. She vowed in that moment, no matter how difficult it would be, she would keep her baby.

Vera knew his words were true. Abortion was illegal and a risk to Ellen's life, so it wasn't even under consideration. It was all very well sending Ellen away, but how could she explain it to Norman? But she sensed the doctor had done as much as he could for them.

He handed Vera a piece of paper with an address and telephone number on. "Ring them up, and see if you can go for a visit soon. In the meantime, Ellen, you have to visit a doctor regularly so they can check that all is well with your pregnancy. But not here; we are an emergency department for injuries and accidents only."

"Yes, thank you, doctor," said Vera. She stood up and walked out from behind the curtain, with Ellen following her. "It's time to go home."

Chapter Three

Ellen lay in her bed, tossing and turning. There was no chance of sleep tonight. She felt like everyone was trying to take her over and decide what would happen. But she wasn't going to let them. She was going to keep her baby, no matter how hard it might be. In her naivety she believed that she would find a way, even though she would have to leave home, and at seventeen, as she was now, she had no experience of the world. If she could only think of one person that she could stay with until she got herself sorted with a job and somewhere to live, but who was there?

Unbeknown to her father, Ellen and her mother were in contact with Tom. They knew his current address, and Vera wrote to him regularly. But he couldn't help, because his life was in the army; that was his home now. Ellen had always been close to her brother, and was glad of the photo she had of him in his army uniform. It was hidden away in a drawer in her bedroom because, like her mother, she didn't want to risk her father's wrath if he found it.

Her granny lived in Wales; her mother's mother. They didn't see her that often, as granny didn't much like Norman. Nevertheless she did love her grandchildren. But Ellen wondered if granny would still love her when she found out about her pregnancy.

Vera was having the selfsame thoughts herself as she tossed and turned in the big bed. It had been a relief to find Norman not at home when they got back; his dinner uneaten and dried up. Sometimes he went drinking after work, but in over twenty years he had never let her know how late he would be. He didn't consider it important.

Vera wished she had the courage to stand up to him. She knew he had used her as a doormat. Trying to hold a home and family together when there was no love between the parents was so hard. And now, with Ellen being pregnant, he would feel he had a just cause for being angry. She couldn't help wondering if she spoke to her mother, whether Ellen could go and stay with her for a few weeks. School was now finished, with exams already over. If Ellen stayed there for a while, it would give Vera time to get her head around this situation. She wasn't that close to Elizabeth, her mother, but Ellen was. If they travelled there together, away from Norman, maybe with Elizabeth's support, Ellen could go into the home at Wrexham to have her baby. It was fairly close to where Elizabeth lived. She plumped up her pillow, and turned over; now she must try and get some sleep.

Norman rolled off Faith, feeling completely sated. This sexy curvaceous beauty was just what he needed. Nobody could blame him for sharing her lust and her bed. They only had to look at Vera; only thirty-seven years old, never wore make-up any more, always dressed in a nylon overall, with her hair scragged back in a bun. Whatever beauty that had attracted him to her at eighteen had gone. She always looked tired, and her blonde hair was already turning grey. She did absolutely nothing to help her appearance. She could have coloured her hair and put some stockings and heels on instead of carpet slippers. He had always admired her legs, but her skirts were so long he couldn't even see them now. No wonder he had fallen for Faith. She had been wearing a gypsy type blouse when he had first seen her walking down the road, her high heels clicked, and her voluptuous breasts wobbled, threatening to escape from the confines of the blouse.

Faith was a widow, although not yet forty. Apparently her husband had been much older, and Norman couldn't help wondering if Faith had been too much for him; she was sexually liberated, and a very demanding woman. Anyway, the old bugger

19

had conveniently kicked the bucket, which suited Norman very much. He could come and visit whenever he wanted, enjoy a night of passion, and there were no strings attached.

He knew he was a hard nut, always had been, and maybe not capable of warm feelings, but lately he had found himself wanting to be with Faith as much as he could. He was aware that she was a free agent, but he didn't like to think she might be putting herself about. He wanted her for himself.

His home life had been a disappointment to him. He had married Vera because it was the right thing to do, and anyway, her father had a vile temper. But when his son Tom was born, looking at him just reminded Norman that he had been forced into a marriage with a girl he didn't love. Vera had been a very pretty girl, and Ellen reminded him of her mother at that age, with deep blue eyes and curly blonde hair, and his happiest time had been briefly just after his daughter was born. But it wasn't long after that when Vera started to let herself go; and she was so timid, with absolutely no personality, unlike Faith, who knew she was attractive and had so much confidence. There was no way he could take control of Faith. She was her own woman, with her own money and a house, and in fact she was in control of him. If she didn't want to see him, or had other plans, she told him so, and he had to accept that whether he liked it or not.

He put his arm gently over her shoulder. She was already asleep, and there was no way he was going to leave the warmth of this bed, get dressed, and then drive home. Vera probably wouldn't even bother to ask him where he had been last night, and if she did, he could soon make up a suitable story. He curled into her warm back, and a feeling of contentment swept through him. Before long, he too was fast asleep.

After a sleepless night, Ellen had made up her mind; she was going to leave home. Today was the last day of school, and there was going to be some sort of leaving party. She had already told her mother that they were not going in uniform, so when she came downstairs wearing a summer dress it would not be thought unusual. All she had in money was a ten shilling note, which would not get her far. Living near to Croydon, in rural Shirley with very few shops or offices, would not help her to have a future. Going to London to seek her fortune, as depicted in many story books, would not work; it cost a lot of money to live in the capital city. So she decided to head for the coast. It was early summer, the weather was warm, maybe she could get some work for the summer.

The nearest places on the Kent coast were Whitstable and Herne Bay. They had travelled there as a family when her father had bought his car, and they had also visited Margate, and stayed in a boarding house. They hadn't seen much of her dad, as he had found a pub to drink in, but with Tom and her mum, they had walked down to the slot machines and spent their loose change, then got some chips on the way home. They had laughed and been happy, and she cherished those memories. She didn't have enough money for a train fare, so she would have to hitch-hike to the coast.

Now that she had made a decision she felt more relaxed. She sat calmly eating a slice of toast, watching her mother bustling about in the kitchen.

"Well, your last day, how do you feel?" enquired Vera, taking off her overall. "I was thinking we might go and visit granny, you and I, that is. We could go on the train tomorrow."

"I am fine. Dad won't like it if you are not here," said Ellen, with a twinge of guilt. But she knew why her mother wanted to take her to Gran's, it was because of the mother and baby home; and this is why she had to run away now.

"I will explain to your father. You know I have to do something!" said Vera desperately. She put on some shoes, and picked up a shopping bag. "I am popping out to get a few bits for us to take, and also to make sure your father has enough food."

"OK Mum," said Ellen, not quite believing her luck. Now she could pack a few things in her haversack, so she would at least have a change of clothes.

"Have a nice day," said Vera, as she exited the front door, and she was glad Ellen couldn't see the turmoil that was raging inside her. She had to get Ellen away from her father, and hopefully with the help of her mother, who she planned to telephone later, they could persuade Ellen to go into the home when her time came and have her baby, and then get it adopted. She would come back home on her own. She knew she could not leave Norman for long, he would only drive down to her mother's and cause trouble. She would have to pretend that Ellen was not well, so staying with granny was giving her a chance to recuperate.

Ellen finished her toast. Her mother had to get a bus to the shops, so she would be at least an hour. This gave her time to fill her haversack; but she would have to travel fairly light, and maybe when she had made herself a home, she could then think about having her own belongings. She looked around her for the last time. This had been her home since she was born, and the lump in her throat was because she was leaving her mother and she was scared of the world out there. Her conscience was bothering her now. She couldn't possibly go without telling her mother, but she did not want that to be a reason for her dad to bully her mother, so she sat down and wrote a note:

Mum,
   I have to do this because I want to keep my baby. I am leaving home. No need to tell Dad why.
         I DO LOVE YOU!
         Ellen XXXX

She then put it in the drawer where the knives and forks were stored. Her father would never see that because he never laid the table. Tears were streaming down her face.

Ellen felt so vulnerable, but for her baby's sake she had to be strong. So she blew her nose, and wiped her face, then picking up her haversack she hitched it onto her shoulders and strode out of the door.

She walked along the main road which led towards West Wickham and Bromley; this was the direction to take when going to the Kent coast. Many cars passed her, but although she hailed them for a lift, none of them stopped. After walking for an hour she was getting very tired and her haversack felt so heavy. She sat on a wall.

22

She had reached West Wickham High Street, and after a short rest, she took the road which was an unmade one which led down the hill to Coney Hall.

A big lorry was coming towards her, so she did her best to flag it down and it ground to a halt just past her. She ran up to it, noting the driver was smiling in a friendly way.

"Where d'ya wanna go, lass?" he asked. She guessed he was about mid-twenties. His blond hair was styled in a crew cut, and he had a pleasant and friendly face.

"Well I am heading for the Kent coast," she explained.

Frank Wilson could not believe his luck. A nice bit of crumpet had just flagged him down. She was probably about seventeen or eighteen, maybe running away from home, so he would be well set up for tonight.

"Well, lucky for you I am going to Dover to pick up some freight off the ship, which comes in early tomorrow. Then I drive back to London."

Ellen hadn't planned to go to Dover. She didn't know it. It was a sea port, and she was so grateful for the lift, maybe when she arrived there she could sort something out.

"Thank you so much," she murmured, climbing up into the passenger seat. "Maybe you could drop me off somewhere between Whitstable and Dover."

"Are you visiting someone?"

"No, to be honest I have just decided to take a holiday. Having just left school, I might stay a while and get a holiday job."

Frank smiled to himself. So she was a teenage runaway. She would be so grateful for his help. He was sure that when he offered her a bed in the back of the lorry, where he had sleeping bags stored, she would jump at it, and they could make a night of it. Suddenly his day had got a lot more interesting.

"Right, off we go."

He put the lorry into gear, and off he drove.

By the time Vera had returned from shopping she was ready to put her plan into action. She could probably only stay at her mother's for a couple of days, as Norman would expect her to be at home looking after him. It was now eleven o'clock, and there was no sign of him. His car was not outside, but maybe he had come home, got changed and gone to work.

She put the kettle on to make a cup of tea, opening the cutlery drawer to get a teaspoon out. She spotted the folded piece of paper; but before she had a chance to read it, there was a knock at the front door. She was not expecting anyone, so when she opened the door, she was surprised to see a policeman in uniform with a female companion. Something about their faces worried her, and fear seized her senses; was Ellen OK, and Tom?

"Good morning. Are you Mrs Vera Payne?"

"Yes, I am, what's wrong?"

"I am DI Andrew Foster, and this is my partner, WPC June Brooks. Can we come in and speak to you? I am afraid we have some very serious news."

Vera took one look at their grave faces, and as if on autopilot, she silently opened the door wider to admit them. She was obsessed with the idea that one of her children was hurt; terrified at what they might tell her, yet desperate to know.

"You need to sit down," said DI Foster. He was a man probably in his thirties, but his eyes looked kind, although sad.

"My children, are they all right?" she whispered desperately, sinking into a chair in the hall.

Andrew glanced quickly towards his WPC, then clearing his throat, he spoke. "Is your husband Norman Payne?"

"Yes, that's right."

"A car was discovered up at Shirley Hills. It appeared to have come off the road and bounced along rough ground then hit a tree. It may have happened very early this morning. The driver had died at the scene, and in his pocket was a driving licence in that name. I am very sorry Mrs Payne, to give you such tragic news."

Chapter Four

Ellen was grateful that she had finally got a lift. The lorry wasn't that fast, but her companion, who had introduced himself as Frank, seemed a jolly sort of man. He had the radio on, and tapped his hands against the wheel to the music.

"Do ya like rock and roll Ellen?" he enquired. "You can see I do."

"Oh yes, Elvis especially. I would love to see him in concert."

"Well you need to go to the States for that. He ain't comin' over here."

"He doesn't like flying maybe?"

"Waal I reckon he has his reasons."

Ellen was beginning to feel more comfortable in his company now. Frank appeared to be a very easy going person. She guessed him to be in his twenties, which to her seemed quite mature.

"I am so glad you stopped. I had walked quite a way."

"Don't expect to be down the coast for at least a couple of hours. We have to drive through Sittingbourne, and it's always busy. So we may get there late afternoon."

Ellen could feel her tummy rumbling. All the walking had made her hungry. She wasn't sure if she should break into her ten shillings, as she would need to spend it on a bed and breakfast place tonight. Tomorrow she would have to go job hunting. It all felt quite scary, but she reminded herself that she was carrying a new life inside her, and so she had to see this through.

Frank was planning his next move. He had made her feel relaxed,

b

and if she had been walking for a few hours she was probably hungry. He could take her to the service stop, treat her to a fry up, and the little wench would be so grateful she would sleep with him. He had done it before, and it always worked. Women just loved his cheeky smile and laid back manner.

"I am stopping off in about an hour for some grub. Do you fancy some too? My treat of course."

Ellen was glad he couldn't hear her tummy rumbling above the noise of the engine, but his words hit just the right spot. "You are so kind. I would love that; thank you so much."

"I will have to refuel then. So if you can wait for an hour; and in the meantime here's a snack."

He opened his glove compartment, then handed her a packet of crisps and a Mars bar.

Ellen took them gratefully. These would be enough to calm her grumbling stomach for a while. She couldn't believe how lucky she was to be given a lift by such a kind man.

"You are a life saver!" she said tucking in.

"My pleasure, luv," grinned Frank. She was just like putty in his hands.

Vera found herself struck dumb with shock. Norman killed in a car accident; surely not? What was he even doing at Shirley Hills? He never visited the pub up there called the Sandrock. He said he didn't like the people who went in there, but she had never asked him why. She was only too aware of what a difficult man her husband was to like.

He was a frequent visitor to their local pub, The Shirley Inn, and that is where she had thought he was last night. He could walk there from the house. But he hadn't brought the car home; if he had, maybe he would still be alive. She had been so wrapped up in the problems Ellen's pregnancy was going to cause, she hadn't really thought much about him.

She felt guilt rush through her, but then common sense told her that there was nothing she could have done to change any of it. Whatever had taken Norman to Shirley Hills, had ended in his

26

demise. He had not contacted her by telephone, so whatever secret he was hiding had died with him.

As if reading her mind, Andrew asked, "Do you know why your husband was out travelling so early in the morning? Presumably he was on his way to work."

"No, I don't. He works in Croydon, so I have no idea what he was doing up there. He had not come home the night before."

"I see, so were you not worried about him?"

"No, he had done that before, and he often forgot to let me know."

"I see."

Andrew spoke gently to her. The poor woman looked stunned, but it sounded as though she had a very uncaring husband. He had already been told that the body still contained a great deal of alcohol from the night before, which had probably caused him to crash, as forensics had suggested he died at about five o'clock in the morning. Maybe he had been with a lady friend, but there was no need to upset this timid looking lady any more than they already had.

"When you feel you are up to it, we will need you to identify his body."

"Is there anyone we can call to come and be with you? You don't need to be alone right now," said June kindly.

Vera stared into space whilst she collected her thoughts. Guilt flooded through her because right now she was feeling as if a great big boulder had just been removed from her chest. No longer would she be in fear of Norman. Now she could cope with Ellen's pregnancy, and finally Tom would come home for a visit. As sorry as she was about Norman's death, she could already feel her life would be changing so much. She must let them know she could cope. She turned towards June.

"You don't need to worry about me. My daughter will be back from school this afternoon, so I won't be alone. In the meantime, I haven't got a car, but I can come and identify him now."

Andrew admired her courage. To be given such a shock, and then show such bravery in going to identify the body was admirable.

"Do you want to call at your daughter's school? We can pick her up on the way, and she can come with you?"

"Absolutely not! I will break it to her in my own way when she comes home."

"OK," murmured June, "but don't forget we are here for you."

Vera picked up her cardigan and put it on. "I will be warm enough with this. Let's get it done."

Frank had found a stop off for lorry drivers at the services near to Sittingbourne. He knew he could murder a fry up, but he hoped Ellen wouldn't mind a greasy spoon.

"Well, if you are hungry, they do a great all day breakfast here," he said grinning.

If he had asked her in the morning, Ellen probably wouldn't have been able to stomach it, but at four in the afternoon her stomach definitely needed feeding. After all, she was eating for two.

"Do you know if they do omelettes?" she asked innocently, having never been in a place like this before. As they entered, a whiff of cooking oil from the deep fryer assaulted their senses.

"You can ask them." grinned Frank, going up to the counter.

He winked at the lady behind the counter. "I will have an all day special with everything, and bread and butter with it, and a cuppa."

"Certainly," said the young woman, who Ellen noticed had long red gold hair which was tied back in a ponytail. "And you, luv?" she enquired, smiling.

"If you do omelettes, that would be nice."

"Ham, cheese or mushrooms? With chips or without?"

"A ham omelette sounds really nice, with a few chips."

Ellen could feel her mouth watering; she couldn't wait to eat.

"What are you having to drink?" asked Frank, bringing money out of his pocket.

"Can I just have water?" asked Ellen. She had gone off tea and coffee. The doctor had said that apparently this often happened in pregnancy, but he had told her she must drink water.

"Yes, if you both go and sit down I will bring your drinks over," said the young woman. Frank put some money in her hand, and Ellen felt so grateful. She had certainly found a kind person.

"Thank you so much," she said, and he grinned back at her.

They sat at a table by the window. It was very hot and steamy, and the smell of deep fried chips seemed to fill the room. The door was open, and the May sunshine only added to the heat.

The waitress brought their drinks over, and Ellen noticed that Frank winked at her and she seemed to quite like it.

After she had gone, she whispered just loud enough for Frank to hear. "I think she likes you."

Frank grinned. He liked to think that all women did. Ellen was feeding his ego very nicely.

"Why would I look at her when you are sitting right next to me," he said, grinning.

Ellen looked at him in horror. In her naivety she had only imagined that he was being kind to her. It had not occurred to her that he liked her, or was he just joking? Suddenly she felt scared; what had she got herself into? She realised she had to make it absolutely clear that she did not feel the same way. In fact, she was going to have to say she was pregnant.

"I hope you are joking, Frank."

The waitress appeared with his fry-up in one hand and her omelette in the other, placing both plates down next to them, and a plate of bread and butter for Frank.

"Any sauces for you?" she enquired.

"I'll have some ketchup, ta," said Frank, winking again. She dutifully brought it over, then left them to eat their food.

Although Ellen's mouth was watering at the sight of the food, she persisted. Frank had not replied to her, and she was no longer feeling sure of herself. "I think you should know that I am pregnant. I have just had a very unhappy break-up with my boyfriend, so I certainly do not want to get involved with anyone else."

Frank choked on his mouthful of sausage. This was the last thing he was expecting! So the little tart had been knocked up, and now she had a bun in the oven. No way did he want to get involved with her. If she had split with the father, he might find himself roped in if she was looking for a partner. She might be very pretty, but not that pretty that he wanted to get involved in this mess!

"Well you best go and make it up with your boyfriend then. If you had told me this I wouldn't have given you a lift," he said in a harsh voice. He certainly didn't want to get his leg over now. He wanted to steer well clear of this little tart.

Ellen winced at his tone. He was no longer smiling or winking. In fact, he had a bullying tone to his voice, which scared her even though there were other people around them.

"Did you think I bought you dinner out of the kindness of my heart!" he thundered, causing a driver at another table to look over.

Suddenly Ellen realised why he had been so charming. He wanted to sleep with her, and she felt dislike of him; he was a loud mouthed bully, and all she wanted to do was get away from him.

"No, I don't want it," she said, ignoring her groaning stomach. She got up from the table, and said quietly, "Thank you for the lift. I am going now."

"You bitch! Get out of my sight!" he shouted at her.

This was all too much for a man and woman at another table. The man strode over.

"Is he bothering you, luv?" he asked.

Ellen was about to reassure him that she was all right, but as she stood there, a feeling of dizziness came over her. She tried to ignore it, but one moment she felt as if she was floating, and then a grey mist descended, her body crumpled up, and she fell to the ground.

Vera was dropped off at her home by police car after identifying Norman's body. It was the first time she had seen a dead person, and it felt most unreal. She comforted herself with the fact that he had a serene look on his face, even though there were marks and bruises, so she hoped he had not suffered. No matter what had happened in their marriage, nothing could change the fact that he was her husband and the father of her two children.

The lady police officer didn't really want to leave her alone, and Vera was grateful for the empathy they had shown towards her. But now she just wanted to sit down quietly in the comfort of her own home and collect her tumbled thoughts.

"Don't worry about me. My daughter Ellen will be home from school in less than an hour."

"Do you want me to stay whilst you explain to her?" said June gently.

"You are very kind, and I am grateful for your support, but I think it will be less distressing for Ellen if she doesn't see a police uniform when she comes in the door."

"Yes, you are right," agreed June. "But don't hesitate to pick up the phone and ring if you need us."

"Of course," said Vera, showing them both to the door, "and thanks again for everything."

She shut the front door and returned to the kitchen. Now for that cup of tea. The kettle was still plugged in from earlier when she had filled it up, so she flicked the switch on, and got herself out a cup and saucer from the kitchen cabinet. Then she found a small teapot, just enough for two cups of tea, and opened the cutlery drawer to get a teaspoon.

The folded piece of paper still lay on top, so she picked it up, curious to see what it was. When she read it, she couldn't believe it. Ellen had left home, she didn't know where she would have gone, and she couldn't tell her about her dad's death. Suddenly Vera felt so alone, and fear passed over her that her pregnant daughter was out there somewhere with nowhere to live and no money. It was not safe out there for a girl of seventeen; and it was all her fault, she had driven her away. How could she ever live with this guilt?

Chapter Five

"Look, she's coming round now."

Edna Wilmot heaved a sigh of relief. The young girl had gone very pale. They were now in a back room of the cafe, away from the abusive lorry driver and prying eyes of customers. Sam, her husband, had carried the girl into the room, and she was laid out on a shabby couch.

"Are you OK now, dear?" said Edna kindly, as Ellen's eyes fluttered open. The waitress was poised at the door, waiting to be told what to do.

"Where am I?" asked Ellen, feeling confused.

"You are in the staff room of the cafe. You fainted, so Sam had to carry you into here, away from the bad tempered lorry driver."

Ellen remembered then; she had thought he was kind until he changed and started shouting at her. "Oh yes, he gave me a lift, bought me dinner, and then started trying to flirt with me. So I had to make it clear I wasn't interested."

"You and many others," said Sam, wryly. "I've seen him at it before. He offers young girls like you lifts, but his intentions are not honourable. Where are you actually hitch-hiking to?"

"I wanted to get to the Kent coast. I have just finished school, and felt like a holiday. I fainted because I have not eaten since this morning, and now I feel very sick."

"There's a toilet out the back if you need it," said the waitress, pointing.

"In the meantime, you must eat. Maybe then you won't feel sick. We'll get you another omelette," said Edna, gently. She turned towards the waitress, who nodded and left the room.

Half an hour later, Ellen was feeling quite a bit better. She had eaten the omelette, and drank a glass of water. The feeling of sickness had subsided, and Edna had struck up a conversation with her. Evidently Edna and Sam were on their way home. They lived in a little bungalow on the Studd Hill estate at Herne Bay. They had been up to London. When he was at work, Sam also drove a lorry, and this is how he knew about Frank's reputation. Edna had a little wool and haberdashery shop in a secondary parade of shops in Sea Street. "Yes, I had to close it today," she said ruefully. "I didn't have anyone who could run it for me."

"You have been so kind to me," said Ellen gratefully. She was now feeling very weary, and had no idea what would happen to her next. Maybe she should try and find a bed and breakfast here at Sittingbourne.

An idea was forming in Edna's mind; she wanted to run it past Sam first, so she took the opportunity whilst Ellen was in the toilet to broach the subject.

"Sam, don't tell her we went to London to see the specialist."

"I wasn't going to," he said indignantly.

"You heard her; she's pregnant and on her own. Obviously not on holiday, but probably been thrown out. If we give her a home for the next few months, and maybe a job in my shop, when the baby is born she won't be able to keep it, so we can adopt it."

Sam gave a long whistle. "You make it sound easy, but she won't want to give it up."

"She won't have a choice. She'll be homeless, with no partner, and nobody will rent a flat to an unmarried mother."

Ellen had by now rejoined them, and Edna spoke gently to her. "Ellen, would you like to come to Herne Bay with us, and stay in our bungalow until your baby is born?"

"You are so kind, but I have no money to pay you."

"Well, I need an assistant to help me in the shop."

Ellen couldn't believe her ears; all of a sudden there was hope.

*   *   *   *

Vera picked up the telephone to ring her mother. She had to let her know about Norman. It rang out, and she was just about to clear down when Elizabeth answered, quoting the number.

Vera drew a deep breath, trying to remain calm whilst speaking. "Mother, it's Vera. I have telephoned to tell you that Norman was killed in a car crash very early this morning. I know it's true, as I have just returned from identifying his body. But in the meantime, Ellen has told me she is pregnant. We visited the hospital yesterday, and it was confirmed, and this morning she pretended to go to school for the last day, but left me a note to say she has left home."

Elizabeth had just been expecting a call asking how she was, and a general catchup. Vera dutifully rang her once in a while, but they had not been close for years due to Elizabeth's dislike of Norman. It had been a shotgun marriage. Her late husband Ted had insisted that Norman married his daughter, but Norman had proved to be just as bad tempered as his father-in-law. She knew Vera tried to hide how bad the marriage was. She had done the same, until mercifully Ted had died of a heart attack, some three years previously. Since she had been free of him, her life had been much happier. But now was not the time to make ill-judged comments about Norman. She felt far more concerned about Ellen leaving home. History had repeated itself, but with her father now gone, if the baby's father wasn't going to do the decent thing, surely Vera could stand by her daughter. She had been in the same position eighteen years ago. She chose her words very carefully.

"Oh Vera, what a shock! Was he on the way to work? And Ellen, what a silly girl. Have you any idea where she is?"

"No, he stayed out the night before, and he forgot to let me know. I think he had been drinking, and was on the way home, and misjudged the corner. Ellen left before I was given the news. I had suggested to her that we came to see you, and was going to ask you if she could stay for a bit."

Vera didn't mention the mother and baby home being nearby. She was full of guilt because she knew that she had pushed her daughter into a corner, but if only she had known about Norman, they probably could have worked something out. Just one day would have made all the difference.

34

Elizabeth bristled inside. So the silly idiot had precipitated his own death. She had no sympathy for him. Ellen was her main thought. "How about I get the train and come and stay with you for a bit. If you contact Tom, he might be able to get leave too. Together we can sort the funeral arrangements. We could even contact the police and see if they can help us to find Ellen."

Vera had tears of relief rolling down her cheeks at the other end of the phone. She had never felt so close to her mother for years, and she knew why it was. Now that Norman had passed her mother was there for her to support her, and at this moment she needed her so much.

"Thanks mother. I will come up to London on the train to meet you and we can travel back together. Your support means everything to me."

Elizabeth, who prided herself in usually keeping a stiff upper lip against what life threw at her, heard the catch in her voice, and she felt a warm glow in her heart. Vera needed her, and with that violent and spiteful man, who had beaten his own son over virtually nothing, and controlled his wife for all of their married life, now gone, she had no doubt that their relationship would become much closer.

Tom Payne took the news of his father's death with mixed feelings. It was a natural instinct to love your parents, they gave you life in the first place, but most of the memories he had were of a grumpy and bad tempered man who rarely smiled. He had stepped out of line the day he went scrumping with his friend, but, at thirteen, he had thought it was clever. That day his father had given him a beating, so after that he toed the line, worked hard at school, and did everything he could to stay out of trouble.

As he grew older he couldn't help noticing his father's lack of respect towards his mother. He could only feel warmth from his mother and Ellen. This was a house where his parents didn't appear to care much about each other. His mother was a dutiful wife, and she took her role very seriously, but his father seemed to care about no one but himself and he shouted and bullied his way through life.

35

Tom was glad to join the army when he was old enough. It was a hard life, with no home comforts, but it forged lasting friendships. He missed his mother and Ellen, as the house had always felt much happier when his father was not around, but he knew that if he had stayed, he would have borne the brunt of his father's temper. He could feel Norman's dislike of him, but he had no idea what he had done wrong; it couldn't just be about the scrumping. He had put his hurt aside and strived to make the best of his new life.

He felt sadness when Vera told him about the fatal accident, because he had never been able to have a proper father and son relationship, but he also felt relief that he could now visit the two people who meant everything to him. There was also a feeling of guilt that his father's death was making him feel relieved.

"Oh Mother, I'm so sorry; it's so sad. I do hope he didn't suffer."

"They believe it was instantaneous, so hopefully he didn't."

"I must get some leave and come home, then I can help you with the funeral. You shouldn't have to deal with it all on your own. How is Ellen?"

Vera swallowed before speaking at the other end of the phone, knowing that her next words were going to devastate him.

"Tom, she got herself pregnant, and we were both so worried about your dad finding out. So earlier today, before we knew about your dad's accident, she left home. She has no idea he had an accident, and what is worse, I have no idea where she is."

Tom couldn't believe what he was hearing. He had always thought of Ellen as his baby sister because she was three years younger than him. His protective feelings rose.

"So who did this to her? Presumably they have run away together."

"No, I think she is on her own. I don't know who it is. She said he didn't know, and she didn't want him to know because they broke up and he is with someone else."

His heart lurched with fear. His baby sister was somewhere on her own, pregnant and scared.

"Right, Mother, I will be home tomorrow, and we will leave no stone unturned to find Ellen and bring her home."

"Yes, and Granny is coming to stay as well."

"Well, Mother, no matter what the world thinks, we must stick by Ellen."

"Yes, I agree, and so does Granny. I don't want her out on the streets. She has no money and no home; we must all stick together."

Tom put the receiver down; his money had run out. He was now going to get permission to go home. They would grant him compassionate leave because of his father's death, but his mind was full of his sister right now. He was already making plans to visit the local police station in Croydon and ask for their help in finding Ellen. To him, nothing was more important than his sister's safety and his mother's peace of mind.

Chapter Six

Edna was humming to herself as she got dressed to go to her shop. After being married for seven years without conceiving, and then being referred to Guy's hospital in London, the problem had been diagnosed. Sam had a very low sperm count. They had both left the hospital feeling heartbroken. They were still young enough to have a family, both being thirty years old, but now it seemed very unlikely. That is until they had met Ellen.

Edna chose a full skirt with black flowers on a white background from her wardrobe. Her long dark hair flowed around her shoulders, framing her doll-like face. Then she found a white top with short sleeves edged with broderie anglaise. She didn't need stockings, as it was a warm day, so she slipped on a pair of wedge heeled sandals, and then looked at herself critically in the mirror. She still scrubbed up quite well.

"Oh, I love your skirt and top."

She turned to see Ellen framed in the doorway of their small lounge, her blonde curly hair looked tousled, which was hardly surprising after the day she had endured yesterday.

"Oh thanks, Ellen, I was going to leave you to sleep in. I have to go to the shop. How do you feel today?"

"I feel much better, and I am so grateful to you and Sam for giving me shelter. But I do want to work. I want to help you in the shop."

"Well I can take you in if you like, and show you around, but no need to work today. If you go and get a quick shower. Did you bring a change of clothes?"

"Only one set," said Ellen awkwardly, as she stood there in the baggy tee shirt that she had slept in.

"I think we are about the same size. I have a pleated skirt with an elasticated waist that you can borrow until we get ourselves sorted."

"Oh, thank you," said Ellen, feeling so grateful.

"Right, you get your shower, and I am going to do some toast. We don't want any more fainting," said Edna briskly, and Ellen disappeared into the bathroom

Half an hour later, feeling refreshed after her shower and marmalade toast, Ellen got into the car and sat next to Edna. It was just a short journey to Sea Street, and when they reached the old fashioned little shop, Edna drove the car up an alleyway beside it and parked at the rear of the shop. Then they walked to the front, and Ellen could view it through the window. The shop was well stocked with knitting wool and patterns, as well as everything a needlework woman could possibly need from cottons, buttons and silks, down to scissors, needles and crochet hooks. In the window a couple of willowy models sported full-skirted cotton dresses, one had buttons all the way down, and the other had a white shiny belt which accentuated the fitted waist.

Edna unlocked the door and they went inside. Once the lights came on, Ellen looked around her wonderingly. It was so quaint and full of character; there was even a drawer full of buttons in all shapes and sizes, which customers could buy just one of if that was all they wanted.

"It is a lovely shop. You have everything that knitters and sewers could possibly want, even down to a single button," Ellen said warmly.

"Oh yes, I inherited this from my mother. We have lots of local customers, and being accommodating when they only want one button encourages them to come back and buy other things."

At the rear of the shop was a small kitchen with a sink and facilities for making tea, and at the end of a narrow corridor was a toilet. Then a back door which led out to the area where the car was parked.

"Do you like the idea of working here? I can school you a bit about what we are selling."

"I would love to!"

"OK, if you sit behind the counter and watch me, we will call it your induction day," smiled Edna.

Ellen smiled back, marvelling to herself that she had found such a kind person. Sam had not said much, he was leaving everything to Edna, who explained that he did long trips to and from the continent, and left her to deal with every day matters. Ellen had found him to be a kind man, who seemed to understand her predicament as much as Edna did. Right now she had a job, a home and friends. In a few months her baby would be born, but right now she wasn't thinking about the future. She was taking each day at a time.

Vera stood in the police station, with Tom and Elizabeth standing on either side of her. Andrew smiled kindly whilst she explained how Ellen had left home.

"When did this happen, Mrs Payne?"

"Two days ago. The day my husband crashed in the car."

Andrew's face showed concern. "Oh, the shock of her father's death you mean?"

"No, it was before we knew." She held back from telling him about the pregnancy. It was a family matter.

"How old is Ellen?"

"Seventeen."

"I see. Well there isn't much we can do, as she is legally old enough to make her own decisions."

"But she is a vulnerable girl," said Tom protectively. "She has never done this before."

June was at the desk, and she looked up. Seeing their worried faces, she turned towards Vera.

"Is it possible now that school has finished she might have gone to stay with a friend?"

"No, we have tried them all," said Vera desperately.

June decided to take over. "Well, if you have a photograph of

Ellen, and also a description of what she was wearing when she left the house, we will keep a look out for her if that helps. As DI Foster has already explained, we can't stop Ellen from leaving home, but if we do happen to see her, we can ask her to let you know she is OK. She may well then be ready to come back home, especially when she knows her father has passed away."

Vera's hopes had been dashed, and Tom and Elizabeth felt the same. Their mission had been thwarted, and all they could hope for was that Ellen would return home of her own accord.

"Well, thank you," said Elizabeth, putting her arm comfortingly round Vera.

"Let's go home Mother, we have a funeral to plan," said Tom, taking her arm, and they all walked out of the police station.

Sam was at the wheel of his lorry deep in reverie. It had been a shock being told by the specialist that he had been firing duds all this time! After being married to Edna for seven years, their love life had become a bit like a military exercise. The joy seemed to have seeped out of his marriage. It was nothing to do with Edna, she was still as beautiful as ever, with her lovely dark hair, slim figure, and gorgeous tawny eyes. But now he knew that the fault lay with him, it had rocked his confidence.

He had arrived at the port of Dover now, ready to pick up a shipment of perishable goods first thing in the morning, which he would be delivering to Ashford. Tonight he was booked into a modest bed and breakfast, as his company did not go overboard when paying for accommodation, but as the back of his lorry was kept cool for the goods there was no way he could sleep there.

Sam parked in the allotted space, and climbed out of his cab. The place where he was staying was just across the road, and right opposite was a pub, so he could get himself a pint and unwind. The door was open, and sounds of laughter came from inside as he walked past. Outside on the pavement people were sitting at wooden benches sipping drinks, all taking advantage of the mellow summer evening.

After booking himself in, he put his holdall on the candlewick

41

bedspread which covered the single bed. He sat down, noting the mattress felt a bit lumpy as he had expected. He had to share the toilet, and next to it was a bathroom, so he decided to slip in there hoping to take a shower, but all it contained was a large hand basin. After a wash and shave he was feeling much better, so he put on a clean pair of trousers, and a short sleeved check shirt, then a dash of aftershave. He combed his dark brown hair, and applied some Brylcreem to keep it in place. Satisfied that he looked OK, he went downstairs. Now it was time to get something to eat. His hostess for the night had seemed delighted to tell him that she didn't serve dinner, so he had to go out, and if he returned after eleven, the door would be locked, and she didn't take kindly to being woken up.

He crossed the road and went into the pub, which had a man at a piano doing his best to entertain the noisy crowd of people, who were laughing and joking, and clearly very merry. He smiled cordially, then ordered his pint. The girl behind the bar smiled in a friendly way at him; she was blonde and petite, with very blue eyes.

"Here you are. I haven't seen you in here before," she said boldly, leaning forward and exposing a low cut top, from which her rounded breasts were doing their best to escape.

"No, I am just passing through. I don't suppose you have anything to eat other than a packet of crisps? I am staying over the road and she doesn't do evening meals."

The young woman leaned provocatively towards him, and laughed, showing her white and even teeth. "Nobody gets a meal at Florrie's, and I hear the breakfast is very greasy. I finish in about half an hour. I can show you somewhere if you like. My name is Lorna."

Sam gulped, no woman had ever thrown herself at him like this, but it soothed him to know even if he wasn't fertile, he was still fancied by someone. He could feel lust rising inside him. Oh, how he wanted to unveil those beautiful breasts and stroke them. He pushed down any thoughts of guilt that he was being unfaithful. His confidence had taken a huge dent, and here was someone who wanted him; not just to try and make a baby, but to have sex with.

"OK Lorna. I am Sam. I am all yours in half an hour, and I am very hungry."

"So am I," she said seductively, putting her hand over his, and Sam felt his senses rising. His body was tingling, and the touch of her hand sent spasms right through him. He quickly drained his beer glass and got her to fill it again. What a night he was in for!

Chapter Seven

November 1961

"Sorry Ellen," said Edna over the telephone, "I am held up and I can't get back until tomorrow, so can you lock up and get a cab home. I will pay for it. Use the petty cash."

Ellen sighed. She wasn't stupid, she knew what was going on, but she really had no choice; with her baby due in about a week, she just had to stay put. Sam was away most of the time, so it was like living on her own. She was struggling to complete a day at the shop because she was so tired, the weight of the baby was holding her back, and Edna was no longer around very much to give her moral support. She had heard Edna on the phone making plans to meet someone, and judging by her comments it was not a woman, the coyness and the blushing when she had come out into the hall after the receiver had been put down was a dead giveaway, and then the muttered explanation that she had to go and buy some new stock for the shop.

"Yes, I will lock up. If I wasn't so far gone I would walk home, but I am so tired."

"Yes, you must be." Edna tried to sound soothing, but her mind was full of Henry. She had thought she loved Sam, but now Henry had come into her life, and it must have been meant to be. He was a representative from a haberdashery company, and the moment he entered the shop to take her order, she had fallen deeply in love with him. She tried to bring her mind down to earth.

"Have you taken much money today?"

"Not too bad, in spite of the rain. Ten per cent up on last year's total."

"Oh, well done. Have to go now, but don't forget to put your feet up tonight."

Ellen was just about to reply when she heard the receiver go down. It was amazing how much had changed in the last few months. In the beginning, Edna had been very supportive and protective towards her. She had been with her on hospital and doctor's appointments, and made sure she was booked into the cottage hospital for the birth. In the absence of her mother, Ellen had been grateful. Edna was like an older sister. But in the last three months, everything had started to change.

Edna had become pre-occupied. She was often absent, particularly overnight, and Ellen could feel her lack of interest in herself and the forthcoming baby. She had always known that the bungalow at Studd Hill was not going to be her permanent home. She had planned to find herself a small flat, big enough for herself and her baby. Now that she had the experience of working in a shop, she was hoping to get a job in another one, and maybe they would let her take the little one to work with her. Ellen's determination to keep her baby, no matter how hard it would be, completely overrode any negative thoughts that she might have had about whether it would be possible.

It was almost closing time, so she telephoned for a taxi, and then took some money out of the till. She wasn't sure how much it would be, so she would have to fill out the petty cash voucher tomorrow. She got herself ready to go, knowing that as soon as the taxi stopped outside, she could lock the door and go home. She was relieved, as she was feeling very tired.

Suddenly she felt a sensation of water dripping, and she looked down in horror. Oh no, her waters had broken, baby was on the way. She must be in labour! The taxi pulled up outside, and suddenly she was scared, but she had to see it through.

After locking the door and turning off the lights, Ellen walked slowly towards the car. The driver had jumped out, and was holding the back door open for her to get in. She got in awkwardly, as her bulkiness made bending so much harder.

"Where to, luv?" asked the taxi driver cheerfully.

"The maternity hospital in Margate, as soon as you can. I think I am in labour."

Roger Daly could see this was an emergency, and he knew nothing about delivering babies, so he stepped on the accelerator. There was no time to argue; he must get her to the hospital in time.

Edna couldn't believe it. After trying for seven years to get pregnant with Sam, she had fallen pregnant with Henry after just three months. The longing for a child had dominated her life for so long, it had in the end destroyed her marriage. When Sam had found out his sperm count was low, she had not felt loyalty towards him, only huge disappointment that, as she felt, he had let her down. This craving had made her selfish, she knew, and now she was going to leave Sam. Hopefully in time he would divorce her, and then it would leave her free to get married to Henry. She had only just had her pregnancy confirmed by the doctor, so in about six months time their child would be born. In the meantime, Sam was away, so tomorrow she was going home to collect her clothes, and then Henry would be waiting for her to join him in his spacious house at Broadstairs.

She did have a bit of a conscience about Ellen, but the thought of having her own baby, something she had almost given up on, meant she was no longer interested in adopting Ellen's. Ellen had repeatedly spoken about how she wanted to keep her baby, so now she could. Edna thought she was actually doing her a favour. She was putting up the shop for sale, as Henry didn't want her working any more, he had said, but the solicitor and estate agents would take care of all that. She would pop home tomorrow, whilst Ellen was at the shop, pick up all her stuff, and leave Ellen a note explaining it all. As for Sam, they had drifted apart, and she had already written a goodbye letter to him; it was in a sealed envelope, and she would leave it under his pillow.

Edna was squashing down any feelings of conscience she might feel about either of them. Being pregnant may have made her selfish, but being a mother had been her dream since she was a little girl, and now she had the chance. Taking the coward's way out meant she didn't have to face them both and feel their pain. Touching her slightly rounded stomach, she caressed it gently. All this would be worth it when the baby came.

It had been a huge relief to Vera when Norman's funeral was over. Her mind had been distracted by Ellen's disappearance, so having the support of Tom and Elizabeth at this time had helped her to hold herself together. She had been taught to hide her emotions. It wasn't dignified to let people know you were suffering mentally, and having been married to a man who didn't appear to have any emotions, meant that she had to keep hers hidden. Now that he was no longer around, she could only feel relief, but her heart ached to know that Ellen was out there somewhere; pregnant, and most probably alone. Elizabeth had voiced her distress because they had no idea if Ellen was safe or not, and Tom had taken his car and gone riding all over the place with photos of his sister, but it appeared that Ellen had disappeared into thin air.

The police had not seen or heard of Ellen either, and whilst Vera understood what they meant about Ellen being seventeen, and old enough to leave home if that is what she wanted to do, none of this could stop the persistent ache inside her heart. How many times had she said to herself, 'if only Ellen had waited for just one day', after her father passed, before she left home. Vera knew that, no matter what the neighbours thought, she would have stood by Ellen and she would still be safe at home with her.

The funeral had been very simple. Norman didn't have any friends. It had just been herself, Elizabeth, Tom and the director of the company where Norman had worked, who gathered together in the church to say farewell to him. He was now buried in the grounds of the local church, and she couldn't help remembering that when they had first bought their house in Shirley, she had asked him if they could get Tom christened there. Norman had angrily told her he was an atheist, and had no intention of setting foot in any church. At the service it had just been Vera and her parents, and Vera's friend Gladys, who had been his godmother. She hoped that God had forgiven him, as his body now lay in hallowed grounds, and that was because Vera had always been an active member of the church, and she had done her best to bring her two children up to be God fearing.

As the months slipped by, Vera settled back into some sort of life again. Tom came home much more often now, but he shared her anguish about Ellen being missing. She was aware that Ellen's baby must be due very shortly, and she continued to say a prayer for her daughter every night, wishing that God would keep her safe, and one day she would come home.

Vera was alone now, as her mother had gone back to Wales but was thinking of selling her bungalow and moving nearer to her daughter. Vera had discovered a closeness to her mother since Norman had passed, and she welcomed the idea of Elizabeth being much closer.

Tom felt a mixture of relief and anxiety, which had not improved since the funeral of his father. He regretted that his only relationship with his father had been dominated by fear. He had always felt close to his mother, Vera had doted on her blond, curly haired son with the laughing blue eyes. Tom didn't have a mean bone in his body, but Norman was jealous of his handsome son, and he made sure that Vera put him first at all times.

When he had come home to support his mother after hearing about his father's death, he had been devastated to know that Ellen was missing and pregnant. He did not judge her in any way. She was his kid sister and somebody had done this to her, and by all accounts they didn't even know. She was taking all the responsibility upon herself, and knowing how biased people were against unmarried mothers, all he hoped for was that she would come back home.

It was during one of their conversations that Tom found out just why his father had not liked him. His mother had told him she had been in the same position as Ellen and her own father had insisted that Norman married her. Now Tom understood why his parents' marriage had never been a happy one. It was a gunshot marriage, and his father had not loved his mother, and had become an angry and embittered man.

48

But Ellen didn't know her father had passed away. She was out there somewhere. Tom had looked in all the places he knew she liked going, visited some of her friends to see if anyone knew, and even driven up to London, scouring the bars and cafes for any sign of her. But she appeared to have vanished into thin air. So he kept close contact with his mother, and came home on leave whenever it was possible. He had wished so many times that he knew her address, so he could write and tell her about his father's fatal accident. Then he could reassure her that if she came home she would have the support of himself and his mother.

Tom was seriously thinking about leaving the army and taking a job in the police force. He had done his two years, and he now felt his mother would appreciate him living with her, and with a regular job he could contribute towards food, rent etc., and that would help Vera to keep a roof over her head. He had voiced his feelings to her, and his mother had explained that granny was also thinking of moving closer. He loved his granny too. The house was quite a big one, with four bedrooms, and he had suggested they keep a bedroom free for Ellen and the baby, and his mother's face had broken into a smile. She had hugged him close, and she asked emotionally, "Do you really think she might come home?"

"I do," he said firmly, and he knew he had to believe it. It was only by thinking this, as a family, that they could hold themselves together. Meanwhile, life had to go on.

Chapter Eight

"Come on now, Ellen. The head is there; one final push!"

Janet McCarthy's voice was a little harsh. Here was another teenager got herself up the duff. Young women these days seemed to have no morals. There was no wedding ring on her finger, and she had come to the hospital unaccompanied. As the tiny body slithered into the world, instead of marvelling at the joy of a new life, she was deciding when she should telephone the adoption society to let them know.

Her assistant gently made the infant comfortable whilst she cut the cord.

"You have a daughter," she said brusquely.

Ellen was weak from her exertions, and the pain had made her perspire, but hearing the cry meant everything to her, and all the agony she had just experienced for all these hours was immediately forgotten.

"Can I hold her?" she said, overcome with emotion.

Janet was a tall, very well built woman, who stood no nonsense from anybody. Her bulky frame seemed to fill the room, and her purpose in life was to deliver a healthy baby, and in the case of an unmarried mother, which Ellen clearly was, make sure the girl did not get too attached to the infant that she would not be bringing up.

Her assistant looked questioningly at her. It didn't do to go against Janet! Janet took the baby from her and wrapped her gently in a cotton sheet. The poor cow had been in labour all night, so begrudgingly she would let her have a few minutes with her baby daughter.

"Here you are. Just a couple of minutes because we need to wash her and make her comfortable."

Ellen sat up in bed, ignoring the feeling of weakness inside her. A tiny face was framed inside the cotton sheet. The very blue eyes opened briefly, and Ellen stroked her face gently, marvelling at the shock of very dark hair which sprouted in all directions. Her baby had Jeremy's dark hair and straight nose, and she felt the tears roll down her face. She had never missed him more than at this moment. Her beloved Jeremy, who didn't even know that he was a father.

"You are beautiful. I am going to call you Grace," she said through her tears.

"That's enough now!" said Janet, and reluctantly Ellen relinquished her very precious little bundle.

The next events were a bit of a blur to her. Overcome with weariness she had fallen asleep, and when she woke again, she found herself in a ward amongst other new mothers, but where was her baby? Panic swept through her; she had a daughter, but where was she? She propped herself up on her pillows and called for a nurse.

Edna was happier now than she had ever been. She was so driven by the new life growing inside that she was oblivious of anything else. She had moved in with Henry now, the shop was closed and up for sale in the hands of agents. As for the bungalow, they had only been renting it, and Sam had moved out, and was currently driving backwards and forwards from Europe. She didn't want to think too much about Sam or Ellen, who she assumed must have moved on now, and maybe even had her baby. She could not allow her conscience to bother her. Her pregnancy needed to be protected; having a healthy baby was all that mattered to her.

Henry lived in a big detached house at Broadstairs. It was Victorian in style and it had a garden which sloped upwards, which had been divided into terraces. Her baby would be born next summer. Right now, in November, it was too cold to go out and enjoy the garden, but she was looking forward to next year, and being so close to the seafront.

Henry had bought her a ring. This was so the neighbours would think they were already married if she met any of them whilst out. Her pregnancy would soon be very obvious, and she glowed with happiness when she remembered how protective he had been towards her. He had introduced her as his wife when she met the elderly couple next door as they were going out one day. George and Mabel Roberts, who were probably in their mid-seventies, both dressed very smartly had apparently both worked in the medical profession. George was a retired consultant and Mabel had been a staff nurse. They were now enjoying their retirement, and Edna was glad that they didn't know she was not married to Henry yet, as she didn't want to be judged.

As far as she was concerned her divorce could not happen soon enough. She could then marry Henry and become mistress of this lovely house. Unlike her marriage to Sam, who had not earned much as a lorry driver, she would never need to work again. Henry might only have a modest job as a haberdashery representative, but being an only child, he had inherited the family home when his parents died. She had already settled into this house and was enjoying living here. Shaking herself into reality, she gently touched her stomach, now becoming rounder each day. She was enjoying the opportunity of being a housewife, and tonight she planned to cook a steak pie for Henry just as if she was his wife.

Ellen had been in hospital for ten days now, and she couldn't wait to take baby Grace home. She had made friends with Sarah, the young nurse who was taking care of her. As she had been treated for a slight complication after the birth, it had necessitated her staying in hospital. Janet was not around, she had been transferred to another hospital where there were more babies to deliver.

Sarah was only nineteen, not much older than Ellen, and she had a lot of empathy for her. She had found Janet very intimidating, and her assumption that Ellen wanted to have her baby adopted, she knew was wrong. Ellen had told her where she lived. She might not have a husband, but she did have friends who cared about her.

Ellen had told her how she worked in the shop right up until Grace had been born, and she was planning to return to shop work as soon as she could. Sarah felt she was very inspiring, so when Ellen had told her she wanted to breastfeed her baby, she had brought Ellen's daughter to her. Seeing how well the baby fed, and the way she clutched her mother's finger as she nestled into her, made Sarah feel quite emotional. Already Ellen and her beautiful baby were forming such a close bond, and it had been wrong of Janet to assume Ellen would want her to be adopted.

Ellen looked up from nursing Grace, as Sarah made her way towards her. She was grateful for Sarah's friendship. Someone close to her own age, who didn't judge her, unlike some of the mothers in here who were married and had other children.

Sarah was tiny, with a doll-like face and big green eyes. Her brown hair was tied back from her face in a ponytail. She was engaged to Clive, and they were getting married next year. She had told Ellen that she couldn't wait to get married and become a mother.

Ellen had buried a slight feeling of guilt that she had told Sarah a white lie. She had expected that when Edna finally came home, she would realise that Ellen was in the hospital, and would be straight up there to see her and Grace. Every day she had hoped Edna would come, and a feeling of hopelessness had swept through her on the realisation that maybe Edna had left home. She had to have a stable home to take her baby back to until such time that she could find somewhere else, so in the absence of a visitor, she had told Sarah that Edna's mother had been taken ill, and Edna had gone away for a while to take care of her.

Sarah smiled brightly at her. "How are you feeling today, Ellen?"

"I am fine, and look how well Grace is feeding."

"Yes, you have certainly got the hang of breastfeeding, which is good. I think after doctor has done his rounds, he might ask if you want to go home."

"Oh yes, I really do!" Ellen brushed aside any worries about where Edna was.

"Have you got anyone who can come and pick you up? We want to know you get back safely so soon after childbirth."

Ellen's mind whirled, and an idea came to her. "My friend's husband owns a cab company. He has always said I can call on him whenever I need a lift. They are practically family."

"Well wait until doctor has done his rounds. There is a phone in the corridor, and you can ring your friend, what's his name? Then he can send a cab for you."

"John, his name is John."

"Great. I will leave you to finish feeding Grace."

Telling lies was not something Ellen had done before, but right now she was living on a knife-edge. She was feeling much stronger now, so she wanted to go back to the bungalow with Grace. Then she would start looking for a job and somewhere to live. She had no idea what was going on with Edna and Sam, but she could not help feeling let down; and because this made her feel vulnerable, she wished that her mother was here. She had never stopped missing her mother, ever since she left home. But now she had her own baby to care for. She was a mother, and as she looked into the innocent eyes of her daughter, sucking gently at her breast, she reminded herself that she must grow up quickly because Grace depended on her.

Chapter Nine

"Thank you very much."

Ellen stepped out of the cab, with Grace wrapped in a shawl, her tiny face shielded from the strong wind which was blowing with all its might, causing fences and gates to rattle. The sky was dark, clouds forming and ready to pour with rain. She had already paid the driver before attempting to get out of the car, balancing her holdall on the other arm had not been easy, but her tiny daughter had slept on, oblivious of anything other than the safety of her mother's arms.

She watched the cab drive away, and then turned towards the bungalow, hoping that Edna might be there to greet her. It was only just after three in the afternoon, but it looked deserted, no lights were on; and then she froze. There was a big sign outside which read TO LET.

Then the rain started. It was soon lashing down, and she knew she would have to get inside. But when she tried her key in the lock, it didn't open the door. Oh no, the locks had been changed! In desperation she opened the shed door; that was not locked, and with a beating heart she slipped inside.

It was almost as cold as outside in the shed, but now Grace was stirring. It was time for a feed, and at the same time it was also getting dark. She was desperate now; she had not expected this. She carefully laid Grace onto a workbench whilst she opened up a deckchair, then she sat down and proceeded to feed her daughter. Meanwhile the rain was lashing on the shed roof. This was like her worst nightmare!

After she had finished feeding Grace, she changed her into the one towelling nappy that she had, and discarded the hospital one into a bucket. She had just a small amount of cash on her, so as soon as it stopped raining, she needed to find somewhere to stay. It was so cold in the shed. She could not subject her baby to a night here, she might not survive.

Grace was now feeling clean and full, so she went back to sleep to Ellen's relief. She was just beginning to realise what a precarious situation she was in; she was actually homeless with a newborn baby. She missed her mother more than ever now, and in a rare moment of weakness she allowed the tears of desperation to roll down her face. The sobs shook her body, but no one could hear her above the raging wind outside.

After she had shed her tears, there was a voice inside her, telling her to pull herself together for Grace's sake. She felt inside her pocket for a handkerchief, and wiped her face. The rain had stopped banging against the window, so it was time to make a break. It was completely dark now, and she wondered if the next door neighbour Betty would help her, even if it was only for one night.

She clutched her precious daughter close to her. She was stirring now, so she pulled the shawl round her face, leaving just a tiny bit exposed. She walked along the path which led to the front gate, and then approached Betty's bungalow. She could see there was a light on, even though the curtains were drawn, so she took a breath and knocked on the door.

Betty appeared at the window. At the age of sixty, she no longer left the house after it became dark, nor did she open her door to strangers. But she could see this was a tragic situation. The young girl Ellen from next door was standing out there on a cold and windy night, and clutched in her arms was a baby. Edna had told her before she had gone away that she was only eighteen, and Edna and Sam were taking care of her. But not any more, the bungalow was empty, and even though she didn't approve of taking in an unmarried mother, her conscience would not allow her to leave them out there.

She opened the window slightly, and said loudly against the wind, "You can't get in. Edna has gone, and it's going to be let."

"I know. Please can you help me? Just for tonight. When it's daylight I will go. It's so cold my baby might die."

"Well only tonight," Betty said firmly. She didn't want the infant's death on her conscience. "I will open the front door."

Ellen was so relieved to get inside the house. Betty took Grace whilst she took her wet coat off and left it in the hallway. She followed Betty into the small lounge, where a coal fire was burning brightly. It felt so homely.

Betty was a retired teacher. A tall thin woman, with her grey hair scraped quite severely from her face. But she wasn't made of stone, and even though Ellen was obviously a teenager without any morals to have allowed herself to be in this position, she could not harden her heart to this innocent little child nestling in her arms who had not asked to be born.

"You can stay for tonight, but tomorrow you must go. My sister is coming to stay with me, and I only have two bedrooms," she said brusquely.

Ellen could see that she didn't approve of her, but she was so grateful, and she was desperate to keep Grace safe. "Thank you so much. I promise we will move on tomorrow."

"When did you last eat?" asked Betty. The girl looked so pale and tired that her conscience wouldn't allow her to ignore the distress she was in.

"Not since lunchtime. I had a sandwich before I left the hospital."

"Right, well I have some home-made chicken soup and some soft rolls. This little one is asleep. We can make up a temporary bed for her with cushions on the sofa, and you can come out in the kitchen and eat," said Betty firmly. "After that, I will keep an eye on her whilst you have a hot bath, so you are clean when you go from here."

"You are so kind, thank you. I have a nightdress in my holdall, and a change of clothes for tomorrow, but I have no more nappies. I had bought some before I went into hospital, but they were in the bungalow."

"Well you have to forget about them. The bungalow was emptied recently and everything is gone. If you have nappy safety pins, I can cut up a towel to use until you get to a shop tomorrow."

Ellen was grateful for the chicken soup. It was thick and nourishing with lumps of chicken and vegetables. As it slipped down her throat, she could feel the pleasant warmth enveloping her, and at the same time weariness was creeping over her. She could hear Betty running a bath. When she had finished eating, she got up from the table and took her bowl and spoon to the sink. There was some soapy water in the bowl, so she washed them up and put them on the draining board. Being with Betty felt a bit like being at home with her mother, so she was happy to obey her orders.

Betty had a spare single bed in the other bedroom, which was already made up. She realised that Ellen had lost any baby equipment that she may have accumulated whilst at the bungalow, so she improvised by taking the bottom drawer out of a large oak chest, padding it out with towels and a blanket, and making it as comfortable as she could for Grace.

Ellen was feeling much better after a bath, so she sat on the sofa next to Grace and watched television with Betty. She was watching a comedy programme, but the humour went over her head, as she was just beginning to realise it was the depths of winter and she was an unmarried and homeless mother, and she only had a reprieve until tomorrow.

Betty always went to bed after the news at about ten thirty, so she left Ellen to give Grace her last feed, realising that such a young baby would probably wake in the night to be fed. The girl looked absolutely shattered, but tomorrow she was going to suggest she went back home. She had obviously either run away or been cast out, but once her mother saw the baby, might she not soften? She didn't strike Betty as being a promiscuous girl, just a silly one who had let herself down.

As she lay in her bed, she wrestled with her conscience. She had no room for this girl to stay, and having a young baby in the house would turn her life upside down, but her conscience argued back, reminding her that it was a very cold November, and neither of them would survive out there without a home. Before she went to sleep she promised herself that tomorrow she would get involved; she would urge Ellen to go back home, and if it helped, she would herself speak to Ellen's mother, and persuade her to forgive her

58

daughter, and let her come back home. She wasn't the first young girl to get herself into trouble, and she wouldn't be the last.

Whatever had happened to cause Edna to move out and leave Ellen at a time when she needed her most must have been something really important, but she could not understand how anyone could leave a young girl in such a situation; especially to arrive from hospital with a new baby, and then find out the house was empty and the locks had been changed. She felt annoyed with Edna. That really was a shabby thing to do to Ellen, to go off without a word of explanation. With her mind now made up, she turned over, pulling the blanket up to her chin, and fell into a troubled sleep.

Inside the other bedroom, after feeding Grace, Ellen fell into an exhausted sleep. She was woken up again at three in the morning, and she sat up sleepily, lifting Grace out of the makeshift bed, and then nursing her. Her daughter fed eagerly, seemingly unaware of all the drama surrounding her. It was now almost four o'clock, and still dark, but Ellen was unable to go back to sleep. Fear about her future, and how she could safely care for Grace, dominated her senses, so in the end she got up and dressed, and packed her holdall.

By the time it was six o'clock, she lifted Grace again, and fed her, using the small towel Betty had given her as a makeshift nappy. Betty had laid the table for her breakfast, with cornflakes and bread for toast, so after eating and making herself a cup of tea, Ellen prepared to leave.

It was now past seven o'clock and beginning to get light. She found a ten shilling note in her purse, and left it on the table with a note thanking Betty so much for helping her out at such a difficult time. She then tucked Grace into a warm shawl, and with one arm protectively holding her close, and the other one carrying her holdall, she quietly closed the front door behind herself and set off towards the main road that led into the town of Herne Bay.

Betty was dreaming that she was walking down a road, but she never seemed to get to the end of it. Somehow her legs seemed to

59

have a mind of their own, and they kept trying to take her a different way. But she didn't want to go the other way, and she was angry that her legs seemed to have a will of their own. Then she woke up suddenly, and moved her legs. She tried to get out of bed, and was so relieved to find her legs were fine, it was just a silly dream. It was daylight now, just about, but another grey and sombre day, and when she glanced at her bedside clock, she was amazed to find it was gone eight o'clock. She was usually up about seven every day, but she had overslept.

Yesterday evening had been a bit hectic, and even though she had told herself she wasn't going to get emotionally involved, she could not get the image of that young vulnerable girl, with her tiny baby wrapped in a shawl, out of her mind. She had decided to have a chat with her, and even telephone her mother and see if she could help. The best place for Ellen and her baby was the safety of home.

She got herself dressed. It was quiet everywhere, so maybe they were both still asleep. She walked quietly past the other bedroom and into the kitchen. She could see right away that Ellen had eaten, and washed up her plate and bowl after herself. Then she spotted the note next to the kettle and the ten shilling note. She unfolded the paper, and with a heavy heart she realised it was too late. Ellen had gone out into the cold with her baby, and all she could hope now was that she had the sense to go back to the safety of her home.

Chapter Ten

"No, we are fully booked, and we don't take young babies!"

The middle-aged woman glared fiercely at Ellen. She had a big house which was let out as bedsitter apartments. But no way was she going to let a room out to an unmarried mother! She didn't care if it was November and extremely cold. The silly young girl should have kept her legs together in the first place. It wasn't up to her to provide her with a home, and she had to think about her other tenants, they wouldn't want to be woken up in the night by a crying baby. She pointed up at the notice on the wall. "See, it says no children under 12 years old."

Ellen turned wearily away. She was exhausted and reality had hit her; she had absolutely nothing to offer Grace, and no money left. It was slowly dawning on her that she was going to have to give up her darling daughter, because keeping her out in this cold weather might kill her. She had visited virtually every shop that was open in the town to see if she could get a job, but the shopkeepers had explained to her that most of their trade came in the summer, they didn't need anyone right now, and on some days it was a waste of time even opening the doors.

Then she had tried all the bedsitters advertised in the newsagents' windows, but nobody wanted to know. She went into the local library for a while. It was a bit warmer in there, but then she was getting curious glances from the staff because she wasn't looking at the books, so she had come out and sat in a cafe in the high street, trying to make a cup of tea last forever, as she was running out of money.

The only place she could feed Grace was in the public toilets, which were neither warm nor comfortable. She had spent the last of her money in a little shop that sold hand-knitted baby clothes. Grace was now dressed in a pink outfit with a warm hooded jacket, as well as leggings, bootees and mittens to match. She had also managed to pick up some terry towelling napkins, but she realised she could no longer roam around the neighbourhood like this.

She tried to contain the tears, because in that teashop, she made an agonising decision; she was going to have to give her beautiful baby up for adoption. If Grace had been born in the summer, she may have stood more chance, as the shops and cafes had so many visitors in the summer and the weather was warm, but her one fear was this extreme cold might cause her baby to die. It was the last thing she wanted to do. She had fought everyone in a bid to keep her little girl, but she felt she was being selfish, and had to put the needs of Grace before her own. No matter how much she wanted to keep her, she had to do what was best for Grace.

She had just enough money to get on a bus to the hospital at Margate, so she stood at the stop waiting for it, doing her best to keep the wind off Grace's tiny face. Her baby was so good. She rarely cried, and already she had formed such a bond, which soon was going to be cruelly ripped apart. No more breastfeeding, no more cuddling her tiny daughter. She could feel the tears unashamedly streaming down her face.

When the bus arrived, she got on, and the conductor took her money and gave her a ticket. She wished they could stay on the bus forever, together, but she knew that soon she would have to say goodbye to her beautiful daughter, who she felt was the one good thing she had in her life; her last link with Jeremy. And once again she sat in the seat at the rear of the bus, desperately trying to hold back her tears.

The bus stopped outside the hospital, and she got down, cradling her daughter, and the conductor, showing a rare moment of kindness, picked up her holdall and handed it to her.

"There you are love, don't stay out in the cold too long," he said kindly.

Ellen thanked him, and did her best to compose herself. She couldn't walk into maternity drowning in tears. She stopped off in the ladies toilet, washing her hands, and then carrying her precious bundle into the maternity department, which she had left only twenty-four hours previously; but it felt like a lifetime. As she entered the ward, Grace was stirring. It was time for a feed, and Sarah, who was on duty, came up to her, her face showing concern.

"What's wrong, Ellen? Is Grace OK?"

"Grace is fine. Right now I need to feed her, and after that I need to speak to someone about having her adopted."

After she had spoken those words, which made it real to her, because previously her heart had been in constant denial, Ellen crumpled onto a chair. Her sobs were loud, as she was completely unable to control them, and without even thinking about it, a bewildered Sarah wrapped her arms around Ellen's trembling body in an effort to comfort her.

The matron had seen the distressing scene unfolding, so she came over and led Ellen into a side room. "Here you are dear, feed your baby in here. It's more private," she said gently.

"Thank you," whispered Ellen huskily, and she sat down and prepared to feed her daughter for the last time. Sarah hovered uncertainly until the matron called her outside.

"What is all this about, Sarah?" asked Sonia the matron, who was a plump lady in her forties with a kind face and a friendly manner.

Sarah explained how Ellen had been desperate to keep her baby, lived in Herne Bay, and had the support of her friends when she left hospital the day before. "I have no idea what has happened since," she said.

"Well, when she has finished feeding the little one, maybe we will know more. In the meantime, make sure she gets a hot cup of tea. It's cold outside, and it will also help her with her milk flow," said Sonia.

Sarah went to get the drink. She much preferred Sonia to Janet; she had a much kinder attitude. When she brought the tea to Ellen, she put it on a table next to her.

"Matron thought you might like a cup of tea, it's so cold outside."

Ellen's head was bent towards her baby, and the little mite had her fingers outside the shawl she was wrapped in. Her tiny finger was clasping her mother's as if to make sure nothing would part them, which gave Sarah a rush of emotion.

"Thank you, that is kind," said Ellen, and then she held Grace upright, gently patting her back to get her wind up.

Sonia tapped gently on the door. "Can I come in?"

Sarah opened it quietly, and Ellen looked over. "Please come in. I need to explain why I am here." She gently passed Grace to Sarah, who continued to pat her back, and Sonia sat down in a chair next to her. Ellen then proceeded to explain how she had gone back to the bungalow only to find her friend had moved out. And as she was now homeless, and had been unable to find anywhere that she could take her baby to, she had returned to the hospital because she realised that she had no choice but to have Grace adopted.

"It's so cold out there. I cannot walk around the streets with her. She will be warm and safe here," she said through her tears, trying not to look at Grace. She felt like somebody was plunging a dagger deep into her heart. Her beautiful baby; nobody could possibly understand the heartbreak she was suffering right now!

Sonia felt tremendous empathy for this poor young woman. It was a situation she had seen so many times. Young mothers who were single really had no choice other than adoption. Society did not accept them, and it just wasn't possible for them to keep their baby and make a life for themselves, unless, of course, there was any support from parents.

"Do your parents know you have given birth? Can we help in any way?"

Ellen looked at her in horror. "No, my father would never have me back home, and he would punish my mother and blame her. You must not contact them!"

"OK," sighed Sonia. "Well you can certainly leave her with us. She will be safe and warm, of course, but we have to wean her onto a bottle. When you have finished your tea I will have to ask you to fill quite a few forms in. There is quite a process involved in placing your child up for adoption."

"Let's get it done then, as quickly as possible," said Ellen, mustering every bit of strength she could into her voice.

Sarah turned towards her, intending to hand Grace back, but Ellen turned away quickly. She could feel waves of nausea inside her stomach. She rushed towards the toilet, but was unable to stop herself from vomiting before she slumped to the ground and fainted.

After three days in hospital, the doctor had said Ellen was now fit to leave. Because it had been so soon after giving birth that she had been wandering around outside in the freezing weather, she had been found to be suffering from exhaustion. Following rest and regular meals, she was feeling much stronger. Grace had been taken to the nursery, and weaned onto a bottle, although at first she had refused to take it. Nobody had told Ellen about that. She had not asked to see her daughter, and the abruptness of the separation had only added to her depression.

Sonia had done her best to help this young woman, and a place had been booked for her at a local hostel until such time as she was able to get back on her feet. If Sonia had been able to keep her in for longer she would have done, but there was now an epidemic of flu, and beds were needed for elderly and vulnerable patients.

Sarah came to say goodbye to Ellen, who was now dressed and ready to go. All the self control that Ellen had done her best to maintain was crumbling, and she knew she had to see Grace for one last time. "I need to say goodbye to Grace," she said, and her eyes implored Sarah to understand.

"Well I hope it doesn't upset you. She is going to be adopted now, you have signed all the papers."

"I won't change my mind. I have nothing to offer her. But just one more time," she pleaded.

"Come on then." Sarah knew that Sonia was at lunch, and hopefully would not find out.

When they entered the nursery, Ellen moved over to the crib where Grace was laying. She was awake, kicking her arms and legs, and her deep blue eyes appeared to focus briefly on her mother. Ellen scooped her into her arms, and automatically Grace's tiny hand clutched at her mother's little finger, which stirred Ellen's emotions, as she was convinced her baby was telling her they must not part. She held back the tears, because she knew if anyone heard her crying, Sarah would be in trouble. She gave Grace one last kiss on her soft little cheek, and even though she had not fed her for three days, she could feel her breast hardening as the milk was coming in. Her body was not accepting this parting from the baby who had thrived on her milk ever since she had been born.

Ellen could not prolong this pain any longer. She put Grace back into the crib, and then turned and left the room without another word. After thanking Sarah, and hugging her friend, she picked up her holdall to go. "Don't worry about me, I will be fine," she said bravely.

"You do know where the hostel is?" asked Sarah anxiously.

"Yes, of course, and I will write to you."

Ellen was aware of Sarah watching her as she left the ward and went out into the corridor. With her head held high she walked down the corridor until she got to the toilets at the other end. Glancing back she was now satisfied that she could not be seen. Just one woman was in there washing her hands, so Ellen walked into a cubicle, and then allowed herself the luxury of weeping her heart out behind the closed door. When she finally stopped crying, she left the cubicle and washed her face with cold water. It was done, and she could not go back on it. She knew her heart was broken. She had lost Jeremy, and now their beautiful daughter, and no matter what happened, life could never be the same again.

Chapter Eleven

Six Months Later

Tom had been up to London so many times in an effort to find Ellen. He had showed the photo of her to so many people, but it seemed that nobody had seen her. Usually London was the place young people headed for, believing that was where they could get a good job, and earn money, but Ellen's situation was different, and this is what worried him and his mother. How could she work with a baby to care for? How could she even find somewhere to live, because unmarried mothers were not welcome anywhere?

As she had not disclosed the name of the baby's father, their only hope was that she had reunited with him, but his mother had said he was with someone else. How many times had they both wished she had not left that fateful day. She had no idea that her father had died. Now, without Ellen, it really put everything into perspective. Becoming an unmarried mother was not as devastating to a family as being harmed or even killed because she was a runaway teenager. His mother had actually said that she really didn't care what the neighbours said about Ellen. If she came home, she would have family support to bring up her baby. They both knew Ellen was not a bad person, and they felt she had been led astray by her boyfriend. If only she would come home, then everything would be all right.

They had sat and discussed all the places that Ellen had liked visiting in the past. As a family there hadn't been too many outings, but one year Norman had gone away for a week fishing. He liked being on his own, he said, and Vera had taken Ellen and Tom on the train with her and spent a week in Margate. Ellen had loved going on the beach. There were donkey rides, and lots of sand, and she had swum in the sea with Tom. He could still remember her laughing when he splashed her. They had gone to Dreamland and enjoyed all the rides, and then ate fish and chips wrapped in newspaper. Vera had booked a caravan. It was on a site at Reculver, where there was an old fortress named Reculver Towers, overlooking the North sea. The views along the coast had been spectacular. They had been able to hire bicycles and ride along the promenade to Birchington and Margate. In the other direction they cycled along to Herne Bay, stopping off to admire the bandstand, which dated back to the last century, and to enjoy a walk on the pier dating from 1899, which was famed for being the second longest in the United Kingdom, with Southend being the longest. Then they had cycled on to Whitstable, famed for its oysters and artists, and enjoyed walking round the local boutiques. The sun had shone, and it was the best holiday they had ever had. Was there a chance that Ellen had gone back there to try and recapture some of the happiness she had enjoyed that week?

"I think it's worth going on a trip to the Kent coast, Mother. Ellen loved it there."

"Yes, she did," mused Vera. "We went down there on the train. What a lovely week that was."

"Well this time we will go in my car. It will be easier. We can start at Whitstable with her photo, and then move along the coast until we reach Margate."

"Thank you, Tom. You are such a good son to me," Vera said gratefully.

Tom smiled at her. The unspoken words between them didn't need to be said, they both knew that this closeness was because Norman was no longer around to rule the roost. Vera had a loyalty towards his father, and she didn't believe in speaking ill of the dead. If they could find Ellen and her baby, they could bring her home where she would be safe.

"How about tomorrow then? We can book a couple of rooms at a bed and breakfast and stay a couple of nights."

"Oh, Tom. That is using your holiday up," said Vera anxiously.

"I don't mind, Mother. Police training college is hard work. A few days at the sea in the sunshine sounds a really good idea."

So the next morning they set off. Elizabeth was also with them, and Vera let her mother sit in the front next to Tom, as she would be more comfortable. His car was a Morris Minor, and a few years old, but it was his pride and joy because he had saved up his wages to buy it soon after he had passed his test. It might look like an old banger to other people, with maybe a bit of rust on it, but for Tom it had been his passport to freedom. No more relying on buses and trains, or hoping for lifts from other people. It was his set of wheels, and he intended to put them to good use.

The journey took over two and a half hours, mainly because they had to drive through Sittingbourne which was an extremely busy town. The first stop was Whitstable, and Tom tactfully suggested that maybe they would like a little walk around the shops, and he would go and make some enquiries, then after that they could meet in a tea shop. His grandmother walked slowly now, and his mother enjoyed window shopping, so he could sprint off up the road and see what he could find out.

He parked the car halfway down the high street, and then popped inside a few shops with the photograph, but people were shaking their heads. Nobody seemed to know anything about her. Then he went round to Whitstable Station. It was by now late afternoon, and there was a man standing just outside selling newspapers. He went up to him and showed him the photo.

"Have you ever seen this girl? It's very important."

The photo showed Ellen laughing. It had been taken about two years previously. Her golden hair gleamed in the sunshine. He had taken it himself in the garden, one day when Norman was not there.

"No, but I would like to," quipped the man, but seeing Tom was serious, he added: "Sorry guv. A pretty one like that, I would remember. How long has she been missing, she looks very young?"

"She's been away from home since last year. She would only be nineteen now." Tom couldn't bear to mention the word missing, because presumed dead sometimes followed it. "She is my young sister."

"My mate Andy sells newspapers at Herne Bay Station, and nothing escapes his notice. She could be somewhere there, you know."

"Thank you, I will check it out," said Tom politely. Then he got in his car and drove back to the high street. He found his mother and grandmother in the tea shop, and they were just ordering tea.

"We have to be quick as they want to close soon," said Vera. "Did you have any luck?"

"Not really, but we have to move on to Herne Bay tomorrow, and find somewhere to stay tonight."

The waitress arrived with a tray of tea and cakes, and after they had eaten, Tom went up to the counter to pay the bill. Apart from them, the tea shop was empty.

"Is there a bed and breakfast near here where we could stay?" he asked the waitress, who seemed quite a friendly girl.

"Well, as it's not summer season yet, you should get in at this one," she said, handing him a card from the counter. "We get asked all the time."

He picked up the card and thanked her. 'Haven House', it sounded nice. It was in a side street not far from the high street. He could telephone them, but as it was only a little way away, they could drive round there.

"Let's go," he said, and Vera and Elizabeth followed him out, and got in the car.

When they pulled up outside the house, he noted the board with the name on it. He jumped out of the car to go and check that they had two rooms available.

"Come on Mother and Gran," he said genially when he returned to the car. "You two have the bigger room, and I am next door. The bathroom is opposite your room if you want to have a wash before dinner."

"Do they do an evening meal here?" asked Elizabeth. "I can only eat small portions now."

Tom hid a smile. It was a well known fact that Elizabeth was enjoying being a senior by eating small amounts of anything savoury, and then filling up on the sweetest desserts she could find. She had reached an age where she could behave like a child, without being disciplined, and she loved it. She had never suffered with a weight problem, so didn't feel the need to curb her habits.

"Yes, they are going to do us a meal. I think the lady said it was beef casserole, so you can have it as little or large as you want."

"What about dessert?" asked Elizabeth boldly.

"Jelly and blancmange," he said, winking at Vera.

"That is all right then," said Elizabeth, following after them.

Tom's bedroom was quite small, but he was not bothered, just as long as his mother and gran were comfortable. The main thought in his mind was tomorrow, and going on to Herne Bay. Would Ellen be there?

The young woman huddling inside the shelter with a dirty grey blanket barely covering her, stirred as day was breaking. She had once been very pretty, but her face looked emaciated, and she was painfully thin. It was no surprise for early morning joggers and dog walkers to see her there. She had been living in the shelter for a few months now. Various people had tried to help her, but she didn't appear to want to speak; she made pushing movements with her hands, making it clear that she didn't want to communicate with anyone.

The local policeman had even come round, but she wasn't harming anyone. During the day she left the shelter, and wandered along the cliff top path, keeping herself to herself, but with such a vacant look in her eyes. Rob Gilbert felt very sorry for her, and it appeared others did too, as little packets of biscuits, crisps and other items were left in the shelter during the day, and nobody attempted to steal them. But Rob couldn't help wondering how long could this fragile looking young woman, with matted hair, and such a strange look in her eyes, survive like this. He knew that in May it wasn't too bad, but what would happen to her when the winter weather came? He couldn't help wondering if she had any family anywhere, and he had tried to get through to her, but she seemed locked away in another world. Some people just chose to live like this, but some were victims of circumstances. Being a husband and father of a teenage daughter probably made him more sensitive to the situation, but she wasn't breaking any rules and nobody had complained about her. Nevertheless, he found himself regularly checking to make sure she was OK.

The thought of his teenage daughter ending up like that was so repulsive to him. That girl was somebody's daughter, and if only she would let him in and speak to him, then maybe he could help, but so far she had resisted any form of communication.

Tom was up early next day and having his breakfast when Vera and Elizabeth came into the breakfast room. It was a beautiful sunny May day, and the birds could be heard singing outside in the garden. Tom had opted for a cooked breakfast to set him up for the day, but Vera and Elizabeth were happy to have cereal and toast and a pot of tea.

After they had finished, Tom explained to their hostess just what the mission was, but she also had not heard anything about Ellen, so he guessed there was no point in staying another night in Whitstable. "Thank you so much for your hospitality and the lovely food," he said warmly.

"Yes, it was lovely, and I will settle the bill," said Vera, smiling at the hostess. "If you give me your card, we will recommend you."

After they had all made themselves comfortable in the car, Tom headed for Herne Bay Station. It was situated on the curve of the road, with grass verges and flowerbeds outside it. The forecourt to the station was very wide, so he drove up, and then spotted the newspaper man standing just outside the entrance. "You two don't need to get out. I will go and speak to him," he said, quickly jumping out of the car.

The man he approached he guessed to be about forty. He was stockily built, his hair was balding and he had a moustache. "Good morning, are you Andy?" he asked. "Yes, I will have a Daily Mail."

"Yes, I am Andy," grinned the man handing him a newspaper, and Tom put some money in his hand.

"I have been told you know everything that's going on in Herne Bay. So tell me, have you ever seen this girl?"

Andy grinned at the recognition, took the photo, and studied it.

Then he looked at Tom, noting how worried he looked. "Is she a friend of yours?"

"She's my kid sister, and we are desperate to find her. I have my mother and grandmother in the car with me."

Andy looked at him with empathy. He knew this young chap was in for a nasty shock.

"Well mate, yes I do know where she is, but she don't look like that any more. I guess your sister is pretty sick in her mind."

The colour drained from Tom's face. Whatever did he mean?

"She's living rough in a shelter down by the King's Hall. Won't let anyone near her or even talk to her. The local copper Rob Gilbert is very concerned about her, as we all are. She needs to be taken home."

He then proceeded to give Tom exact details about where he could find her, and although he was stunned at the news, relief flooded through him; at last he was getting somewhere. He thanked Andy, and ran back to the car, wondering how he could prepare Vera and Elizabeth for such news.

After jumping in the car, he started it, and without looking at either of them, he said tensely:

"We are going to the King's Hall. That newspaper man has just told me Ellen is living rough in a shelter down there. She isn't well, and we are going to have to tread very carefully. Also there was no mention of a baby."

He glanced in the mirror as he pulled out, and saw the look of horror on his mother's face, and he felt guilty at having to tell her such devastating news.

"No baby?" queried Elizabeth. "Did it die?"

Tom did not reply to this. He felt sick inside. He drove towards Herne Bay seafront, turning right as directed, and driving up Beacon Hill until he reached the back of the King's Hall. He spotted the shelter, but decided it would be better if he tackled this alone. Too many of them might make it worse. He parked and put the handbrake on.

Ellen lay in the shelter huddled in the blanket at the end of the seat. She had not gone for a walk this morning, as she had pains in her stomach, but she no longer cared about herself. She had such guilt inside her, which dominated her every thought, and such grief for the baby she had been forced to give up. She believed she was a bad person and deserved to die. She was not fit to be a mother, and death would be a welcome release from all the turbulence that raged away inside her head. She didn't deserve any kindness from anyone, nor help, they must all leave her alone to die. She was a sinner and not fit for this world.

Somebody was approaching her, so instinctively she drew her blanket up closer; but he took no notice, he spoke to her: "Ellen, it's me, Tom."

His face was familiar, so was his voice, and a memory stirred deep inside her. She could feel emotional pain which seemed to link to her past, but in her confusion all she could do was weep, and she had no idea why she was crying.

Tom was feeling desperate. This frail emaciated girl bore little resemblance to his beloved sister. But instinctively he knew it was Ellen, and he could see how sick she was. Whatever had happened to make her end up like this?

"Ellen, where is your baby?" he asked gently, fearing the worst. Maybe it had perished whilst she was living like this.

"I am not fit to be a mother!" she said weeping. He had asked the one thing that had struck a chord with her.

Tom acted swiftly. Picking her up like a little child, he held her closely to him. And although she felt confused, Ellen offered no resistance, his arms holding her felt comforting. He carried her carefully to the car, and Vera helped him to put her in the back next to her.

"Right, don't question her yet, Mother. Let's all go home," he said, very firmly.

Chapter Twelve

1968

"Eric Burdon and the Animals are appearing at the Orchid on 20th May, and Kathy wants me to go with her, but I am not sure that I can."

Vera glanced anxiously at Ellen, who sat twisting her fingers together in the kitchen. She knew exactly what Kathy was trying to do, what they all as a family had tried to do, and it had taken so long; to help Ellen get back to leading a normal life. And they were not there yet.

Ellen had been in hospital for several months, then finally she had been allowed to come home. Vera had been so sad to see how frail and gaunt she was, and when she finally started to eat again, and show signs of wanting to live, they had all breathed a sigh of relief. Losing baby Grace had broken her completely. Her breakdown had robbed them of the happy smiling girl she had once been, and in her place was a nervous twenty-five year old young woman, who did her best to avoid going out or having the sort of life she should have at her age.

Kathy had always been her best friend from childhood. She hadn't known about Ellen's pregnancy, but after she had come home, Kathy had been there, encouraging her, telling her she was beautiful, doing her hair, and helping her to choose new clothes.

Vera was so grateful to Kathy. Giving up Grace had been so damaging to Ellen, she doubted whether her daughter would ever truly recover from it.

Last year another step of progress had been made when Ellen got a job in Shirley Library. But that was because it was just up the road, and each afternoon she returned home at five o'clock, and made no effort to socialise with the staff there, even pretending to be unwell when they went out for a meal together at Christmas.

Some women would have been married at twenty-five, or at least had a steady boyfriend, but Ellen showed no interest, and she never went out and had fun.

In a way Vera and Ellen had changed places. At the age of forty-four Vera had started wearing make-up again, and coloured her grey hair with a blue rinse, which really suited her. This was because she had met Eddy, a man of fifty who had been widowed a couple of years earlier. Eddy was everything Norman had not been; kind, gentle, and he always treated her with such respect, and understood why Ellen was so fragile. She was happier with Eddy than she had ever thought possible, but she couldn't really think about remarrying because of her responsibility towards Ellen.

"Ellen, why ever not? Kathy has been such a great friend to you. If you won't do it for yourself, do it for her. She won't want to go on her own, and when you get there you might even enjoy it."

She wondered if she had gone too far. It was like walking on thin ice with Ellen; a step forward sometimes, and then two back. She had been told by the doctors not to pressure her, and to let her make her own decisions, but it was heartbreaking to see someone so young and pretty just going to work and coming home again, with no social life, and no friends other than Kathy.

Ellen untwisted her fingers, and looked up at her mother. She knew she had been stuck in a rut for a long time, but the day she had parted with Grace had felt like the end of her life, and she had not cared whether she lived any more. But lately she was realising that life did have to go on. Her family's love had helped a lot. Tom was now engaged to Linda, and doing well in the police force, and her mother seemed to have a new lease of life since she had met Eddy, who Ellen had found to be a kindly man, who had suffered his own heartbreak when his wife had died, but was now getting on with his life. She could feel a bit of the old Ellen returning, and she might need help with it, but she too wanted to get on with her life. Kathy was the truest friend anyone could have; she had never judged her. So now it was her turn to give something back.

"Mother, I will go with her. I have never been to the Orchid, but I hear it's very nice."

"It's a lovely place. Johnny Kid and the Pirates were on there once, a few years ago. I always liked them, but your dad thought I was mad. Apparently they have a revolving stage, and the musicians come round slowly, and the fans get so excited. It's a shame I couldn't go, as Johnny Kid was killed in a car crash in 1966."

"Yes, I remember that. He was only young. What a waste of all that talent," said Ellen.

Vera said nothing, but after losing Norman in the same way; one minute he was there, and then he had gone, it was a shock for any family. How many times had she wished that Ellen had waited one more day to leave, because, with Norman gone, they could have cared for baby Grace together.

The fact that society condemned young unmarried women, as well as the wrath her father would have shown, was what had caused Ellen to leave that day. But by trying to save her family from what was considered a disgrace, it had broken Ellen, and she had nearly died. All the pain she had suffered, and now it was too late. With Tom's help, Vera had gone back to the hospital to try and trace who had adopted Grace, but they had refused to give out any details, other than the fact that Grace had gone to a loving home.

"What are you going to wear?"

"I suppose I should get a new dress maybe?"

"Kathy will let you know what to wear. She has been before."

Ellen smiled at her mother, and Vera saw a glimmer of the carefree girl she used to be. Maybe all was not lost; time was a great healer.

Jeremy was enjoying being back visiting his parents. He had got his degree, and passed all his exams, and was now aged twenty-seven. He had been offered a job at Croydon General hospital, starting as a junior doctor, but he was ambitious and determined to rise to greater heights in the future.

His parents' home at Shirley Hills was plenty big enough for him to stay, as both of his brothers had now left home, but he planned to get a flat in Croydon, close to the hospital. He wanted to be independent, but in the meantime he could relax and enjoy some of his mother's home cooking.

He had decided to have a night out with Clive, an old schoolfriend. Clive liked a drink, but the police were getting pretty hot about drivers being over the limit, so he couldn't risk either of them being stopped. In his job it would look really bad, so rather than drinking all night, they decided to go to the Orchid, sharing a taxi both ways. He liked the idea of listening to some great music and having a laugh.

He dressed in a stone coloured suit with its own waistcoat, which looked great on his lean frame. He wore a chocolate coloured shirt, and shoes to match. He enjoyed dressing smartly, as he had aspirations to be more than a junior doctor, and wearing stylish suits gave him an added confidence. Clive, on the other hand, would be wearing jeans and a check shirt. He favoured the way Americans dressed; the casual look. But did it matter that they were opposites? Jeremy could never imagine himself wearing jeans, even if he was gardening, as he had to wear a suit to work, and then a white coat over it. Clive would probably rib him about his clothes, but it was only banter and he didn't mind.

The taxi had arrived, so he went out to get into it, and Clive grinned at him. "It's all casual tonight, man. You are dressed up like a dog's dinner. Who are you hoping to meet?"

Jeremy could feel himself reddening, but he was never going to admit it. It was eight years since he had last seen her, but he had never forgotten Ellen. Parting with her had been the biggest mistake of his life, because none of the women he had ever met since could hold a candle to her. That smile which lit up her face, her giggle, and the way her curls bounced when she moved her head. But maybe she was married now with children. She was so beautiful, she would never remain single. Someone would have snapped her up by now, he was sure.

He wished he had the courage to look her up. Perhaps to go and knock at the house, because her parents would know where she was. But he wasn't sure it was the right thing to do. He had hurt her badly when he dumped her, then he had gone away to university and tried to put her out of his mind. But for him the saying 'absence makes the heart grow fonder' had certainly been true. He was just hoping that, because everyone local seemed to be going, she might be at the Orchid tonight. But if not, there might be someone there who knew whether she was still single and living around in the area.

"Oh, you know me, got my own style," he quipped. "And you are more like Tommy Steele than Elvis, even though you are wearing the same gear."

"I know," sighed Clive, ruffling his fingers through his tight blond curls, and wishing he had the dark Latin looks and tanned skin that Jeremy had. "We are in for a great night."

Kathy and Ellen were sitting on the bus, which was not in a hurry as it trundled from Shirley into Croydon and then onto Purley. Ellen had decided it was time she learned to drive; it would be much more convenient if she was going to start going out. Kathy didn't drive, but Ellen felt she wanted to try. Her mother never had. If she could pass her test, and get a little run around like Tom had, it would be her first step towards independence. She didn't expect to live with her mother forever. Her wages from the library would not cover a mortgage, but in time maybe she could find herself a small flat. She was conscious of how much her mother had done for her during the last few years, but now Vera had Eddy, and Ellen didn't want to be the reason her mother would not remarry.

"We are there now. I've rung the bell," said Kathy excitedly, disturbing Ellen's reverie.

Ellen followed Kathy down the stairs, amazed to see the amount of people heading towards the doors of the Orchid, which were now open. It was almost like they were visiting royalty.

"Are you sure my dress is OK?" she asked shyly. Kathy had taken Ellen to C&A in Croydon and together they had settled on a turquoise blue dress. It really complemented her very blue eyes, and the nipped in waist and full skirt with a frilly petticoat was just right for a night at a dance hall. Kathy had also done Ellen's hair. It was a bit longer now, and the curls bounced as she walked.

"Are you kidding? Ellen, I don't think you realise how gorgeous you are. The fellas will all want to dance with you," declared Kathy, who was dressed in a full red skirt which was also gathered at the waist. Her gypsy style white blouse showed off her brown arms and neck, as Kathy tanned easily, being partly Spanish from her mother's side of the family. Her dark hair looked sleek, with a short urchin cut, as her elfin face and petite frame were similar to the actress Audrey Hepburn and she wore her hair in a similar style.

Ellen found herself blushing. She was only just getting her confidence back. It had taken some time to feel normal again, whatever normal was, and she was beginning to like her life again. She enjoyed working at the library. People who came in there were interested in books and reading, so she could help them find what they wanted. It was mostly women, and it was helping to build her confidence again. Coming out tonight was a big step for her; into a social situation where there would be people of both sexes. There had not been anyone since Jeremy, and she didn't want there to be. She knew she could not cope with all that emotional pain again.

"I don't want a boyfriend. I am not ready," she said solemnly.

"Neither do I. They are more trouble than they are worth, but we can have a chat and a laugh tonight. I want to see that smile back on your face," said Kathy firmly.

"Of course," said Ellen, making a supreme effort to smile, and it wasn't as hard as it had been before.

"Come on then," said Kathy, linking her arm through Ellen's, and they joined the queue of people who were all waiting to enter the ballroom.

Jeremy brought the two pints of lager over to the table where Clive was sitting. Eric Burdon and the Animals were performing 'The House of the Rising Sun'. It was a familiar sight, young men sitting at tables having a drink, the music pulsating, and young women all jiving together on the dance floor, pretending not to notice the boys, but hoping some would venture out to dance and break them up. Jeremy had scanned the dance floor, but the lighting was not bright in there, except on the stage, and he realised how unlikely it would be to see Ellen. Even if she was there somewhere, there were such a lot of young women. Meanwhile Clive had spotted a dark haired and very exotic looking girl, who reminded him of someone he had known at school. She was walking past their table with two glasses of wine in her hand. He turned towards her eagerly.

"Is it Kathy Laurence all grown up? You were in another year at my school a few years ago."

Kathy stopped right in her tracks. Of course she remembered Clive, and glancing over she saw him, which meant the other man must be Jeremy. They had always hung around together at school. She felt a stab of fear for Ellen. How would she ever be able to cope with seeing Jeremy again after everything that had happened?

"Hi Clive, nice to see you. Must take these drinks over; my friend is waiting. Have a good evening."

Jeremy was feeling a bit light-headed, and more courageous than before. Chances are if Kathy was here, so would Ellen be, and he had a burning desire to know whether Ellen was still single. Thoughts of her, the girl with a ready smile and sparkling eyes, who had captured his heart forever without him even realising it, had dominated his thoughts ever since he had come home to visit. He was full of Dutch courage right now.

"Is Ellen with you? How are you both? "

He stood right in front of her, and as it was crowded, and she didn't want to push him out of the way, she had no choice but to answer him.

"She is with me; but Jeremy, you don't understand, you can't just go barging up to her. She is very vulnerable, and seeing you might upset her."

He stared at her without comprehending her words. "Upset her? She is the love of my life. I could never upset her." He had not been able to control his words; they came straight from his heart, but Kathy was having none of it.

"You have a short memory, Jeremy. You dumped her, and broke her heart!"

He stared at her, scarcely able to believe what she was saying.

"But that was years ago. We were just teenagers. Has she never forgiven me?"

Kathy felt awkward. It was not up to her to give Ellen's secrets away, and here was Jeremy, slightly the worse for wear, getting all nostalgic. When he was sober tomorrow, he probably wouldn't have meant a word of it. Men really were the limit at times!

"If you care about her, you will leave her alone. All I can say is she is very vulnerable. I have to tread carefully."

Jeremy felt alarmed, but a sixth sense told him it wouldn't be a good idea to force himself onto Ellen. Kathy was clearly uncomfortable with seeing him, so at that moment he vowed to himself that he, too, would tread carefully.

"OK Kathy, you have your reasons, but just one more question: Is she still single?"

Kathy swallowed uncomfortably, but she could see sincerity shining from his eyes. Maybe he did love Ellen, and maybe Ellen needed him, but not tonight, it was too soon. He was certainly a catch for any woman; his lean Latin looks had always reminded her of Elvis Presley, and he was very smartly dressed. That suit was well cut and really looked good on him.

"She is still single, and now I must take this drink to her. If you really care you can always write to her, then she can decide if she wants to see you."

The crowd parted, and she took the opportunity to walk past him. Ellen had gone to the cloakroom, but might be back at their table by now. Being careful not to spill the drinks, she wove her way back towards the table. When she arrived Ellen was seated, but she was smiling and swaying to the music.

"Oh, Kathy, there you are. This music is great. I am really enjoying myself."

Kathy handed her the glass of wine. There was a sparkle in Ellen's eyes that had been missing for a long time. It gave her a glow of happiness to know that tonight Ellen was happy, but would telling her about Jeremy add to her happiness, or set her progress back again?

Chapter Thirteen

The next morning Vera asked Ellen, "Well, how did your night out go?"

"Yes Mum, it was lovely. We had a great time."

"I knew you would."

Vera refrained from asking her whether she had met a nice boy. She could always check with Kathy, but she knew she must not pressure Ellen. Each day there was a slight improvement, and she was so glad that Eddy understood that right now Ellen must come first. She knew now that she could have the sort of happiness with Eddy that she had not had with Norman, and she need never be afraid of him. The prospect of a life with him was very appealing. Maybe when Ellen was more stable, she could consider it, but right now they took it in turns to stay at each other's houses, as she never left Ellen for longer than a weekend.

Tom and Linda were planning to get married next year, and then they were going to get their own flat. Linda worked at an insurance company in Croydon, and Tom also worked there at Croydon Police station. So a flat in that area would obviously suit them, which pleased Vera, as it was only a short way from Shirley. Of course, having Tom at home had been a great support for her, and she would miss him, but if she could look forward to a life with Eddy in the not too distant future, that would be great.

"Right Mum, I am off to work now. Kathy wants me to meet her at the coffee bar in George Street after she finishes work at 5.30, if that's OK?"

"Of course it's OK. Will you be out for the evening?"

"I am not sure. She wants to chat apparently, but don't worry about cooking me anything. I might pop home at lunchtime and have something."

"OK dear," smiled Vera. "Cold chicken and salad in the fridge if you fancy it. Eddy's got a few days holiday, and we are off out into the country for a ride, and then a pub lunch I think."

"Enjoy Mum, and don't worry about me," smiled Ellen. She gave her mother a quick hug, and headed out of the door, her stiletto heels clicking on the concrete path.

Jeremy was at work. He was helping out in the casualty department, which meant he had a variety of different people of all ages to treat and make more comfortable. Some of them had been sitting in the waiting area for a long time, and could be quite short tempered, but he understood that. They were in pain, and anxious, and in between treating patients, he was also busy reassuring others that they would be seen soon. His calm manner allayed many of their fears, and after a visit from him there was a distinct air of optimism in the waiting room.

Before he knew it, lunchtime had arrived, so he went to the canteen to grab a sandwich and a coffee. He only planned to be away for about fifteen minutes, and he found, as soon as he left the working environment, thoughts of Ellen invaded his mind and refused to go away. On Saturday night she had actually been at the Orchid, but he had not got to see her. Yesterday he had sat down to try and write a letter to her, but he had no idea what to say. She was now a woman in her mid twenties, not the teenage girl he remembered. Would she have changed, and would she even bother to read it?

He thought going round to her house to try and look her up was not a good idea. Maybe she was single, but she might have a boyfriend, so her parents would not take kindly to a blast from the past turning up. Kathy had said she was vulnerable, but he could not believe it would have been because they broke up; it was years ago. So what else had happened in her life to make her that way? Why was she suffering emotionally? His doctor's head wanted him to help her, but maybe he was the last person she would want help from. He quickly gulped down his coffee and demolished the sandwich, but not before making a vow that when he got home tonight, he would put pen to paper in an effort to get Ellen back.

He rose from his chair. It was time he returned to the ward. He was going to make sure that the young girl who was sitting holding her arm, and clearly in pain, was seen immediately. Somebody needed to check whether she had broken anything and make her more comfortable.

Ellen crossed the road and headed towards the coffee bar. The jukebox was playing 'What becomes of the broken hearted?' by Jimmy Ruffin. The words struck a chord with her, but she brushed the thought aside when she saw Kathy waving cheerily from a table near to the jukebox.

The coffee machine was in full flow, and a pleasant aroma of coffee was circulating in the air.

"You sit down, and I will go up and order our coffee. Do you want anything to eat?" said Kathy, hospitably.

"No, I am fine, but I am intrigued. What did you want to talk to me about?"

Kathy smiled gently at her, and then went to order the coffee. When she returned, Ellen looked expectantly at her, and Kathy had no wish to delay it any more; it was time to enlighten Ellen. She took a sip of her coffee, and then leaned over the table, brushing her hand against Ellen's shoulder.

"When we were at the Orchid on Saturday, if you remember, I went to get us both a glass of wine."

"Yes, whilst I was in the ladies."

"I bumped into Clive, you remember him? He was a year or so above us. . ."

". . .Jeremy's best friend!" said Ellen, and immediately a very sad look came into her eyes.

Kathy plunged on; she really had no other choice now. "Yes, and then Jeremy came over to me. He was a little bit merry, and very nostalgic. He reckoned he still loves you, and realises he should never have broken up with you."

Seven years ago they were exactly the words she would have wanted to hear, but after all the emotional pain she had suffered, Ellen couldn't cope with it. She had lost Jeremy and beautiful Grace, who would be seven years old now and at school. Too much had happened, and she found her eyes filling with tears as the memories came flooding back to her.

Kathy saw the tears, and wondered if she had gone too far. But warning Ellen that Jeremy was around, and planning to write to her, was surely the best thing to do so that it would not be a total shock.

"I am sorry to bring it all up, but it's only fair you should know. He was even talking about looking you up, but I told him if he has to make contact, it would be best if he wrote to you."

Ellen wiped her eyes. She was determined to cope with the situation. Jeremy was not going to wreck her life again. Her voice became firm. "I certainly do not want him coming round. You, Kathy, are the only person who knows he is Grace's father. I never told my family, and they never mention it now, and as for him trying to make up for the past and getting back together, it might not work out, and there is no way I could go through all that pain again."

"I agree. It's a huge risk because you are both older now, and you might not even be attracted to him any more."

Fat chance of that, thought Ellen. Those feelings would never go, and because of those feelings, and the hurt he had caused, it had left her unable even to try to get to know anyone of the opposite sex. They may have only been teenagers, but he was also Grace's father. They had made a baby together, and her feelings of guilt for giving up her baby had continued to haunt her and define her life ever since the day she had done it.

"So what happened to Simone then?" she said bitterly, and Kathy could see she was hurting.

"Not even mentioned. So I assume it didn't last long."

Ellen didn't want to think about him, but her heart was not listening. She remembered the gentleness of his touch, the joy of being his girlfriend, the laughs they had shared together, and all the things that had made him so special to her. Oh, how she wished she could turn the clock back and be the carefree seventeen year old girl she had been, who was always laughing and enjoying life, and trusted everyone, including him.

But her head was reminding her that he had dumped her for someone else, and even though he claimed that he had never stopped thinking about her, he had not made contact with her for over eight years. How could she possibly trust someone as unreliable as that?

"No, he is history, and it will never work," she said very abruptly.

Kathy was relieved to have told her, but she was not convinced with the last sentence. It was clear that Ellen was still very much in love with Jeremy.

Jeremy had retired to his room early, and was absolutely determined to write the letter to Ellen. The only problem with staying with his parents was there was no privacy, so he had feigned being extra tired tonight, saying he would have a bath and an early night in order to be fit for work tomorrow. Soon he was going to start looking for a flat in Croydon, hopefully fairly near to the hospital, but at this moment all he could think about was writing to Ellen. He was going to try and keep the letter light, so as not to put fears into her head about meeting him. He sat thoughtfully, chewing the end of a pencil, eventually picking up a notepad to write a rough draft.

Dear Ellen,

I met Kathy at the Orchid last Saturday. I expect she may have told you. I have had many years to reflect on the unfeeling way I ended our relationship, and I am deeply sorry. I wouldn't blame you if you never wanted to see me again, but I am hoping I can take you for a drink and apologise properly, as I am no longer that pathetic school boy with no manners.

Looking forward to hearing from you.

Jeremy x

87

He then added his parents' telephone number and address, which she might still have from the past, but where she would not have known he still lived.

He wrote it out on some notepaper, trying to keep his handwriting legible, as he had been teased at work that he would make a great doctor because his handwriting could be difficult to read. Then he put it in an envelope, and sealed it. After adding a stamp, he knew he had to post it quickly or he might never do it, so he walked to the post box and deposited it. He had thought of maybe delivering it by hand, but then dismissed this idea as she might feel that he was invading her space. He returned to the house, and then ran himself a bath. All he could do now was see if she responded.

Chapter Fourteen

Ellen could not stop herself from checking the post daily. She told herself that it was because she wanted to leave the past behind, that she was now well over him and she would tell him so. But her heart argued back; she needed to see him, to see if he still had that magical effect on her, because she was certainly in love with a memory. Over seven years had passed now, and it was time to move on for both of them.

But when the envelope arrived with his familiar and slightly untidy handwriting, she felt her heart miss a beat. Was he about to confess his undying love for her? When she read the note, she almost felt disappointment sweep through her. He simply wanted to apologise for being a teenager. She had made up her mind she was going to be strong; she would meet him, and accept his apology. They were both different people now, and she doubted that he could have the devastating effect on her that he had in the past. Her head was doing a really good job at convincing her heart that this was true.

She penned a quick reply to him, saying she would meet him in the Shirley Poppy, a local pub, at seven o'clock on Thursday evening. If this was OK, he need not reply. She said nothing to her family, nor to Kathy, about the meeting.

After arriving home from the library on Thursday, she told Vera not to bother with any dinner, as she had used her luncheon vouchers in the local cafe earlier. She was not hungry because her heart was doing somersaults, but she was not going to allow him to get to her again.

"I am meeting an old school friend for a drink, Mum. I won't be late," she said smiling.

Vera was pleased to see Ellen going out; it was so rare. She had taken pains to look nice. That cream crimplene dress with the tie belt really suited her, and the stiletto heels. Her hair looked lovely; it was framing her face, the curls bouncing energetically. Could she possibly be going to meet a man? She decided not to ask.

"Have a lovely evening," said Vera.

She watched Ellen striding rapidly down the path. There was something different about her, and Vera couldn't quite put a finger on what it was. She didn't seem as vulnerable any more, and she was getting on with her life. Judging by the way she was acting, her life was becoming more bearable. Slowly they were getting there.

After all day wearing a familiar dark suit with a pale blue shirt and tie and a white coat over the top, Jeremy was pleased to get out of what he classed his 'work gear'. He took a shower, and then ate the meal his mother had prepared for him. Tonight it was a beef hotpot, and he sat down with his parents, expressing his enthusiasm when he had eaten it, which made his mother beam with pride. He would certainly miss all her spoiling when he got his flat, he thought ruefully.

"You look nice son, are you going out?"

Mary kept hoping that Jeremy would find himself a nice girl and settle down. A boy as handsome as Jeremy would surely be in great demand, but he only seemed to go out socialising with Clive. In the past he had brought a couple of girls home, but neither had lasted, and he didn't tell them much.

"I am going to meet an old school friend that I have not seen for years."

He was careful not to say 'her', as he knew his mother wanted to see her youngest son married like the other two. Mary nodded, seemingly satisfied with that, and he rose from the table, dusting imaginary specks from his light cotton trousers. He wore a blue shirt and tie and a navy blazer, which felt much more casual than his suit.

"Make sure you have your key. We may not be up."

"I won't be that late, mother. But yes, I have it."

Jeremy smiled as he jumped in his car; all the while he was living at home he realised that even though he was twenty-seven years old, he was the youngest son and his mother just couldn't help herself, she still thought he needed looking after. Being at home and having a fuss made of him was all right in small doses, but maybe he should make the most of it now, because once he got his own flat, it would stop.

He arrived at the Shirley Poppy at fifteen minutes before seven. He couldn't possibly be late for Ellen. Not only that, he wanted to have at least one drink inside him before he saw her. What a fool he had been breaking up with her, because in the years in between, young women had come and gone, but none of them had reached his heart in the way that Ellen had. It was true they had been childhood sweethearts, but that memory had stayed with him.

He took his pint of lager to a table, and started to drink it. It was quite warm on this summer evening and some people were sitting at tables outside, but he stayed inside, hoping that she would spot him as soon as she came in.

Ellen got off the bus at ten minutes to seven. She didn't go into pubs on her own very often, but she knew the landlord here as his wife frequented the library quite a lot, and they were both a jolly couple. As she entered the door, she saw him immediately, and everything else was forgotten. She could only feel admiration that the skinny gangly youth that she remembered had become this very handsome well dressed young man. Her heart flipped as he looked up at her and his eyes softened. It might be several years on, but what was she doing to herself? Those feelings were very much still there. However she was wary of not making a fool of herself; he simply wanted to apologise.

Jeremy's eyes took in everything about her, and what a beauty she had turned out to be! Her beautiful big blue eyes widened when she saw him. Her lustrous hair that she had tried so hard to straighten was flowing just above her shoulders, and it looked stunning. But there was something different about her; that ready smile and schoolgirlish giggle that had captured his heart was missing. She seemed to have become a more solemn person. He stood up, and took her hand.

"Thank you so much for coming, Ellen. What can I get you to drink?"

His touch felt like an electric shock to her; thank goodness he could not see how wildly her heart was beating. She smiled politely at him. "Thank you, Jeremy. A glass of white wine, not too dry, would be lovely."

He gestured for her to sit down, and then went up to the bar to get her drink. When he returned she was seated opposite him. Somehow the years between didn't seem to matter. He immediately felt comfortable in her company, and after she had enquired what he had been doing since she last saw him, he explained how he had worked hard, passed all his exams, and was now working at Croydon General Hospital.

For Ellen, as he spoke, she could feel that easiness they had always enjoyed in each other's company. Nothing had changed, and as she listened politely, she knew there was one thing that she could not keep from him. He had to know about Grace.

"How about you, Ellen? Has life treated you well since I last saw you?"

Ellen gulped, it was almost as if he knew there was something, and she was sure he might well be angry with her, but he needed to know that he was a father. She spoke falteringly, telling him everything, and when she got to the part when she had to part with Grace, she had to stop because she could feel the tears in her eyes and the pain in her heart. She had too much guilt to bear.

Jeremy sat listening to this revelation, and he became white with shock. It was such a harrowing story. He had come here to apologise to Ellen for dumping her, but it was even worse, she had been carrying his child, and she had to deal with it all on her own. He felt sick inside to know what she must have gone through. He held her trembling hand in an effort to comfort her.

"Ellen, I am so sorry. I wish you had told me you were pregnant."

"You were with Simone, and also just about to go to university; it would have ruined your life!"

"Simone lasted all of three weeks. She just wasn't you, and there are no excuses, I should have stood by you. But I admire you for trying to be independent!"

"Yes, and I failed!" He could hear the bitterness in her voice, and he realised why she had lost her smile. Having her baby adopted had changed her; she had never got over it, and he had gone on with his life, blissfully unaware of what a trauma she was going through.

"Ellen, I know you have probably lost all trust in me, but can we start again, and take things slowly? I know I can never make you heal from the pain and loss you have suffered, but I do love you with all my heart."

She had planned to be strong, and hold him at arm's length, but when she saw the tears in his eyes she knew he was sincere. Being with Jeremy would help her to heal. She needed him so much. She took out the only photo of Grace that she had, all dressed up in her pink outfit, and with trembling hands she passed it to him.

"This is Grace, but she would be about seven years old now."

"She is beautiful," he murmured. "Can you come and sit in my car; it's more private in there."

Ellen put her empty wine glass down, and with Jeremy holding her hand, she left the pub. Once inside the car, she could not stop the tears from falling, and he held her close, murmuring words of comfort, telling her he would always be there for her, and maybe one day they could go and find their daughter. After a while, she was able to compose herself, but she still stayed within the comfort of his arms. She spoke falteringly.

"I don't think we can ever find her. My brother tried to help, but it was like a closed book. We were told that since she had been adopted, it left me without any rights."

Jeremy lifted her tear-stained face up, and kissed her gently on her cheek.

"Ellen, you have every reason to hate me, but please let me spend the rest of my life trying to bring that smile back to your face. I love you, and I hope you will marry me."

Ellen smiled through her tears. She had so much guilt inside her, but with Jeremy beside her, sharing her pain, suddenly that huge burden on her shoulders had become lighter. She had accepted that her life could never be the same again, but with him by her side the pain would be easier. This man was her world, and it seemed they were meant to be together.

Chapter Fifteen

Grace 1971

"Mrs Hart, I am afraid that Grace is having one of her tantrums, and we don't know how to calm her down."

"I am so sorry. I will be there as soon as I can to pick her up."

Pearl Hart put the phone down and picked up her handbag. Outside on the drive was her little red Ford Fiesta, so she jumped into it and headed into Canterbury to the school. She knew the sort of scene that would greet her. Grace trembling and upset, sniggering children from her class, and an overwrought and flustered teacher who would be doing her best to hide her anger.

Right from the moment she had seen Grace, on a cold winter's day, dressed in a pink knitted outfit and just a few days old, the love that she felt for this little girl was akin to a mother who had given birth to the baby herself. After suffering three miscarriages, and with very little hope of being able to carry a baby full term, being able to adopt Grace had been like an answer to her prayer. Roger had understood how much it meant to her, and had always been supportive of all her decisions.

Pearl never having had a child had nothing to base her experiences with Grace upon, and no matter how hard the road ahead would prove to be, she loved her daughter with all of her heart. Right from the beginning, both Pearl and Roger thought she should know that she had been adopted. So they both made a point of telling her how special she was to them because they had chosen her to be their daughter.

Grace was now ten years old, and was blossoming into a beautiful girl. She had an abundance of dark hair when she was born, but as she grew it changed to more of a strawberry blonde colour, which was very striking. She wore it long, and it flowed around her shoulders in bouncy curls. Her hazel eyes were framed by beautiful thick and long lashes, and she was tall, which made her look older than her ten years.

Pearl had once been a nurse, so had developed a great deal of patience. As Grace grew from a baby to a little girl, she learned how to look after her. Grace had always been very bright. She had walked at an early age, she had an amazing memory, and was reading well before her fourth birthday. But apart from Jamie, who had always been there, because he lived next door and idolised the ground that Grace walked upon, Grace did not have many friends.

But this did not seem to bother her because she enjoyed her own company. She was always reading, or doing sums, and she really enjoyed learning at school. What she didn't like was being touched. She liked her own space, and although it had never been a problem at home, at school it was. Children jostling her in the playground could easily freak her out, or even a teacher trying to take her hand and lead her somewhere that she didn't want to go. Grace very much had a mind of her own, and that didn't go down well at school where pupils were all expected to conform to the rules.

This was not the first time that Pearl had been called to the school to free Grace from a difficult situation. Although it had been the intention of both Pearl and Roger to encourage Grace to have friends, even though there were many other girls in her class, it hadn't worked, so it seemed the only solution was a home tutor. They had tried to resist this in the past, because Grace was a loner. Jamie was her only friend, and that was because he made all the effort. To her Jamie was like a brother, he had always been a part of her life. Their mothers were friends, so the children had played together and spent a lot of time with each other, and to Grace that was normal.

As a baby, Grace was cuddled and cared for lovingly, but she was not a particularly demonstrative child. When Pearl did get a cuddle from Grace, it felt very special, and Roger too. At family get-togethers, Grace did not hug her uncles and aunts, because she didn't know them that well. It could be two years since the last time she had seen them. Pearl had tried to explain how shy she was because she didn't want them to think that Grace was rude. She had always hugged Jamie; it was normal, as she had done it since they were babies. And the whole world could see, even at the age of ten, that Jamie was absolutely besotted with her.

Pearl had arrived at the school now, so she drove through the gates, and parked in the visitor car park. She was glad she hadn't been at work today and had been able to come straight away. She had a part-time job as a doctor's receptionist, so her calm and patient disposition had stood her in good stead when coping with people who were feeling ill or stressed, and not in the best frame of mind.

She hadn't stopped to put any make-up on, but her hair looked tidy enough. She wore it short with a side fringe, and had recently had it permed. At forty years old, she had looked after herself, retaining her slim figure, and her chestnut brown coloured hair was sleek and shiny. Her skin had a healthy tan due to her walks along the Kent coast in the sunshine.

Brenda Williams was the headmistress of this school. An elderly lady nearing retirement age, with grey hair tightly drawn back from her face with kirby grips. She never wore make-up, or stockings, and her every day dress was a grey skirt and a white blouse with chunky black lace-up shoes.

Pearl and Roger were comfortably off, so a private school seemed to be the best option for developing Grace's talents. They had assumed because she liked learning, and had a quick mind and a good memory, she would do very well. But with Grace's apparent lack of social skills, and perceived unfriendliness to other pupils, all that had happened was she had developed disruptive behaviour. Of course, children being children, once the others had realised she didn't like being touched, it became a huge joke touching her to antagonise her.

As Pearl mounted the steps to the main reception area she saw

Miss Williams already standing there waiting for her, and she looked very annoyed. Her heart sank. They just didn't understand Grace here, not like she did, and she felt sad for her daughter; she was so misunderstood.

Grace was curled up in a ball with her head on her knees underneath the table. She had her hands over her ears to shut out the laughter from the other students in her class. She was in her own safe world.

She had always known from a small child that she was different from other girls. She didn't want to make friends or play with any of them. She didn't like being touched, and she knew they had deliberately done it to make her get angry, and she did get angry. All of a sudden she felt she could make no sense of the world around her, and she found herself screaming and covering her ears to shut them all out; and when she got under the table, she could not see them any more.

Her mother had told her she must learn to control her temper, that it wasn't acceptable behaviour, and she knew it was true, and for her mother she would try. She had vowed to try, but the teasing and sniggering, and then the deliberate touching, had wound her up again, and it felt like her whole world was falling apart.

Miss Williams had said that she was calling her mother, and she hoped that she would be taken home. Once there, in the familiar atmosphere, she would be all right. By now somebody had come along and taken the students to another classroom, so she cautiously peeped out from under the table to make sure they had all gone, and then, satisfied that the room was empty, she crawled out and sat on a chair. She could hear the sound of footsteps in the corridor, and judged by the sound of the stiletto heels clicking, that her mother was with Miss Williams.

Brenda Williams ushered Pearl into a side room. She was trying to remain composed, but there was always one who couldn't behave, and she simply had no time for disruptive students!

Pearl picked up on Brenda's manner immediately. She had not

97

even greeted her, and she sat in the chair opposite feeling very much like a naughty schoolgirl herself.

"This is the third time in three months we have had to call you in, Mrs Hart. I am afraid Grace is completely out of control."

"I am so sorry. She is no bother at home. She reads a lot, and is very willing to learn."

"We know that Grace is bright, but she makes no attempt to socialise with the other students. As for her temper; well we find her volatile."

"She doesn't like being touched."

"With all due respect, Mrs Hart, when you have a class of thirty or so children who work and play together all day, she is bound to be touched. None of them are going to hurt her."

"I know that, and I have explained to her that she must expect contact. It's inevitable."

Brenda nodded, and then stared directly at Pearl, who continued to feel very uncomfortable. She shuffled some papers on her desk, and then spoke again. "I know you told me that Grace is adopted. Presumably if you told me, you have also told her?"

Pearl wondered where this conversation was going. Her defensive instinct rose inside her.

"We have always told Grace she was adopted, and we explained that she is very special to us because we chose her to be our daughter."

Brenda's face took on a look of sympathy. "Well I think that is where the problem lies, Mrs Hart. Grace feels different because she is adopted. Not that any fault lies with you and your husband. I believe that this is why she is acting up."

Pearl looked at her in horror. It couldn't be true, surely. They had showered Grace with love right from the beginning. She had never asked anything about her mother; whether she was alive or dead. She had not appeared to be interested, and she had always called them mum and dad. She drew a trembling breath, and spoke rapidly.

"We have always loved Grace as our own child, so that does not make her different. At home we do not get these displays of anger, so regrettably I think we may have to have a private tutor for her. But, of course, I need to speak with my husband before we make a final decision."

This was music to Brenda's ears. It looked like Grace's parents were going to take her away from the school anyway. None of the teachers knew how to deal with her. She could not wait to lose such a difficult pupil. She injected a soothing note into her voice. "Of course, Mrs Hart. Right now you need to take Grace home, and when you have discussed it with your husband, we can move forwards. I, too, believe that Grace would thrive much more if she was tutored at home."

Pearl rose from her chair, still feeling emotionally wounded by the references made to Grace's adoption. "I want to collect my daughter now please," she said quietly but firmly.

"Of course, Grace is in the classroom." Brenda was beaming now, as she took Pearl to the classroom where Grace was sitting on a chair waiting, her head was bowed. She was waiting to be reprimanded, but Pearl did not rebuke her. Something in Miss Williams' manner didn't sit right with Pearl. It was clear the headmistress couldn't wait to see the back of Grace, and she was not wanted at this school.

"Come on, Grace, I am taking you home now. Thank you so much for calling me, Miss Williams," she said, and Grace rose from the chair and walked over to her mother.

"Goodbye," said Miss Williams, smiling. Grace did not reply, and Pearl muttered a polite response, and then ushered her daughter out of the room.

Chapter Sixteen

Jamie was waiting outside in the playground for Grace. He always travelled home from school on the bus with her. Now they were ten years old, her mother had agreed they could travel together as long as they were sensible. The only time she picked Grace up herself was if she had a dental appointment.

Grace had been a part of his life for as long as he could remember. To her he was a brother figure, but to him she was so much more than a sibling. He was the one person, apart from her parents, who understood Grace. Their families lived in houses next to each other, overlooking the bay at Hampton. Pearl and Roger had moved in with newly born Grace ten years ago, and Jamie had also just been born to Sybil and George, who had also just moved into the area, so it was no wonder the two families had become friends.

Jamie had memories of their first day at school. Grace had not wanted to go in and mix with children she didn't know, but when Jamie took her hand and walked in with her, all had been well. Now they both attended the private school in Canterbury, and were in the same class. Jamie was considered an oddity, because ten year old boys did not like ten year old girls usually, but he wore his heart on his sleeve where Grace was concerned, and was the butt of many jokes and sniggers; not that he cared.

He didn't understand why people did not get Grace. She was unique. Unlike some of the other girls who stood around in groups giggling and making spiteful remarks about others, Grace always spoke the truth, she was direct and honest, but never spiteful. She was not a chatty person, but he was, and his ability to make her laugh created a connection between them.

As the pupils streamed out, they pointed at Jamie waiting patiently and dissolved into laughter, until one of the girls spoke up: "Grace went off with her mother a while ago. She had a meltdown."

"So what did you load of bullies do to upset her then?" he said angrily.

"Oh, just touched her, that is all. She is weird!"

Jamie drew a deep breath. His first instinct was to slap that smile right off her nasty gloating face. But boys did not hit girls, that had always been instilled in him by his parents.

"She's worth one hundred of you!" he retorted angrily. Turning on his heel, he left to go and get his bus. Knowing that lot they had not accidentally touched her, they had goaded her until she snapped.

Such bullies, and the girls were every bit as bad as the boys.

When he reached home, his mother was sitting in the lounge overlooking Hampton Bay, drinking tea and chatting with Grace's mother Pearl. She greeted him with a smile.

"Did you have a good day, son?"

"Yes OK," he smiled.

"Jamie, I am sorry. I went to pick up Grace today, and of course you wouldn't have known, so must have waited for her."

"It's fine," he said lightly.

"If you want to go round and see her, she would be pleased to see you."

These were just the words he wanted to hear. His heart ached for her, and he wanted to cheer her up. "How about I ask her if she wants to go over to the swings?"

The play area could be seen from the house, and it was somewhere Grace really liked to go. Up until 1966 there had been a small boating lake, and as a small girl riding the boats with her dad Roger in charge, this had been one of her favourite things. In the beginning, when it had gone, Grace had been very disappointed. But afterwards, when the playground was empty, she had wandered over to acquaint herself with all the fun things to do there, and Jamie had enjoyed it with her too. Now it was a familiar fun zone for them both, and right now, because it was teatime, it was virtually empty.

Pearl took a fifty pence coin out of her purse. "Jamie, you are a godsend, and buy yourselves some ice cream too."

Jamie thanked her and sped off to get Grace.

"That boy is a credit to you," said Pearl, smiling. "He always makes her laugh."

"He's a good lad," said Sybil, warmly.

"Yes, he understands Grace. I wish her school did. The others tease her, and then she has a meltdown. I am going to talk to Roger about having her home tutored. Because she has always been a bit of a loner, I thought being with other children would help her with social skills, but it hasn't worked," Pearl said sadly.

Sybil's heart went out to her friend. Having known Grace since she was a baby, she knew how hard Pearl had worked to understand her daughter's complex character, and keep her home life harmonious. She was also aware of how much affection Jamie held for her. He might be her only friend, but he was incredibly loyal to her.

"Pearl, Grace is blooming into a beautiful girl, and she is bright and intelligent, which is probably why she gets teased. With an understanding tutor she will probably do very well, and we both know Jamie will always be there for her."

"Yes, but what really hurt me was the insinuation Miss Williams made that Grace is acting up because she feels different knowing she is adopted."

"What utter nonsense!" interjected Sybil. "Grace is being bullied, and the school are sweeping it under the carpet, and looking for another reason to blame Grace for her behaviour."

Pearl leaned forward, her eyes cloudy with apprehension. "With Grace being an only child, I don't have another daughter or son to compare her with. Tell me the truth, Sybil, you are my best friend. Does she stick out like a sore thumb as being different?"

Sybil felt uncomfortable. Having known Grace for all of her life she hadn't really thought about it. Grace to her was a shy girl, without many friends, but her intelligence and hard working nature had never been in doubt. Sometimes Grace did her homework with

Jamie, as he was not as dedicated to learning as she was, and Sybil was pleased to see him getting on with it, so she didn't have to keep on at him to do it herself. She had heard that sometimes Grace had meltdowns, but never actually experienced them, as she mostly saw her in the company of Jamie, who seemed to have a calming effect on her.

"Pearl, you are asking me, who only has one son who spends most of his life joking about, and your daughter Grace has been the inspiration behind him actually doing his homework! The only way I see Grace as being different is her lack of friends, and I would hope that is not because Jamie is monopolising her."

"Jamie has always taken her as she is. But the bullying just goes on, and so I think a home tutor would be the answer. Thank you for your honesty, dear Sybil," said Pearl warmly.

Sybil patted her friend's hand. "Come on, I will make some fresh tea. Let's have a few minutes to ourselves whilst they enjoy the playground," she said, pointing over to the green opposite where the figures of Jamie and Grace could be seen running into the playground.

Later that evening, when Grace was in bed, Pearl explained to Roger exactly what had gone on with Grace that day. Roger was a man in his early forties, and his hair was beginning to grey but was still thick and curly. He worked at a local engineering company in Herne Bay as a quality control manager, which gave them a comfortable income to live on. His kindly disposition and patience had not only helped him to climb up the ladder of success in the company, but also endeared him to anyone who worked with him.

As Pearl recounted the events to him, his face took on an expression of empathy. Grace had always been very dear to them both, but he realised that owing to him being at work a lot, it had been Pearl who had borne the brunt of many of the difficult situations that had presented themselves over the years. He had a close relationship with his daughter. Like Jamie, he had the ability to make her laugh. Maybe he had been guilty of spoiling her a little because she was so precious to them both, but she had never been demanding. She was not tactile, she chose the people she wanted to be affectionate towards, and as he could see she was growing into a real stunner that surely wasn't a problem, because he didn't want any Tom, Dick or Harry pawing his little princess!

"Well kids will always tease each other. I was like it when I was young, and if they know she isn't tactile, they will exploit it. Maybe we should go and have a word with this Miss Williams?"

"That was my first thought, but Grace won't thank us for doing it. She is very shy, we know, and doesn't find it easy to mix. We also know she is very bright, and wants to learn, so how about getting her a home tutor?"

Roger considered her words. Money was not a problem and they could afford a tutor, so it seemed a good idea. "Why not, my love, as long as Grace is OK with it."

"Well yes. I know she is only ten, but she is very mature, and I think we should let her sit in on the interviews, and then tell us which tutor she likes."

"Brilliant!" beamed Roger. "All we have to do now is see what she thinks about having a tutor in the first place."

Grace had enjoyed her trip to the swings with Jamie. He could always make her laugh, and after the events at school she needed that. He had explained how he had waited for her without realising she had already gone home, and although she would have usually said nothing, she found herself telling him how she had a meltdown because they all kept touching her and laughing at her.

"They made me feel as if I wanted to hit them; but that's wrong, then suddenly I had to let it all out. Am I a strange person, Jamie?"

"They are the strange ones, Grace. They are so jealous because you are cleverer than them, and much prettier."

"If I tell you something, Jamie, I don't want my parents to know." Her expression was very serious.

"Of course, I promise."

"Mum and Dad told me I was adopted. I have always known, but it has never worried me, because they are the only parents I have ever known, and they love me. . ."

". . .of course."

"The gang at school have found out. No idea how, because none of us would have told them, but they call me a freak, and say my real mother didn't want me."

She had her head bowed, and Jamie lifted her chin gently, and saw the tears in her eyes. It was so rare for Grace to display emotion, so he knew she must be really hurt. Without giving it a second thought he wrapped his arms comfortingly around her, and Grace did nothing to resist him.

"Grace, we both know it's not true, and now we have to be one step ahead of them. No, you can't hit them back, but you can stand up to them verbally. Don't allow them to walk over you. When you feel anger brewing, think to yourself that you won't let them win."

"That's what Mummy tells me, and I am going to try really hard. It's just sometimes I feel like my world is being ripped apart, and I cannot make sense of the world around me."

"I know," he said gently.

"Because of what they have said, I am wondering if it might be true. Do you know why my mother had me adopted?"

"Grace, I don't, but you need to tell your mother what you have told me. I am sure she will answer anything you need to know."

"Yes, I will ask her."

Jamie released her as the sound of the ice cream van playing its familiar tune could be heard.

"Your lovely mum has treated us to ice creams. So come on, I will race you to it!" he shouted, and they both ran off along the sea front.

Chapter Seventeen

"Mummy, I am sorry about my temper yesterday." Grace looked anxious, and Pearl moved to reassure her that everything was all right.

"I know we spoke about you having more control, but I also know how spiteful schoolchildren can be. I am not angry with you Grace."

"But I am angry with myself. Yes, they tease me and call me different, and then a red mist comes down on me. How can I cope with it? I do not want to be known as 'that girl with a temper she can't control'. I have to do something to stop it!"

Pearl looked at her set face. Poor little Grace, only ten years old with her whole life ahead of her, and yet determined to tackle her own faults head on. But maybe she didn't have to.

"Daddy and I had a chat last night, and thought maybe you would like to be tutored at home, then no one can tease and bully you any more, and you will find it much easier to learn."

Grace was aware how protective her parents were, and always had been, but what flashed through her mind was a feeling that she didn't want to be protected, she wanted to learn to fend for herself. And not only that, if she had a tutor, she couldn't travel to and from school on the bus with Jamie, and she really did enjoy that; they had a laugh together.

Suddenly, quite out of the blue, as was often the case with Grace, she changed the subject.

"Being adopted has never worried me, because I have only ever known you and Dad as my parents, and that is all that I want, but did you know my real mother, and why she had me adopted?"

Pearl was quite taken aback by this remark. Being adopted seemed to be a subject that Grace had no interest in previously, but of course, she was growing up now, and might be a bit curious about where she came from. It was only right that she should share the little bit she knew, but hopefully Grace would not have ideas about tracing her real mother, because it might unsettle her. She sat forward, taking Grace's hand gently.

"I never met your mother. She gave birth to you at a hospital in Margate. I was told she was desperate to keep you, but it was winter, and she was homeless and jobless, so had to take you back there because she thought you might die from the cold."

"What about my father?"

"Nobody knew who he was. Your mother had left home because she had a violent father, who might have done something to her or her mother if he found out she was pregnant. They said your mother was just eighteen when you were born."

Grace digested all this, and sat for a while without speaking. So she *had* been wanted, and her mother must have been so desperate. She had left her own parents maybe to protect her mother as well as herself. So it seemed like her mother had been an honourable person, who now had to live with the knowledge that someone else was bringing up her daughter.

"That is all I wanted to know, it's fine," she said abruptly, and Pearl felt a great feeling of relief sweeping through her.

"Now what do you think about a tutor?" asked Pearl, tentatively.

"I like going to school on the bus, and I don't want them to drive me away from school. I have to learn to deal with them!" she said briskly, and Pearl looked at her admiringly. She was a very mature ten year old.

"OK, let's compromise then. We still have half a term left. Let's see how we go for the rest of the summer."

"I have to get my bus now," said Grace, seeing Jamie waiting outside the front gate.

Pearl hugged her gently. "Yes, Jamie is waiting, have a lovely day."

She watched them walk down towards the bus stop together, and thought about what Sybil had said yesterday. Did Jamie monopolise Grace, preventing her from having other friends? But commonsense told her different. Grace just wasn't sociable, and the conversation that she had just had with her was probably the longest and most in depth one she'd ever had, as Grace had always been a thinker rather than a speaker. Jamie, with his carefree and nonchalant attitude to life, was the perfect person for her to be around. He made her laugh and brought her out of herself. Half the reason why Pearl and Roger had made the decision to put Grace in the private school at Canterbury was when they heard that Jamie was going there. All she could wish for now was that they could finish out this term without any more summonses from Miss Williams, and that Grace would be able to cope.

As they travelled together on the bus, Grace explained in a low whisper to Jamie, what Pearl had told her about her real mother.

"There you are; of course she wanted you! It's a very sad story, and whoever or wherever she is, you can't help feeling sorry for her," said Jamie.

"I know, but Mummy also said that the adoption agency didn't tell my real mother who had adopted me, so there won't ever be any birthday or Christmas cards; there never have been. The parents I have are my parents, even if I did not grow inside my mother's belly."

Jamie wasn't sure whether this bothered Grace or not. She was a very deep person, and it wasn't always easy to read her mind. "Your parents are great Grace, we both know that. One day the law may change, and you may be able to trace your real mother, but it sounds to me as though you are very content with the way you are."

"Yes, I want everything in my life to stay the same. I don't like change, all I hope is that my real mother has been able to have peace of mind after having me adopted. It seemed like she had a very traumatic time."

Jamie felt a flash of empathy for her unknown mother. The gang at school had made up those stories about Grace not being wanted, but how on earth had they found out? Neither Grace nor her mother would have said anything. Maybe it was something to do with when they first started school, and they had to bring in a birth certificate, perhaps if one of the 'nasties', as he called them, had overheard, or even their mother. Parents were often jealous if another child appeared to be brighter than theirs, and this was a way to hit back. What a cruel world it was. Even at the age of ten, he was learning that it was dog eat dog.

The bus had come to a standstill now, and it was their stop. The people were thronging off, and Grace gritted her teeth; some would touch her and knock against her, as everyone was in a hurry to get off. Usually Jamie went ahead, holding her hand and guiding her through, but today she sprang up in front of him. It had to be done.

"Let me go first, Jamie."

He looked at her in surprise, but she had made up her mind and she didn't want to be wrapped up in cotton wool any more. Lots of things in life were unpleasant, and for her being touched was one of them, but she held her breath and walked with determination, slipping into line behind others exiting the bus. She was telling herself that this closed-in feeling would not last forever; perspiration was on her face.

A lady in front of her was carrying a small baby, and Grace concentrated on the tiny face and big blue eyes that were surveying her. She smiled, and the chubby face of the baby crinkled into a smile back. Everything was all right. She was now stepping off the bus, and the crowd was parting with people going different ways. By then Jamie had caught her up.

"Grace, that was fantastic!"

"I know," she said proudly, and then spotted Janet Reilly, the leader of the gang, and she knew what to expect. True to form, with a big smirk on her face, Janet knocked against her as they entered the school gates, just in time for all her cronies to erupt into cackling laughter.

"So sorry!" she exclaimed, with a sneer.

Grace drew a deep breath, remembering Jamie's words from the previous day.

"No worries. It must bother you, not being able to stand up straight. It would bother me," she said, forcing a smile to her face.

There was complete silence from Janet, who was a very heavily built girl with a florid face and lank and greasy hair. Her cronies were disappointed to see that Grace did not appear to be upset, so they walked away. She hadn't bitten the bait, what a shame!

"Grace, you've done it. You shut them up!" said Jamie jubilantly.

"I know, now let's get to class. I actually want to learn something today," said Grace. The bell had now sounded, and once again she held her breath as she filed behind the other students from the playground into the classroom. She was learning that some things in life she had to do whether she liked it or not, and this was one of them.

Miss Williams observed her progress along the corridor. It looked like the Hart girl was going to behave this morning; it certainly made a change. Hopefully she would hear from her mother soon that they were taking Grace out of school, but of course they had paid fees for the whole term, so she might have to suffer her until then. It was unbelievable how much the parents had obviously spoilt her and allowed her temper to get the better of her. All she could wish was for this term to finish as quickly as possible.

Chapter Eighteen

Ellen 1971

"Push now, Ellen. You can do this!"

Jeremy held onto her hand tightly, his face etched with worry. He had been married to Ellen for three years now, and right at the beginning she had told him she didn't want to have another child, it would only bring back the pain of losing Grace. He had understood that, and as much as he would love to be a father, it was no contest, Ellen was the love of his life, and he had told her he would never want to lose her again.

He had a lot of guilt about how he had treated her, and the fact that she had been alone when she was pregnant, deserted by everyone. How many times had he wished that she had told him, and that he had never met Simone, who had turned out to be a five minute wonder? But nobody could undo the past, and when Ellen had accidentally fallen pregnant after two years of marriage, he had been with her every step of the way, supporting and encouraging her.

It had not been an easy pregnancy. Sickness had plagued her, not just in the morning, but all the way through. He had known when he married Ellen, that she was never going to be the carefree young woman he had fallen in love with as a teenager. She had too much guilt inside her, and her mental health would always suffer. But finding out how much she had suffered whilst pregnant, and having to give her baby up for adoption, made him want to find out more about dealing with mental health. So as a doctor he had taken courses, in the hope that anything he learned was going to help his wife lead a happier life.

She had been depressed during her pregnancy, and had told him she didn't deserve to be a mother again, and Jeremy understood all her feelings. But now he knew he must encourage her to give birth, as the baby had decided to arrive two weeks early. It was a shock to them both, and he knew that right now, she needed him more than ever.

"I can't do it. The pain is too much. Oh, my God, please help me!"

"Yes you can, Ellen. Just push, we can see the head," he exclaimed.

The midwife was poised, waiting to receive the baby. It had been a long and painful labour, and she could empathise, having been through it herself, twice.

"Ellen, your baby has jet black hair, like its dad."

Those words took Ellen back ten years. Grace had been born with black hair, just like Jeremy. She could still feel the pain of her loss, but here she was again, giving birth. With one enormous push, which made her groan even more with pain, her baby's head was out, and the midwife calmly guided its shoulders as it slithered into the world.

"You have a beautiful little boy," she said, scooping up the infant into a cotton sheet. The baby was not crying, and the silence felt unnerving, and forgetting her own plight immediately, Ellen cried loudly.

"Why isn't be crying? Is he alive?"

Jeremy watched the midwife swiftly cutting the cord, then the tiny infant was taken out of the room. His heart was full of dread. Surely after all these months, they were not going to lose their son?

"It's OK," he is a little bit small, so he is going into a special cot to help him breathe," the midwife informed them.

"I need my baby," sobbed Ellen. Suddenly her tiny son had become very important to her. She believed that God had given her a second chance, and her arms ached to hold him and feed him.

Jeremy put his comforting arms round her. She looked tired and dishevelled after hours of pain and the midwife set to work to deliver the afterbirth. When this was done, a nurse appeared at the door to say that the baby boy was now breathing.

"Thank you so much," said Ellen, weeping with relief, and Jeremy could feel the tears pricking in his eyes too.

"It's OK, honey; he will be OK. Now you need to rest," he murmured gently.

"Yes, we are moving you back to the ward," said the midwife.

"I need to hold him," said Ellen. Nothing felt real. She had been told she had a baby, but she had not even seen him. Surely she wasn't dreaming?

"You will in time. He is very small, and needs a bit of special care, but his heartbeat is strong. Tomorrow you can go to the crib and view him, maybe even get to hold his hand."

"There you are," said Jeremy. "We have to be patient. Our son is getting the best care. Well done, Ellen!"

The porters came into the room to move her bed back into a maternity ward with other mothers. Their babies were brought to them at feeding time, and then taken back to the nursery afterwards. Jeremy followed after them. He wanted to make sure that Ellen was comfortable before he went home.

When they got to the maternity ward, Ellen's bed was placed at the far end, and he tucked her down. "I will be back tomorrow, honey, and we can visit him. In the meantime, he needs a name."

"Oh yes, Charles is a good one," she said sleepily.

"Charlie it is then," grinned Jeremy. Kissing her gently, he left the ward full of pride. He was a father, and he had a son. Life could not get much better!

Ellen remained in hospital for ten days. Charles was a strong baby, and was soon able to breathe independently. It was important for him to be breastfed, and Ellen wanted to do this so much, but had to be content with expressing her milk, which initially was fed to him through a tube. In the beginning he lost weight, but Ellen was informed that this was normal. By the time she left hospital, he weighed just four pounds.

She would have stayed there until he was able to come home, but her bed was needed, and she had made a good recovery. She had plenty of milk, so she told them very firmly that she would be coming back every day to make sure Charles received it, and nobody argued with her. It was clear to see how much she needed this little boy, and in the end the hospital said she could sleep in a side room if she didn't mind sleeping on a fold up bed.

Jeremy understood how important it was for her to be there for Charles. Her new son was going to help her emotional wounds heal. Losing Grace had left a huge void in her life. There could never be another Grace, but Charles was here now, and life had to go on. She had another chance to be a mother, and this time she could keep her child and share his upbringing with Jeremy.

After a month she was able to nurse Charles and feed him from her breast. She marvelled at his tiny but perfect fingers and toes; he was like a little doll. He had a lusty cry, and he fed really well. Every day she could see his little body filling out. His fingers gripped hers strongly as if he knew she was helping him to grow and become strong. Finally, at the age of eight weeks, he weighed five and a half pounds, and the doctor agreed that he was strong enough to go home.

Jeremy came to pick them both up from the hospital. It was a proud day for him. Even Ellen had a glow about her through the joy of being a mother, and the knowledge that he was now a healthy baby. Jeremy very carefully helped her into the front of the car, and thanked the nurse who had accompanied her, for all the care they had given to Charles. The carry cot with a sleeping Charles was on the back seat, and Ellen turned round several times to make sure he was comfortable and still sleeping.

"Right, let's go home," said Jeremy, kissing her gently. He had missed her so much these last few weeks, but it was absolutely right that she devoted those first few weeks to being at the hospital with her baby. Jeremy had kept himself busy. He was now a senior doctor at Croydon General hospital, and was soon planning to set up his own practice.

They had recently bought a house within the affluent area of Shirley Hills, which consisted mainly of private roads and big houses; some of them even had swimming pools. His plan was to use the very large room at the front as a waiting room, and the slightly smaller one as his surgery. Working from home meant he would be as close to Ellen as he could be, and share as much of Charlie's upbringing as he could.

Ellen had worked her way up to being branch manager at Shirley Library, but when she became pregnant, she had battled with the sickness and had to go home from work several times. When it did not improve after three months, she decided to leave her job. It was not a hard decision for her, as her baby's welfare was paramount. Everyone said they hoped she would return after her baby was born, but to Ellen, the future was very clear, she wanted to be a mother, and as money was not a problem, she wanted to be a homemaker. But, of course, she would visit the staff she had shared the last few years of her working life with, and show them her baby.

Jeremy didn't want her to be overloaded with work, as they now had a big house, so he found her a good and reliable cleaning lady. He also suggested that a nanny might be useful, but Ellen was adamant about that, because she wanted to care for Charles herself and she did not want any help. She was happy to have a cleaning lady, but she was looking forward to taking her baby to the clinic to be weighed, and meeting other mothers with babies of a similar age.

Jeremy was excited to see animation back in her eyes. The sparkle was there, and although initially she had said she didn't want another baby, it had given her a new purpose in life; especially knowing that her visits to the hospital were helping her son survive.

Ellen had been evaluating her life whilst she had been in hospital. She recognised that losing Grace had been her lowest point, and her mental health struggles afterwards had made a lasting impact on her. But then along came Jeremy, who would always be the love of her life, and since she had unburdened her grief to him, he had shared her pain. Somehow this had made her pain less, and during the last three years, being with him had been so uplifting; he had always had the ability to make her laugh. This man was going to be with her for the rest of their lives, God willing. They both regretted losing Grace. She had lost a part of herself that day she had given her up for adoption, but life did have to go on.

She now had a second chance with Charles, or Charlie, as Jeremy called him. She smiled to herself. She had a beautiful healthy son, and she was now going to look forward and be grateful for her life.

She had survived a very rough time with the help from her family and Jeremy, but every day now she was getting stronger. She would always miss Grace, but Charles deserved to have a good life with a mother who was not going to steep herself in misery because of a situation that could never be reversed. She turned towards Jeremy, and smiled. "Well, here we are, and I can't wait to get Charles home, and thank you for all your support, darling. I couldn't have done it without you."

Jeremy smiled back. "What a great life we will have. A new home and a new son, and I am married to the girl of my dreams."

Ellen blushed. He was such a charmer, and he always said all the right things, but he did mean them; he was sincere. "Stop all your flannel and drive us home," she quipped, and they both laughed. Jeremy put the car into gear, gave a mock salute, which made her laugh even more, and drove out of the hospital car park.

Chapter Nineteen

Grace 1974

"Grace, are you happy at school?"

Pearl looked expectantly at Grace. She was such a dark horse, that daughter of hers. The meltdowns had been less frequent, but Grace was now in the habit of shutting herself away in her bedroom, and not speaking to them, so she had no idea what that was all about. She still travelled to and from school with Jamie, and Grace seemed to have accepted that people touching her was part of life, which, of course, it was, and she was learning to cope with it.

But it wouldn't be many years before they took their exams, and then as Jamie wanted to be an engineer, it was expected that he would be taking further courses at a college in Canterbury. Ever since she was eleven years old, Grace had declared that she wanted to be a scientist, working in a laboratory. She was fascinated by the idea of discovering medicine and vaccines to cure illnesses, and had already said that she wanted to work at Pfizer in Sandwich. She had read about many illnesses and knew a lot of the information by heart.

It was such an unusual thing for an eleven year old to be fixed upon, but as she was growing up, Ellen's intelligence really shone through. Pearl was not convinced that her school had done their best for her; and because she had unusual choices about her future, she didn't get the right support. Most of the other girls had aspirations to be a hairdresser, model, beautician, or other jobs that seemed suitable for females.

Ten years previously, girls were expected to leave school at sixteen, find a job, then a husband, and settle down and have children. But now more girls were going to university and studying for a degree, which gave them a much wider choice for a career, although not many of them would end up being scientists. Pearl believed that Grace would need to go to university and get a degree if she wanted to be a scientist, so now might be the time to get her a tutor. Now was the time to have someone who could give her their undivided attention, and also an assessment as to whether Grace could get the job she really wanted. At the back of Pearl's mind was also the thought of how Grace would cope at university. She didn't like change, but if she wanted to pass her exams and get a degree she would have to go.

Grace lifted her head slightly, but as always she never made proper eye contact with her mother. "I have never been happy there, but I want to learn."

"Are you still being bullied?"

"No Mother, it's not that. The work I am given is easy. I want to learn more."

Pearl knew what she meant. She wasn't being pushed enough. The thing about Grace is she always spoke the absolute truth, even if it landed her in trouble; she lacked tact. She wasn't showing off and saying how intelligent she was, she was simply stating a fact. She needed more stimulation.

"OK, Daddy and I are agreed, so I will write to Miss Williams and let her know you won't be back next term."

"She will not miss me," said Grace, looking very serious.

Pearl felt very sad. Grace had obviously picked up a vibe that Miss Williams did not approve of her. But it was difficult to know if that upset her, as Grace hid her emotions and she did not wear her heart on her sleeve.

"They have never really understood you at that school," said Pearl, disapprovingly.

Grace made no reply to that. She knew she was different to the other girls, and she had never fitted in, but she didn't know how to change herself, and she didn't really want to change.

"I will not miss anyone there, except Jamie."

"Well, Jamie is like family. But what Daddy and I thought was that when we advertise for a tutor, you can meet them and sit in on the interviews, and as you are such a mature thirteen year old, you can choose your own tutor."

"Yes, I would like that," said Grace thoughtfully. This was another change. Her life seemed to be full of change, which she didn't like. But the passion inside her to become a scientist was so strong she knew she had to carry on with her education.

Pearl had already scanned the local papers to see if there were tutors available to do home schooling, and had found three, one man and two women, so she contacted them, explaining all of Grace's needs, just in case they thought they were in for an easy ride. Two of them replied to her: a man of twenty-seven called Daniel Jones, and a woman of thirty called Vanessa Lloyd.

Daniel was interviewed first. He was a personable young man, very serious by nature, with grey eyes and big glasses. He was average height, and spoke in a rather clipped way. Learning for him was the most important part of life, and he did not appear to have a sense of humour, which Pearl and Roger had found to be a necessity when dealing with Grace, meaning that no matter how qualified he was, he just might not gel with her.

They thanked him for coming, and Pearl promised to let him know whether he had been successful. As he drove away, she turned to Roger and Grace for their opinion. Grace spoke first.

"He was very clever. He had lots of qualifications."

"But do you think you will get on with him?"

"He's not funny like Jamie."

"No one will be like Jamie. You will find that out in life," remarked Roger. Privately he had thought the man to be a bit of a stuffed shirt, having not responded to any banter. Of course, it wouldn't be right to say that. But his princess deserved the right person who would understand her, and that man didn't seem to fit that description. He was too wooden, and had said very little to Grace.

"OK, well in half an hour we have a lady called Vanessa Lloyd. Let's see how we get on with her."

Grace was silent. Her experiences with her own sex were not

119

good, as she had been ridiculed and teased by them. Men seemed to be kinder, and Jamie especially, but this woman was an adult, so maybe she wouldn't be made to feel so different by her. Nevertheless, it didn't stop her from feeling nervous and stressed about it.

Roger pressed her hand, almost as if he could read her thoughts. "Don't worry, Princess, we will find the right person. Nobody is coming here to teach you if you cannot get on with them. You have a good brain in your head, and Mummy and I are very proud that you want to be a scientist, and to help people, so we are going to make every effort to see that happens."

Grace smiled with relief. It was not something she could put into words, but deep in her heart was buried the knowledge that she had the best parents in the world. They were so understanding about her needs, and they never made her feel different. Just because she didn't say it, it didn't mean she didn't think it. In a rare display of affection she went over to them both and hugged them, simply saying:

"Thanks."

Pearl felt her eyes fill with tears. They both loved her so much, and had always accepted that she had her own personality, and had never believed that she should just be dismissed as a bad tempered person. She had worked so hard to control her meltdowns at school. To them she was beautiful in every way. She wiped her face with a tissue, laughing at Roger, who was joking around with Grace as he always did. This type of banter had always worked. It made Grace feel safe and secure, and taught her not to take life too seriously.

"Do either of you want a cup of tea before Vanessa comes, or would you prefer to wait until she is here?"

"I would rather have one after she has gone, when we can properly relax," said Roger bluntly, and Pearl conceded that he did have a point.

Grace could feel her anxiety building again. Meeting new people was not something she ever looked forward to, and she realised that whoever was chosen to be her tutor would be spending all day with her for five days a week. Jamie had promised they could still hang out together after he got home from school, so at least that would

120

not be changing. At the age of thirteen, she didn't even want to think about how her life would change when he went to study engineering. He was very interested in cars, and how everything worked, whereas she was interested in sciences and anything that could help her in studying cures for illnesses. She had read about the life of Marie Curie and found her very inspirational.

She knew that when she was older, if she passed all of her exams, she would have to go to university, and that meant mixing with a whole new set of people she didn't know. But the desire to be a scientist was burning very brightly inside her, so she made up her mind that whatever it took, she would do it; she would get there.

The doorbell rang again. This was it; another interview. She could feel the butterflies inside her.

"That will be Vanessa. I am just going to let her in," said Pearl, rising from her chair.

f

Chapter Twenty

Vanessa Lloyd was thirty years old, and married to a doctor who had a practice at Broomfield, which was the nearest village to Herne Bay. They had been married for three years, and previously to that Vanessa had also worked in the medical profession, firstly as a student nurse and then as a sister, and this was how she came to meet Peter.

She also had a lot of qualifications after studying and getting a degree in sociology and human behaviour. The reason she had taken such an interest in this was because of her brother Max. He was not treated very well at school, and had few friends. He spent a lot of time in his bedroom, much to the despair of her parents when she lived at home, and by the age of seventeen he still didn't have a job, even though he was not lacking in intelligence. Unfortunately, at school he had been left to fend for himself because he was considered odd and difficult.

During her studies, Vanessa found out about autism. It was described in the dictionary as: 'Messages to the brain are confused'. When she read the symptoms, she knew immediately that Max was affected; it was not hard to work it out. So she spoke to her parents about it, and her mother had subsequently sought help from the doctor.

The doctor had referred them to a specialist, and the next part was harder, as it was explaining to Max that he needed to go and see the specialist. He wasn't ill, and so his mother had done her best to explain that the specialist wanted to help him. Max had been quite depressed for a while, being stuck at home and lacking the inclination to find a job. But it was not because he was lazy, it was because he lacked confidence, and he didn't think he had any particular skills. So he assumed the specialist was going to help him with his depression.

After he went to see the specialist, and had his condition diagnosed as autism, a lot of things made sense. His hiding away was due to lack of social skills. His inability to look anyone straight in the eye was not because he was sly and deceitful, it was because he was autistic. Vanessa's heart went out to him when she realised he had been struggling to make sense of life for a very long time, and together with her parents, she vowed to try and get him the help that he needed. Max felt relieved that at last people were beginning to understand him. He was growing into a handsome young man. He shared his sister's hair colour, which was blonde and curly, and innocent looking blue eyes. The one love of his life was his dog Bouncer, named for his love of playing ball. Max and his dog spent hours together, going for long walks and playing ball.

So Vanessa had come up with an idea, if only her parents would take it on board. Until now they had been very protective of Max, but at seventeen, he needed to find his own way in life. He loved all animals, and the local dog rescue centre needed volunteers to walk the dogs. Max never had a fear of animals, but only of humans, he felt that animals did get him and they didn't judge him.

The centre were pleased to have him as a dog walker, and he got on so well, and had such great rapport with the dogs, that he was given more and more responsibility. It had been the making of him, as after a few months, with the encouragement of those that worked with him, he had studied hard and taken exams to become a vet.

Now aged twenty, he was working at a practice at Whitstable as a newly qualified vet. He thrived in the friendly atmosphere, because animals were the priority of everyone working there, from the receptionists and practice nurses, to the vets. Nobody treated him as different or odd, and for the first time in his life, he felt he fitted in. Since his autism had been identified, and acted upon by his family, Max was a much happier person. The junior receptionist at the practice had become his friend, and recently they had started dating. Vanessa had chuckled to see that. Mandy had done most of the running, but she accepted that Max was very shy, and they seemed very happy together with their shared love of animals.

So when Vanessa received the letter from Pearl, who had gone into great detail to explain Grace's needs, she started to wonder if this young girl also had autism, and it sounded as if her parents were totally unaware of it. She was intrigued by the challenge, but if Grace was having the same difficulties that Max had experienced, and her parents hadn't realised, then it was definitely up to Vanessa to help them. They had said that Grace was very intelligent, and had aspirations to be a scientist. She had also been virtually ignored at school, and her teachers did not appear to understand her. But her mother thought that with the right help, she would blossom. The letter had been finished off with a reminder that Grace's special needs must be considered, and if she thought it was all too much, not to worry about replying.

This stimulated her curiosity even more, so she contacted Mrs Hart to arrange an interview. Nothing would please her more than to help their daughter on her way to passing exams which her parents believed she could do.

She wanted to look businesslike for the interview, so she dressed in a navy suit with a pencil skirt. She teamed it with a crisp white blouse and navy stiletto shoes. Her blonde curly hair was piled on top of her head, giving her an air of sophistication.

When she arrived at the house, she was impressed. There was a nice lounge which overlooked the sea. It was a big house with a garden which sloped upwards at the back, and the front garden had a wooden bench in it which must be very pleasant to sit out on in the summer, with a view of the sea, and also a play park which had probably been visited many times by Grace when she was younger.

She pressed the doorbell, and she didn't have long to wait before the door was opened. A lady whom she guessed to be about mid forties, with a pleasant face and a welcoming smile, shook hands with her, and introduced herself as Pearl. Vanessa noticed that as she led her towards the lounge, a look of anxiety was on Pearl's face.

A man rose from an armchair. He had a kind looking face, and Pearl introduced him as Roger. His handshake was firm, and immediately she felt comfortable with both of them.

"Grace, come and meet Vanessa."

A young girl came shyly forward. Her face was slightly averted, and she did not hold out her hand to greet Vanessa; but this is what she had expected. Vanessa was immediately struck by Grace's beauty. Her blonde reddish hair was a mass of curls, and it framed her petite oval face. She had a glimpse of Grace's big eyes; hazel, with a slightly disengaged look in them.

Ever since she was a little girl, Grace had found it difficult to meet the gaze of strangers, and her parents had always encouraged her not to be shy. She was not comfortable being scrutinised, but this lady was smiling, she wasn't too close, so not invading her space, and she didn't have her hand out to shake. Grace did not like shaking hands with strangers, but this time she didn't feel so threatened.

She slowly lifted her head to meet Vanessa's gaze, and said, "Good afternoon, Vanessa."

She noticed that this lady had hair, curly like hers, but it was dressed on top of her head. She also noticed her suit and high heeled shoes. "We have the same curly hair," she exclaimed.

"We do, indeed," smiled Vanessa, and Grace felt the tightness inside her chest subsiding. She told herself there was nothing to be anxious about.

Vanessa sat opposite her. She had declined a cup of tea, so Grace watched her as her mother interacted with her, asking all the questions they needed to know. Vanessa was giving all the right answers, and Grace could already feel a connection with her. She seemed very laid back. Daddy liked her too; he was smiling, and joining in the conversation.

When Pearl had asked all the questions and found out all she needed to know, she turned towards Grace. "Is there anything you want to ask Vanessa?"

Because of everything that happened at school, Grace was not comfortable with anyone of her own sex. Her mother and Sybil were the exceptions, and she loved and trusted them. But she knew instinctively that this lady would not tease or belittle her, or make her feel different. But there was something she wanted to know.

"You said your husband is a doctor. Did he or you ever study infectious diseases and vaccines?"

Vanessa smiled gently. We have both done a little because of our connection with the health services. But like you, I am always interested in learning something new, so together we could delve into the mysteries of disease, and how to prevent as well as cure it."

"Yes, that would be fun," enthused Grace.

Pearl felt relieved, because Vanessa seemed perfect. She was very intelligent and laid back, but also appeared to have patience, which she would need when handling Grace. From what she could see of her daughter, Grace appeared to like her, but they would need to get together as a family and make sure they were all happy before she offered her the position. She turned towards Roger.

"Have you any questions for Vanessa, dear?"

"I don't think so. Everything has been covered," said Roger, smiling.

"Very well. Can we let you know tomorrow? We won't keep you waiting, I promise," said Pearl. She had no doubt that Vanessa would be in demand from other families, but as a family, they had to make sure they were all on the same page.

Vanessa stood up, and shook hands with both Pearl and Roger. "Thanks so much. It's been a pleasure meeting you all." Her eyes took in Grace as well, who had also risen to her feet. Then suddenly, very spontaneously, Grace held out her right hand to shake Vanessa's. She didn't want to be left out; she wanted to be a part of the warmth that seemed to flow between them all.

Her response was very touching for Vanessa. This young girl had accepted her, she felt, and she could tell from the surprise on the faces of her parents that her reaction was an unusual one. She really wanted to work with this family, and help Grace to achieve her dream. Well, all she could do now was go home and wait to hear from them.

Grace stood at the lounge window, and watched Vanessa walk down the path. None of the teachers at her school had ever been as easy to talk to as this lady. Vanessa turned at the gate, sensing Grace's eyes on her, and waved.

"Mother, can we have Vanessa? She wants to study with me, and I like her," said Grace.

"We will see," promised Pearl. Everything seemed so right, and she was sure Roger would agree.

Chapter Twenty-one

"Do come in and sit down, Vanessa. Grace has gone out on her bicycle with Jamie. They like to ride along the promenade into Herne Bay and get an ice cream at the bandstand."

"That sounds nice, and Jamie sounds like a good friend."

"Jamie is like a brother. They have grown up together since they were new born babies."

Vanessa sat down in the armchair in the lounge, and looked out to the sea. It looked very blue today, and there were children in the playground, and plenty of people strolling along the promenade enjoying the sunshine.

"It's such a lovely spot here," she commented, as Pearl handed her a cup of tea and offered a biscuit. She took a chocolate digestive and thanked her.

"Yes, we are lucky to be so near the sea, and, of course, Roger is within walking distance of the Hampton Inn," laughed Pearl.

"Very handy," chuckled Vanessa, and Pearl liked the fact that she had a sense of humour and was always so approachable to speak to.

"Well, I wanted to ask you how it's going with Grace? She certainly seems to like you, and it's been three months now." Pearl looked quizzically at her.

Vanessa had given a lot of thought about what she should say to Pearl. Suddenly telling her that her daughter might be autistic would be a shock, and also might upset her. Some people didn't like to be labelled, and it might do more harm than good. After spending the last three months with her, she was as certain as she could be that Grace was autistic, but it needed to be confirmed by a specialist. She chose her words carefully.

"Grace is doing very well. She wants to learn, which is always a help when teaching at home. She has me also interested in science now, which is great. We are learning together, but she has something that I lack, which is the ability to remember everything. That comes in very handy in exams. I always had to swot and remind myself again."

"Yes, Grace has always had a very good memory, but when she was at school, they didn't bother too much about her. The one to one teaching she gets from you is definitely much more suitable."

"She certainly enjoys learning, and that is not true of all girls, especially at Grace's age. Once they become teenagers, boys tend to be an unwelcome distraction."

"Oh, it's the other way round here. More often than not Grace would be helping Jamie with his homework, and Sybil reckoned without Grace's encouragement, he wouldn't be doing it," said Pearl.

"Ah yes, Jamie. Now Grace no longer travels to and from school with him, yet their friendship is just as strong, so it's all good."

"Yes, they see each other after school now, hence the bike ride," smiled Pearl, then she changed the subject. "I have never asked you, Vanessa, but do you have any brothers and sisters."

"Yes, I have a brother called Max. He has just started work as a junior vet, having finished his training. He is ten years younger than me; just twenty."

"Oh, how nice. An animal lover then. I often thought about getting a dog for Grace, as she loves them, but she suffers from allergies so the doctor said it might not be a good idea."

Vanessa realised this could be her cue, so she launched into the story of how Max had not coped at school, his depression, and just how alone he had been. Then she explained about the diagnosis from the specialist, and the strides he had made since, including his new relationship with Mandy.

As Pearl was listening to Vanessa, it almost sounded like Grace all over again. No social skills, very alone, and being ignored at school as he was considered to be different. The specialist had said Max was autistic, and this was a word she was not that familiar with, but Vanessa explained that it meant that the brain was wired in a different way. When people with autism found it hard to comprehend what was going on around them, a defence mechanism allowed them to retreat into their own safe world, and when everything became too much for them, this could result in a meltdown. It was very easy for onlookers to label them as difficult and badly behaved, but that was because they did not understand. The sad part about it was that nobody realised how much they were struggling to make sense of life. But doctors were beginning to recognise the condition, and offer advice to families whose children were affected.

Pearl had taken in every single word of this conversation. It resonated with her, especially the words that Miss Williams had said to her as long as three years ago. "When Miss Williams called me in one day to bring Grace home after she had a meltdown, she referred to Grace as 'acting up' and said she believed her behaviour was because she felt different to the other girls because she was adopted. Roger and I told Grace right from when she was old enough to understand that she was adopted, and it had never been a problem."

"First of all, Pearl, she was not acting up, and it's clear the school did little to understand her needs."

"This is what I thought, Vanessa, and still do."

"It's nothing to do with being adopted. You didn't spring it on her, she always knew, and as far as Grace is concerned, you and Roger are the only parents she ever knew. So why would that make her feel different?"

"Being autistic would, though," burst out Pearl. Suddenly everything was beginning to make sense to her. They had always known that Grace was not a bad girl, although her character was definitely unique, but the thought of her being misunderstood for so long was very distressing.

Pearl faced Vanessa, giving her an intense look. "Vanessa, tell me the truth, do you think Grace has autism? It will not upset me. Just tell me."

129

Vanessa chose her words carefully. "I have studied autism. It's a relatively new condition that doctors are only just learning about. There seems to be a very wide spectrum, and no two people are exactly the same. A specialist would know for sure. I am just basing it on the fact that Max is affected, and there are definitely similarities between Max and Grace."

"Yes," said Pearl thoughtfully. "I must share this with Roger, of course, and then we will make arrangements to see a specialist." She was thinking that they could go to a private consultant if necessary. For Grace's sake they needed to do this. "Thank you, Vanessa, for telling me all this."

"Well, I didn't really. You worked it out for yourself."

"I wonder how Grace will take the news?" pondered Pearl.

"Only you and Roger can know that. You know her better than anyone. Some people don't like to have a label attached to them. But with Max, once he knew, he started to understand himself and it turned his life around. He is very happy now."

"Well in that case, we need to give Grace the same chances. Knowing her, if I mention the word autism, she will have heard about it. After all, she studies all sorts of conditions, and how to prevent them, but of course autism can't be cured, it's just the way the brain works."

"It's nothing to be ashamed of, either. Grace is a lovely girl, and with the intelligence that she has, if we guide her on the path she wants to take, she will do very well."

"Thank you, Vanessa, I am so grateful that you told me about Max."

Vanessa smiled as she rose from the chair. "Well thank you for the tea, and please do not worry about Grace, she has a bright future ahead of her. I just know it. Now it's time for me to go home."

Pearl saw Vanessa to the door, and as she was saying goodbye, Grace and Jamie came into view on their bikes. Their faces were flushed and happy.

"Bye guys; have a great weekend," said Vanessa, and Pearl stood at the door and watched her until she got into her car.

Roger was sitting in his armchair reading the newspaper. He was alone, as Grace had gone to bed. Pearl had been biding her time, as she didn't want to discuss Grace with him whilst she was still around. She brought him in a cup of tea, and he put his newspaper down and took the cup off her.

"Lovely dear, thank you."

Pearl sat opposite him, sipping her tea, and after a few moments she spoke. "Roger, I have something important to tell you."

"Yes dear."

"You must concentrate. This is very important!"

"I am all ears, sweetheart."

Pearl then proceeded to tell him what Vanessa had told her about her brother Max, and just how many traits he had which were similar to those of Grace. Roger's face registered surprise, and then he became very thoughtful.

"Well I have never heard of autism. I suppose we should look into it. Maybe if we took Grace to the doctor, he could direct us to the right person. A specialist, of course, but if it's quicker and easier for Grace, we could have a private consultation. It's not an illness that she has, it's simply the way God has made her. I have to say, my love, that the way you have handled her difficulties over the years, and the patience and understanding you have shown our princess has been truly amazing! Not even the best specialist could beat that!"

Pearl blushed. "I can't take all the credit for it, you have always given me your full support in every decision."

"Yes, you can. I have not always been available, but your unwavering support has been constant. Basically we are going to see a specialist to get a diagnosis of a condition that few people know about. Grace has a very understanding tutor, and the possibility of achieving her dream to become a scientist. Whether she wants the label of being autistic, we have yet to find out, but I certainly think we should look into it."

"Thank you, Roger dear, I will have a word with her in the morning, and see how she feels about it. I am fairly sure Vanessa will be able to recommend a good private specialist, but I just want to make sure that Grace is happy about it all."

"That sounds perfect to me," said Roger."

"Go on, Roger, now you can read your newspaper," laughed Pearl, collecting both of the teacups and taking them out into the kitchen.

The next morning, whilst Grace was eating her breakfast, Pearl decided to speak to her about autism. She was wondering how to start the conversation, and decided through Max might be a good idea.

She tried to make herself sound as casual as possible. "Yesterday Vanessa was telling me about her younger brother Max. I hear he is a vet now, and enjoying his job very much."

Grace lifted her head up from the exercise book she had been studying. "Oh, I know about Max. He has autism. I looked it up to find out about it, and I think I have it too. It doesn't tell you much in the dictionary, but one of my study books mention it as a new discovery in recent years, and doctors are working on finding out more about it."

Pearl suddenly found herself lost for words. Grace had mentioned it so casually as if she was announcing that she was about to take a bath. She seemed completely unfazed by it. But still she felt she must proceed cautiously. "How do you feel about knowing you might be autistic?"

"I feel nothing except maybe relief that I am not the only one. Max is coping with it and so will I."

Pearl had the sudden desire to put her arms around Grace and praise her for her courage. She could feel her emotions churning away inside her, but maybe she was making a big deal about this. After all, Grace was not ill. She gulped her feelings down.

"Would you be willing to come to a specialist with us, to have it definitely confirmed? Apparently it has helped Max to understand himself better, and it might help you too darling."

"Yes, I don't mind. I also want to make my own study about it, to find out why my brain is wired in a different way to yours. I find it very interesting."

"It doesn't matter to Daddy and I that your brain is wired

132

differently. You know you will always be very special to us," said Pearl huskily.

Grace surveyed her mother. She had never found it easy to read other people's feelings, nor to express emotion, but that did not mean that she didn't care. Deep inside her heart was the knowledge that she had the best and most understanding parents in the world, because over the years she had given them a rocky ride at times, and there had never been any recriminations from them. Right now she could see her beloved mother was close to tears. And in a rare display of emotion she put her arms around her.

"I love you Mum, and Dad too."

Pearl wiped her eyes quickly. This would never do!

"We love you too, darling. Now it's almost time for Vanessa to come."

"Yes, I am going to get my books ready."

Chapter Twenty-two

Ellen 1980

"Mummy, I really want to get into Beckenham Swimming Club. They are holding trials tonight. Please can I go?"

Ellen looked into the pleading face of her son Charlie as he stood before her. She had been sitting peacefully in the lounge, having a few minutes to herself, until the whirlwind who was Charlie Scott, her much loved son, had descended upon her. At nine years old, there was so much about him that reminded her of his father Jeremy. His thick coal black hair and dark eyes, his cheeky nature and his charm. Also his sense of humour. He was incorrigible, and no matter how naughty he was, it was impossible to be angry with him for long. His affectionate nature was his dearest quality, and his ability to say sorry always won his mother over, although Jeremy had tried to be a bit stricter with him so he would not be spoiled. She tried desperately to harden her heart, and ignore the pleading look in his eyes.

"What did Dad and I say to you after you climbed over the fence to Mrs Milton's house and trampled on her flowers?"

"I didn't mean to. My football accidentally went over there."

"I know what happened. But the question is, what did we say?"

Charlie looked abashed, and muttered, "You said I was grounded for a month."

Ellen studied his downcast face. Charlie was a very hyperactive boy. He was always doing something. He had a lot of friends, and was very popular at school. He really loved sport, football and swimming particularly, and Jeremy had made sure he could swim at a very early age. It wasn't because he wanted him to be competitive, but hopefully he had explained it might save his life one day if he ever fell into water.

Now, if he joined the swimming club, she knew for a fact that there would be training sessions most evenings, and also early morning training at Crystal Palace. And if he turned out to be very fast, he would be entered into swimming galas all over the United Kingdom. Of course, she knew she was looking ahead, but as Jeremy was very busy in his job, and not always available, she would have to be prepared to travel about with him and support him.

When she thought about it, she didn't really mind because she believed that having a hobby like swimming in a club would help to keep Charlie disciplined as he grew up, and he would be less likely to hang around on street corners like some teenagers did. She came to a quick decision.

"Firstly, you will go and apologise to Mrs Milton and take her some flowers from our garden, and whilst you are doing that, I will telephone your dad and make sure he agrees with me that you can go for the trial."

"Oh, thanks Mum." Charlie's face lit up with animation, then he impulsively hugged his mother, who did her best to remain aloof, but finally returned his hug.

"Here you are. A bunch of daffodils just cut this morning."

Charlie dashed off to take the flowers next door, and Ellen picked up the phone to ring Jeremy. He was having a rare day off, and hoping to play a round of golf if the rain stayed away. Right now he would be in the club house. He had said they were starting about eleven o'clock, so she rang and spoke to the secretary, who brought Jeremy to the phone.

"Anything wrong, darling?" he enquired anxiously.

"No nothing. It's Charlie, he wants to go for a swimming trial later for Beckenham Swimming Club."

"Of course, you didn't need to ask me about that."

"Well, he is grounded for a month."

"He is, but I did far worse at his age. Of course, let him go, and I will try and be home in time to come as well."

"I know. Enjoy your game of golf."

As Ellen put the phone down, her memory flipped back to the time when Tom had been beaten by their father because he had been scrumping. She could still remember the scars and weals on his back. It had been awful. But nothing like that would ever happen in this house. They had never used physical punishment for Charlie, and they never would. He was just a young boy learning about life, and being naughty sometimes, but there were other ways of punishing without inflicting injuries and pain on a child.

Charlie ran through the door, very breathlessly, accompanied by Mrs Milton, the lady from next door. Ellen wondered what was happening, but the elderly lady was smiling.

"Thank you so much for the flowers, but Charlie didn't squash the ones by the fence, my friend brought her dog round and he did it."

"Oh, I see," Ellen was surprised. "But Charlie knows he should not have climbed the fence to get his ball."

"Yes, Charlie, if you knock on my door in future, I will let you go into the garden to get your ball," said Mrs Milton, a lady of about seventy years old, with grey hair and a lined face which right now appeared amused, as she was smiling at them both.

Ellen sensed she might be lonely, as she was a widow and lived alone. She had a million things to do as usual, but a few minutes chat wouldn't harm.

"Would you like a tea or coffee, Mrs Milton?" she asked.

"Thank you so much dear, but my daughter will be round in a little while to take me shopping. I don't drive any more now. When Michael died, I sold the car because he did most of the driving anyway. I don't mind going on the bus, but Laura likes to take me to Sainsbury's in West Wickham once a week."

Ellen smiled as she saw her out. "Thank you for being so nice about it," she said warmly.

"Well Charlie makes it difficult for anyone to be cross with him. Your son is a charming young boy," she said smiling. "I am sure he will knock to ask next time. I am there most times, but if I am out,

136

I give my permission for you to open my side gate, and let him go through to collect it. I don't lock it except at night; it always feels very safe around here."

"Yes, we are very lucky," agreed Ellen. "Being a private road it only seems to be the residents or their families who come down here, especially as it's a no through road. Thank you so much, Mrs Milton, and I hope you enjoy your shopping trip with Laura."

As she shut the door, Charlie was jumping up and down with impatience.

"Calm down Charlie, you can go for your trial this evening. Dad and I both hope to come."

"Ooh whoopee, will I still be grounded as I didn't damage the flowers?"

"We'll see! Now I suggest you get on your bike and ride off some of your energy. "

"Can I go round and see John?"

"Yes, off you go. Be back for lunch about one."

Charlie was gone before she could even take a breath. She had completely forgotten about his grounding, and it was too late now, he had disappeared down the road. She brought the kettle back to the boil and made herself a coffee. There was washing to be put on, and other chores, as it was Saturday. Her cleaner was not in, but at this moment she was treasuring a quiet moment, and having the house to herself.

Jeremy ran his practice from the house, and Ellen was his receptionist. They both enjoyed working together, and one day a week he also worked at Mayday hospital at Thornton Heath. So the house was rarely empty. As she sat drinking her coffee, she was thinking about just how much her life had changed after Tom had come and rescued her from Herne Bay. She didn't have much memory about that time, only that she had suffered a breakdown. But her family had stood by her, and she had recovered. Then Jeremy had come back into her life, and since then she had never looked back. Nevertheless, there was always going to be that ache in her heart for baby Grace, all dressed in pink, on the day when she had to give her up for adoption, and the guilt would never quite leave her. If only she'd known at the time that had she left it for just one day before leaving home, everything would have been different.

But marrying Jeremy had been a great healing for her emotional wounds, as they then grieved for their daughter together; but they also realised they had to move on. And then when Charlie had arrived, it felt like a gift from God, a second chance to be parents. Charlie, who always kept her busy, who made her laugh, who gave such spontaneous affection. As painful as it was, she had to accept that somebody else was a mother to Grace, and all she could hope for was that her daughter had been loved and cared for properly.

Of course, Charlie had no idea that he had a sister some ten years older than him. This bothered Ellen, especially as they had been unsuccessful in having any more children. He was an only child, and she did her best not to spoil him. Her conscience bothered her for keeping it from him, but the fear that he might look down on her for what she had done kept her silent. Jeremy had left it to her to decide what to do, and every time she thought about it, she just couldn't tell him.

She shook herself back to reality, and picked up her mug and put it in the dishwasher. Her biggest problem was she suffered from too much guilt, and all through leaving home just one day before events would have allowed her to keep her baby daughter. But over the years she had learned not to let it dominate her life. It was time to move on.

She kept herself busy for the rest of the day, and Charlie returned dutifully to eat his lunch at one o'clock. Ellen had cooked him sausages and mash, as he always seemed to have hollow legs. He ate it with enthusiasm, and then did justice to an apple pie and custard that she had made earlier.

"I need to save a piece for your dad," she reminded him, when he asked if there was any more.

"Anyway, what time is the trial? You cannot eat for two hours before swimming."

"We have to be at the pool between five-thirty and six."

"OK, we will eat afterwards when we get home."

"Maybe get fish and chips," suggested Charlie, his eyes lighting up at the thought of it. Ellen couldn't help laughing. Two dinners in one day were no problem for Charlie, although his long lean frame gave nothing away.

Jeremy arrived home at four o'clock. He had managed to get his round of golf in, although it had been slightly interrupted by some April showers. He kissed Ellen when she handed him his cup of tea. "How was your day, darling?"

"Yes, good." She smiled.

"What time are we off to the swimming pool?"

"We leave in just over an hour, then once he has done his trial we can come back. I thought maybe we could bring back fish and chips."

"Of course, as long as I can have a piece of that nice apple pie to keep me going. That's assuming our son hasn't already demolished it."

"He hasn't. I told him you would want some."

Ellen disappeared into the kitchen to get it, and Charlie came into the room. Ellen had insisted that he tidied his room before they went out.

"Hi Dad, it's cool you are coming to watch me swim."

Jeremy studied his son; he was certainly a chip off the old block. Not only did he look exactly like Jeremy had at the same age, he also had his father's temperament; cheeky, funny and very affectionate. Behind all the bravado Charlie was also very sensitive, and he would never want to hurt or upset anybody. He couldn't help being very proud of Charlie. He was quite intelligent, but at the moment showed more interest in sports than in learning. He was still only nine, and if he wanted to get into Beckenham Swimming Club, then Jeremy thought it was a very good idea.

He was aware that Charlie was the apple of his mother's eye, and being a parent again had helped her tremendously with her grief after losing Grace. Jeremy had been sad to think they had a daughter somewhere that they might never know. He had only ever seen one photograph of her in a pink knitted outfit, but it had captured his heart, and stayed inside him for all these years.

"You do realise you have to be a very quick swimmer to get in, son?" he said kindly.

"Yes dad, but I will get in. I am very fast," said Charlie, with great confidence.

139

"Well even if you don't, your mother and I are very proud of you," he reminded him.

When they arrived at the swimming pool there was a long line of boys and girls of all ages. Charlie excitedly got into line with the others. "You can watch from the gallery, Mum and Dad," he said, turning to chat with the others.

Ellen and Jeremy climbed up the stairs to the gallery which overlooked the pool. It was very hot in there, so they took off their jackets when they sat down to watch. For the next hour they saw many children swimming up and down the pool, closely followed by the vigilant eyes of the instructors. When it was Charlie's time, he strode to the edge of the pool confidently, and then, catching their eyes, gave a wave.

With her heart in her mouth in case he didn't get through, Ellen watched him swim up and down several times. It was impossible to tell if one child was better than another from where they were sitting. She told herself not to be so silly, it was simply a swimming trial, but it didn't stop her desire to see him do well.

"We can go down and wait for him now," whispered Jeremy. He had no idea why he was whispering; it wasn't the library, but there seemed to be a great deal of expectancy in the air. All of these children wanted to be in the swimming club, not just his son. Some of them would be disappointed, but he did so hope that Charlie would not be one of the them.

After a while, Jeremy went into the changing room. As usual Charlie would be the last one out. He always talked too much, and played around. Charlie was the last boy in there, and he looked very down in the dumps. Jeremy's heart went out to him.

"Never mind son, you gave it a go," he said, gently.

Charlie burst into laughter. "April fool, Dad. I did get through!"

Jeremy laughed with relief. The little blighter had fooled him again.

"Well done, son. Let's go and tell your mother!"

Chapter Twenty-three

Tom and Linda Payne had been married since 1963, and now had two teenage daughters, Paula and Ava. These girls were very special to Tom. He would not have minded if one of them had turned out to be a boy at birth or not, the main thing was they were both healthy babies, who were now growing up to be delightful young women.

He was pleased for Ellen that Jeremy had found her again, and also that Charlie had been born, because without that happening, he wasn't sure whether Ellen could have recovered from her breakdown and mental health problems. The day they had gone to Herne Bay, and found her at the shelter, was indelibly marked on his mind. The shock of just how mentally disturbed and affected she had been after tragically parting with her baby was something he could never forget, and every time he looked at his girls, he realised how lucky he was.

It was unbelievable just how affected people had been by the disapproval of society in the 1960s if a girl became pregnant. Looking back it wasn't as if they had murdered anyone, or robbed a bank, or even attacked someone, and yet all these young women had been treated like criminals. For what? Having sex with their boyfriend.

To send a girl away from home when she needed her family most was cruel, and then the attitude of society towards them that meant they had to have their baby adopted was inhuman. He was sorry that when he had returned to Margate to find out who had adopted baby

Grace, the authorities had refused to give him any information, other than the fact that she had gone to a loving home.

He never spoke about it to Ellen. Although she was now happily married to Jeremy, the love of her life, and also had Charlie, he could sense a sadness at times inside her and he had no wish to add to her pain. She had never spoken to him about Grace since, but Jeremy had. There was so much regret with both of them for how it had turned out, but also no turning back now.

Tom knew that in 1975 a new law had been passed that allowed adopted children to trace their real parents, but how did that affect parents that wanted to trace their adopted child? So next time he paid a visit to Ellen and Jeremy, he waited until Ellen was not in earshot, and spoke to Jeremy.

"Jeremy, have you thought about going back to Margate to see if you can trace Grace? It would give Ellen peace of mind, wouldn't it?"

"I am not sure, because she has too much guilt inside her for having Grace adopted. She will be scared of rejection, and that might set her back again, and we can't have that."

"Oh yes, I agree, but Charlie has a sister he doesn't even know about."

"Maybe you can understand my dilemma, Tom. I have always left it to Ellen to decide if Charlie should know. We do talk about Grace to each other, maybe to comfort each other, but never in front of Charlie. Vera knows never to mention it, but she is getting on a bit, and her memory is not what it was. Sometimes I feel like we are treading on eggshells, because if Charlie was to find out from the wrong person, I think he would be very upset that we had not told him."

"Well how about you and I go back to Margate to see what we can find out, and if we can get in touch with Grace secretly and pave the way so that Ellen would not get hurt, do you think it's worth a try?"

"Another difficulty, of course, is that when Grace was born, I didn't know about her, and although Ellen got her birth registered, she told me that she left the father's name blank on the certificate."

Jeremy's face looked so sad, and Tom felt great empathy for him.

142

He patted his shoulder consolingly. "I just wanted to help if I could."

Jeremy became very thoughtful. He was aware that they were carrying a very big secret. For all he knew, Tom may have told his daughters that they had a cousin. One slip up from anyone in the family, and Charlie's life could be ruined forever, and his relationship with his parents might deteriorate because they had kept such a big secret from him.

"Well Tom, we spoke about going on a fishing trip together. Let's do it, and see if we can find out any information about Grace. She may still be living at the Kent coast. We will not tell Ellen until we know if there is any chance of tracing Grace."

Ellen was now kept very busy with Charlie and the swimming club. He had turned out to be very fast at front crawl, so had immediately been put into a competitive group. He had made it into the relay team, and also the under elevens freestyle, so they were now travelling around Kent as he was part of the team competing for Galas. This particular weekend he was swimming in the Kent championships at Dover, so Jeremy was coming to see him, which he was thrilled about.

She was very happy that Tom, Linda and the girls were also coming to watch him, and then on Sunday Tom and Jeremy were going fishing. Jeremy had booked them all at a nice hotel in Dover, and Linda and Ellen planned to take all the youngsters to Broadstairs for the day on Sunday, as it wasn't that far. Ava was studying Charles Dickens at school and was keen to visit Bleak House, which had been Dickens' summer residence. Then they were having lunch at the Albion Hotel which dated back to 1760. It overlooked Viking Bay, so it would be such a treat for them all.

Ellen had to smile to herself about the men wanting to go fishing. She could think of nothing more boring than sitting quietly all day waiting for a fish to bite, but as both Tom and Jeremy had stressful jobs, maybe this peaceful occupation was just what they wanted. Tom spent his life chasing after criminals, and Jeremy did his best to cure the sick and wounded.

When the weekend came, they drove to the hotel on Friday afternoon and booked themselves in. They enjoyed a family meal together in the pleasant dining room. Ellen looked around her as they sat at the table. Charlie was chatting with his cousins. They treated him like a little brother, and she felt the warmth of the family bond, but the only thing that spoiled it for her was the thought that Grace had been a part of the family, and should have also been here now. She swallowed down her feelings of sadness, and tilted her glass of wine towards the centre of the table.

"Let's drink to family."

"To family," echoed the others, all chinking their glasses together.

"To swimming," said Charlie, holding up his glass of water. Ellen ruffled his hair.

"You, my son, will be doing yourself proud tomorrow!"

Tom and Jeremy had arrived in Margate, so they made their way towards the centre where Grace's adoption had been arranged. There was an office there which housed details about adoptions spanning back to over thirty years previously.

The lady behind the counter smiled kindly at them. She was used to seeing people who were very nervous and stressed when they came into the office. She was about forty years old, with mid brown hair and glasses, but her expression looked empathetic.

Jeremy nervously explained that he was trying to trace his daughter who had been adopted way back in 1961. Her mother's name had been Ellen Payne, and she had named her baby Grace.

"I can have a look back through the records, of course, but it will take a while. Quite often adoptive parents change the baby's name, so she may not be Grace now."

"How about if we come back in a couple of hours? Shall we ask for Shirley?" suggested Tom. He noticed she had a badge on with her name.

"Yes, that should be long enough for me to look," agreed Shirley.

They headed out of the office, and walked along the seafront past Dreamland. It was a warm day, and the sandy beach was full of people. There were also some venturing into the water; it looked clear, but judging by the cries was probably cold. The blue sky was reflected in the water, making it look very inviting. Children were making sandcastles, and the donkeys were trotting slowly along the sands with children sitting on their backs enjoying the ride.

"It always seems very full of life here," remarked Tom.

"Yes it is," replied Jeremy. Then his emotions surfaced: "You know I hate keeping things from Ellen, but Margate only has sad memories for her."

Tom had been expecting a reaction like this from Jeremy. Obviously Margate could never be a happy place for him or Ellen.

"There was no point in her coming along here. If we can't find out anything it will only evoke sad memories for her."

"I know," said Jeremy. "Let's pop over to the pub and get a pie and a pint."

Two hours later they presented themselves back at the office. Shirley was still on duty, but Jeremy could tell by her face that the news was not going to be good.

"I have found the file. Grace was adopted in November 1961. She was fourteen days old, but I am afraid I cannot give you the names of the family that adopted her. The new law states that adopted children can be allowed to trace their blood parents, but it does not allow parents to seek out their child unless that child has indicated that they are seeking their blood parents. There is nothing on this file to indicate that Grace has been looking for you or her mother."

"I understand that," said Jeremy. "Her mother was traumatised by the whole experience, and I fear she may never have peace of mind if we cannot locate our daughter."

"I am so sorry to hear that, but unfortunately we also have to consider the feelings of your daughter. If she has had a happy life with the family that adopted her, she will think of them as her parents, and not feel the need to look elsewhere."

Jeremy knew what she was saying was true, but it still hurt, so he was glad that Ellen was not with him, and had no inkling of what they were doing. He tried once more to find out something.

"One last question: Did the parents live around here, or were they just visiting when they adopted her?"

145

g

"They lived locally at the time, but don't forget it was nineteen years ago. Who knows where they might be now."

Tom could see they were getting nowhere fast, and Jeremy's face was full of sadness, so he intervened quickly. "Well, thank you so much Shirley for your help, and for looking out the file."

"No worries," murmured Shirley. She could see how disappointed they were, but it was more than her job was worth to give out sensitive information.

The two men went back to the car, and Tom drove them back to the hotel in Dover. They were staying one more night and then driving back to Shirley the next morning. After a quick wash and change into suitable clothes for dinner time, they went downstairs to join the family in the lounge. Most of the excitement was centred around Charlie, who had won a medal for one hundred metres freestyle the day before. He was showing his medal to everyone, and Ellen sat there with such a proud look on her face.

"Hi everyone," said Tom. "Has your day been good?"

"We've had a fabulous day," said Ellen smiling. "How many fish did you catch?"

Tom and Jeremy looked guiltily at each other, chorusing in unison: "None."

Ellen could sense there was something wrong with Jeremy. She had thoroughly enjoyed the weekend away, and the icing on the cake had been Charlie winning his medal, but although Jeremy had told him he was so proud of him, she could sense there was something wrong. When they were chatting in the car on the ride home he seemed detached from them, in a world of his own. Maybe he was worrying about a patient. Although he always maintained that he never brought his work home, her much loved husband was a sensitive man, and if he had a situation where he could not help someone to recover, it did affect him.

She did not say anything to him for a couple of days. His surgery resumed on Monday evening as usual and, as his receptionist, she was also on duty. On Tuesday he spent the day at Mayday Hospital, he came home at six o'clock, and they all had dinner.

146

After Charlie had gone to bed, they sat down together, and Ellen decided it was time she found out what was bugging him. As a couple they had always been very close, and didn't really have secrets from each other, but right now she felt like a cloud was hanging over them.

"Jeremy, darling, what happened to make you so sad at the weekend? It's surely not because you didn't catch any fish."

Jeremy looked at his wife. Her last remark had been meant to be a joke, but he didn't feel like laughing. It was hard to keep anything from her. He certainly was not going to lie, because the closeness that they had always shared did not allow for that.

Before he could think twice about it, he poured it all out. It was a huge weight on his mind that he had to share with her. But the hopelessness that he felt at not getting anywhere was still raw, and he had to let it out. When he had finished, he sat there looking silently at her, waiting for a response. She had every right to be angry with him, as he had gone behind her back, no matter how well intentioned it had been.

But Ellen was not angry with him. She put her arms around him, and spoke gently.

"I am so lucky to have you Jeremy, and my dear brother Tom, and to know how much you care about trying to help me to find Grace is very touching. I must be honest with you in saying she may not want me to find her. She would be nineteen now, and must love the parents that brought her up. I am so scared of rejection, and I don't think I could cope with that."

"This is why I didn't tell you what we were doing. But Tom and I also had a discussion about the fact that Charlie doesn't know he has a sister, and we are worried he might find out in the wrong way."

"It worries me too, Jeremy, my love, but please give me time. I will do it, but not just yet. He is only nine."

Ellen was reduced to tears by now, so Jeremy took his hanky out of his pocket and gently wiped her face. "Of course, my darling, don't be upset. I love you so much. They both hugged each other tightly, united in their grief, but also giving each other the support they both needed.

Chapter Twenty-four

Grace 1980

"Well Grace, you don't need me any more. It's off to Oxford for you."

Vanessa smiled at Grace. She would miss her. She was so intelligent, and she worked so hard. They had shared many interesting experiences together. It had been six years now and, at thirty-six, Vanessa was ready to welcome the baby she was now carrying into the world next spring.

Grace, at nineteen, had turned out to be a stunner. No surprise there, but she didn't have a boyfriend, and she held most young men at arm's length. Only Jamie was allowed to be close to her, simply because he had been there for all of her life and was like a brother.

"I only want to go there to learn," burst out Grace.

"I know why you are saying that. You've been to view the place, and being surrounded by other students all the time can be daunting."

Grace looked gratefully at Vanessa. She did understand, as did her parents, that it was so hard for her to be sociable. She had met a girl on her visit named Belle, but she had never stopped talking, and said because they all worked so hard, they also liked to party hard, and she would, of course, be welcome to join them. Grace knew that wouldn't be for her. She would just stay in her room when the time came.

"Don't let anyone intimidate you. Just be your own person," said

Vanessa. She felt a little anxious now, wondering how Grace would cope, but she couldn't get the job she wanted unless she got her degree. Since Grace had been given her diagnosis from the specialist, to Vanessa's amazement, one of the studies Grace had undertaken was autism. She stated quite frankly that she wanted to discover everything she could about herself and why her brain was wired in a different way. The ironic part about it was that through all her studying, Grace herself knew as much about autism as any specialist would, and although she had very few meltdowns these days, she understood why she suffered from them, and had learned to control them, which was amazing.

She held out her hand to shake Grace's, but suddenly, without warning, Grace ran towards her and hugged her. Vanessa was very taken aback, but also it gave her a warm glow inside; it meant that Grace trusted her, and felt as close as she could be to her.

"Goodbye Vanessa, good luck with your baby."

"You can see it when it's born. I will pop round when you are on holiday," promised Vanessa.

Grace watched Vanessa walk down the drive. She had a funny feeling of loss inside, which she couldn't quite equate, but six years had been a long time, and it had been a much happier time than when she had been at school.

She had another reason for this feeling inside. Jamie had a new friend, and her name was Felicity. She had looked the name up; it meant happiness. Jamie was on holiday from college, where he had been studying engineering. He had always been very interested in how cars went, and now he even had one of his own. It was on old Ford Escort, but he loved it, and had saved up money from his paper round for a long time before he was able to buy it, and then he had passed his driving test.

He had introduced her to Felicity, who was apparently in his class at college and also studying engineering, which was extremely unusual for a girl, and it was a subject about which Grace knew very little.

She had found out a few years ago about how women had babies, and how the man played his part. She was not certain that would be for her, as she still didn't like being touched, but she couldn't help

149

wondering if Felicity was Jamie's girlfriend, and if they had that sort of relationship. Felicity found him very amusing. It almost felt like Grace was losing her brother, and knowing that she was going away to university soon, she would see even less of him.

Grace didn't understand the feeling that was surging around inside her every time she saw him smile at Felicity, but it made her feel as if she wanted to tell her to get lost, even though she knew that wasn't right. She did not own Jamie, and he could have his own friends, so she swallowed down her feelings and told no one about them.

She knew she would also find it strange to be away from her parents. They understood her more than anyone else. But these days, after all the research she had done about autism, she also understood herself, so much she felt she could have written a book about it. Knowing why she reacted the way she did in certain situations made it easier to cope, so she was glad she had found out about it.

She had her suitcase packed and was ready to go. Tomorrow both her parents were driving her to Oxford and helping her to settle into her lodgings. Her bedroom would be next to Belle's. She would have preferred to have her own space, but it wasn't possible, so she knew she would have to discipline her mind to the idea of another student being close by.

Once again, Grace checked that she had all the books and other stationery that she needed. They were leaving just after rush hour in the morning, so as soon as she got there, she planned to unpack her books and put them in a safe place. Learning was a very important part of her life.

She didn't sleep that well on her last night at home. She still had confidence issues, and change was always difficult for her. She was about to leave the home that was so familiar to her, the parents who had always understood her, and go into a strange place with a bedroom which was close to another student.

But she was doing this because she wanted to fulfil her dream and work at Pfizer. She wanted to explore the world of vaccines and preventing disease. It had been a passion burning so brightly inside her ever since she was eleven years old. Her parents had not laughed and ridiculed her for choosing an occupation that was not specifically feminine, but they had supported her. Unlike school, where when she had said what she wanted to do, she was met by a look of incredulity and sneers and laughter from other pupils. Well she was going to have the last laugh on them and become a scientist, so as far as Oxford University was concerned; bring it on!

When she woke up in the morning, she got herself ready, and then went downstairs where her parents were having breakfast. "What would you like, dear?" asked Pearl brightly. Her parents were both tucking into egg and bacon, but Grace knew that with all the butterflies inside her stomach right now, she would not be able to eat a cooked breakfast.

"Nothing Mother, I am good."

Pearl wiped her mouth on a napkin. She didn't usually have a cooked breakfast, but she had joined Roger because she wasn't sure how long it would be before they were free to get something to eat. She was also hoping that when Grace saw them eating, she would have something herself. She had guessed that right now Grace would be feeling stressed, so she must leave the house with a proper meal inside her.

"Grace, you must eat. If you do not fancy egg and bacon I could always do you scrambled egg on toast."

Grace sighed to herself, but she knew her mother was right. She would not see her for about three months, so she wanted to remember that she had obeyed her mother the very last time she saw her. "OK, scrambled egg it is then; but only one egg, and one piece of toast."

Pearl went to rise from her chair, but Grace stopped her. "It's OK, I can do it. You finish your breakfast."

Pearl smiled gratefully, and watched Grace as she prepared her breakfast. She knew why Grace was doing it herself, she would make sure she had only one egg, and one piece of toast. But Pearl contented herself with the thought that a small breakfast was better than no breakfast at all.

Roger had finished eating as well now, so she collected up their plates and put them in the dishwasher. This was a relatively new addition to her kitchen, and she was finding it very useful.

"Any toast, dear?" she enquired of Roger.

"No thanks. I will go up and shave, and then maybe I can have a cuppa when I come down."

"Yes, of course, we have over an hour before we need to leave."

Grace sat down at the kitchen table with her scrambled egg and toast. As it slipped easily down her throat, the slight feeling of nausea faded, and secretly she felt grateful that her mother had encouraged her to eat. She didn't think she was hungry, but actually just that small meal had made her feel better.

After she had finished, she put the kettle on, and sent her mother upstairs to get ready. When it had boiled she made a cup of tea for both of her parents, and then made herself a coffee.

Later when they had reached campus, Belle came out to greet them. She was a naturally friendly girl with a bubbly personalty. Grace returned her smile, and thanked her for being there.

"I just want to unpack and get settled," she said a little brusquely.

Belle didn't appear to notice. She was a tall girl with mid brown hair, and her eyes looked kind.

"Well, I will leave you all to it. We are all meeting in the students lounge for a catch-up if you want to join us later."

Pearl was wondering if she should take her to one side, and quietly make her aware of Grace's autism. Even at the age of nineteen, her instinct was always to protect Grace, because she knew that a meet-up would not appeal to Grace, and to others she would just appear to be unfriendly. But before she could say anything, Grace addressed Belle.

"Thank you, Belle. I am autistic, so meet-ups or parties are not for me. I am here to learn and then pass my exams."

The way Grace had expressed herself actually did sound a little rude, and Pearl felt uncomfortable. She knew Grace was just being honest. But Belle seemed totally unfazed by it.

"Grace, you should speak to Kevin Hayward, our tutor. He encourages us all to share anything that is not work related. If you are happy to talk about how autism affects you, he might suggest you do a talk to the students about it."

Pearl could feel her heart pounding with anticipation. She had no idea what Grace's response to that would be, but she had no need to worry.

"I have done so much research on it, I think I would like to talk about it. I really wanted to try and understand myself, and why I react the way I do in certain situations. I know my brain is wired differently, but it doesn't mean I am odd."

"I think that sounds great. I don't know much about autism, neither do the others, so you can bring us all up to speed."

"Where do I find Kevin Hayward then?"

"You don't have to find him, he will find you, but not until tomorrow. He gives you time to settle in."

Part of Grace's character was that she always wanted to do everything immediately, but she had found that was often not the case with other people, and when she thought about it, she did feel tired. Pearl had already found the thermos flask she had thought to bring with them. She had also packed some cups, and was soon busying herself pouring out tea. There was a dining hall where Grace would eat meals with the others.

After her parents had gone, Grace unpacked her clothes and books. She had her own bedroom, but students had to share the bathroom and toilet. She had brought her own pillow, which she placed on the bed. This bedroom was quite a small room, but she had not expected it to be like her bedroom at home. To her none of this mattered; getting her degree did.

Her mother had done her a packed lunch, which she ate, and by now it was early afternoon. Lessons commenced tomorrow, so today was free, which was probably why there was this meet-up.

Grace decided to go for a walk round, so she left her room and walked along the corridor, passing other students along the way. When she went outside, she noticed a man of about thirty walking towards her, and he was smiling, so she couldn't help wondering who he was.

"You must be Grace Hart. Welcome to Oxford. I am Kevin Hayward, and I will be your tutor."

He was holding his right hand out in a friendly way, but Grace needed to know him better before she could shake hands with him. She shrank back, and he surveyed her with surprise.

"Yes, I am Grace. So sorry I can't shake your hand until I know you better. I am autistic," she explained.

Kevin had heard of autism, but he hadn't had any pupils that had the condition. He guessed that the others might give her a hard time, and he didn't want that.

"Grace, would you like me to explain to the group tomorrow about your autism?"

"You don't need to do that. I have researched the subject because I wanted to understand myself. I am happy to do a talk about it so people can understand me."

Kevin looked at her admiringly. The girl had guts, and he vowed to himself that, if he heard any snide remarks, he would be right down on them.

"Well Grace, I look forward to hearing this talk myself, and I am sure everyone else will too. You can teach us all a thing or two about autism.

Grace smiled. None of this was as bad as she had thought it would be. She was just being honest. There were no sniggers, people were accepting her autism, and even wanting to know more about it. That was definitely a step in the right direction.

"Until tomorrow then, sir," she said, and then she walked off, anxious to discover her new surroundings.

Chapter Twenty-five

Ellen 1983

"I can't keep it a secret any more, Jeremy. I can't live with myself."

Jeremy put his arms around Ellen. She was going through a bad spell, and he understood why. Today was Grace's twenty second birthday, and every year that passed reminded her of their loss. They had never succeeded in giving Charlie a sibling, and he was now twelve years old. But it was on both of their consciences that Charlie did have a sister somewhere that he would probably never meet.

"Darling, I think you are right. It will ease your worry, and mine, because we have never wanted him to find out from anyone other than us."

"I will have to take a chance that he doesn't look down on me," gasped Ellen, with tears in her eyes.

"Honey, I won't let him. I am just as guilty. We were two teenagers in love, but it's not the biggest crime of the century."

"But supposing he wants to track her down?"

"I have thought of that, but I don't think it will ever happen. Grace has had the opportunity to find us, but she hasn't done it, and we don't have the right to be given any information to find her."

For the last eight years, since the law had changed to allow adopted children to trace their birth parents, Ellen had nursed a hope inside her that Grace might find them. She was convinced that it was only a dream, and the reality was probably that Grace didn't want to find them. She was more than happy with her adoptive parents, and she would probably never forgive her real mother for giving her up.

"She will never know how much I wanted to keep her," she said tearfully, and Jeremy held her close, lovingly stroking her tear-stained face.

"Darling, she probably does know. The adoptive parents were told how hard it was for you, and how heartbroken you were to have to part with her, and they will have told her that."

Jeremy's soothing voice, and the warmth of his arms, calmed Ellen. He always understood, and said the right thing to her. Without this man and his support, who knows where she would be now? Then there was Charlie, their wonderful happy-go-lucky son. She had the love of a good man, and the best son in the world, and she should be grateful for all that, she told herself sternly.

"I will go and pick him up from swimming, and we will tell him together," he said gently.

"You do know you are my rock," she said, kissing his cheek.

"Well I hope you know that you are the love of my life," replied Jeremy, and then he started to tickle her, and was rewarded when she giggled just like a teenager. He wasn't normally a romantic person, but his little family unit meant everything to him. Ellen and Charlie were the most important people in his life.

"You best go and get him then," she said laughing. So after a quick hunt round for his car keys, Jeremy jumped into the car and was gone.

Charlie, as usual, was last to leave the changing room at Beckenham. He chatted to his friends, and was easily distracted from getting dressed. At the age of twelve, he was turning out to be a very talented swimmer, and had swum in the under thirteen age group in both the Kent county championships and also at the Southern Counties. He had made up his mind that he wanted to be a professional swimmer.

He was intelligent, and had managed to pass his exams to get into Dulwich College, but swimming was his first love, and he was looking forward to having the opportunity to travel to other

156

countries to swim against other nations. But first he had to do well at the Nationals.

It was a chilly November night, and he had towel dried his hair, so he carelessly wedged his school hat on his head before going out into the cold air. He knew his mother would scold him about going out into the cold with wet hair, she always did. But when he finally exited into the foyer of the swimming pool, it was his father who was patiently waiting for him tonight. This was unusual because he had a very demanding job, and worked long hours, but obviously today he had managed to get home earlier.

"Hi Dad," he said, swinging his satchel in front of him as he got into the car next to Jeremy.

"I was beginning to wonder if I had missed you," remarked Jeremy, well aware of his son's inability to hurry.

Charlie always took the bus from school to the swimming pool, and was supposed to start his homework before his session started. Ellen was usually the one who had to chase him up over that, but today Jeremy was going to check with him, because right now Ellen had a lot more on her mind.

"Did you get any homework done, son?" he enquired. Charlie's silence gave him his answer.

"You know swimming training does take over your life if you want to succeed, and I know you do, but you cannot neglect your school work, because when you are older you will want a career. Swimming doesn't last forever, so you need to pass your exams and get qualifications so you can get a well paid job."

Charlie was silent whilst he thought about what his father had said. He had always been proud of his dad, a man who saved lives and healed sick people. He had thought a swimming career might be fun, and never even thought about it not lasting, but his dad was right, most competitive swimmers were in their twenties, and after that they were often retired.

"I haven't done it yet, Dad, but I will after supper."

"Thanks for your honesty, son."

"Dad, did you always want to be a doctor?"

Jeremy's eyes twinkled. "No, I wanted to be a professional footballer, but I wasn't good enough."

157

"I don't really know what I want to do apart from swimming."

"Don't worry, you have years to decide, but enjoy your swimming in the meantime. You can discipline yourself to do both."

They had arrived home by now. Charlie jumped out of the car, and they went indoors. The main thing on his mind right now would be food. He always arrived home saying he was starving, and Ellen was wise to that. The dinner table in the lounge was already laid up for them, and Ellen urged them to wash their hands as she was just about to serve up.

After Charlie had demolished the chicken dinner, he was about to leave the table, but Ellen, who had struggled to eat her dinner, restrained him gently. Jeremy poured some water into her glass, as he knew her throat would be dry.

"Charlie, I have something very important to tell you, so I need you to listen to me very carefully, and not allow your mind to be distracted by anything else."

Charlie looked at his mother with surprise. "I know I have to do my homework. I was just going to get my books out."

"It's nothing to do with your homework." Ellen looked towards Jeremy, who got up from the table, and came up to her, putting his arm around her shoulders in a gesture of solidarity.

"Listen to your mother, Charlie."

"Back in 1961, on this day, I was not married, but I gave birth to a baby girl. Her name was Grace. But it was winter, and I could not keep her safe, so I had to have her adopted."

Charlie surveyed his mother with interest. He had learned at school how babies were created, and then how they came into the world. It had not greatly interested him. At the age he was now, he felt nothing that drew him towards girls. They were giggly and stupid, and if anyone was caught talking to a girl outside school, they would know about it in class, and they would be ragged. At his swimming club it was a mixture of boys and girls, but they all competed in their own groups, and they all had separate changing rooms. Girls held very little interest to him, but he supposed that might change when he was older, because his own parents clearly loved each other. He realised they must have done the deed, or else he wouldn't be here now, but it was hard to believe that his parents

158

had 'done it'. Right now his dad was holding his mum's hand. They were just like Romeo and Juliet.

"Did you have another boyfriend before Dad?" he asked, trying to work it out.

"No, your dad was always my only boyfriend," Ellen said quietly.

"It was my fault. I left your mum to go out with another girl, but I didn't know she was pregnant," explained Jeremy. "That was a terrible mistake, as I always loved your mum."

"So when did you find out? Surely Grandma Vera didn't want you to leave home?"

Charlie adored his grandmother, who had always done her fair share of spoiling him.

"I know it's hard for you to understand, but in those days, girls were cast out by their families if they got pregnant, especially if they were alone. Grandma Vera was worried about how your Granddad Norman would react, so I made the choice to leave home. I went to live at Herne Bay, but after Grace was born I found myself homeless and without a job."

". . .and to answer your question, I didn't meet up with your mother again until 1968, some seven years later. I had been away studying to be a doctor," cut in Jeremy quickly.

For once in his life, Charlie was lost for words. Somewhere out there he had a sister. He would have preferred it was a brother. Boys were much more fun, and they could have played football and gone swimming together. But somehow the idea of a sister felt cool. Suddenly he was not an only child.

"So she is twenty-two now, an adult," he said, after doing the maths in his head. Why can't we find her?"

"Because she might not want to be found. She might be happy with her adopted parents," said Ellen sadly, and Jeremy tightened his grip on her shoulder.

Charlie could sense his mother's grief. Her face looked sad, and his dad was holding her close. "She would love you if she knew you," he said stoutly. "You are the best!"

His kind words caused Ellen to weep. She had been expecting recriminations for not being told about his sister, but there were none. She had been worried that Charlie would lose his respect for her and look down on her, but she was wrong. Jeremy held out his arms to Charlie, who ran in between his parents, and cuddled in closely to both of them. He was glad his friends couldn't see him being all mushy, but he didn't like his mum to cry.

Ellen dried her tears. She had felt it wasn't right to mention about her father's temper. Granddad Norman had died long before Charlie was born, and Charlie did not need to know details like that. He had a vision of his grandfather being a heroic figure, and he had seen photographs of him. There was no need to use his temper as an excuse, and spoil the image. Nor did he need to know about her breakdown, because she was much stronger now.

"You Charlie, are the best son, even if you do drive me to distraction at times. You are our pride and joy, and now it's time for your homework," she said, gently extricating herself from them both.

"I'll help you to clear the dishes," said Jeremy. "Charlie, don't forget to tidy your room after you have done your homework. You can't reach the bed without falling over all your clothes."

"OK," sighed Charlie. Life was back to normal. He was being nagged again, and he went to unpack his satchel.

Chapter Twenty-six

Grace 1983

"Well Grace, all your hard work has paid off. You have your degree. Daddy and I are so very proud of you."

Pearl's face was alight with happiness, not just because Grace had her degree, that had been a foregone conclusion, but because she had found a way to cope with living amongst other students. Giving talks to others to explain about her autism had really worked for Grace. Students had looked up to her and respected her, and they had all learned something from it. Now her time at the university was over, she had already approached Pfizer, and had an interview scheduled for the following week.

"We certainly are, Princess." Roger's face showed such pride. Grace had overcome so much. She was a total inspiration to many, and her tutor Kevin had said the same. Nobody had taken their condition by the scruff of the neck the way that Grace had, and used it to inspire others.

"There is an end of year celebration. Belle wants me to go to it."

"How do you feel about it?" asked Pearl, cautiously.

"I think maybe I should go for a little while. We are all going separate ways now and may never see each other again."

"True. Are you sad about it?" asked Pearl.

"Not really. University was a means to an end. My life will begin next week."

"Well, you certainly have the qualifications, so you just need to get through the interview."

"I know, Mother, and like you said, I cannot just answer yes or no to the questions. I have to sell myself."

"They will probably ask you why you want this job, so tell them it's been your dream since you were eleven, and say you want to make a difference, then you will be fine," said Roger, very aware of how difficult the interview would be for Grace.

"Yes Daddy. If I am myself, they won't want me, so for that interview I am going to imagine I am an actress in a play, and I need to play my part."

"Good girl, that's the spirit. Now would you like your mother and I to stay at a hotel nearby, and then return in the morning to take you home?"

"If it's OK with you, and once I start work, and earn some money, I will make sure I have a car and pass my test. Then you and Mummy won't have to run me around."

"We don't mind!" interjected Pearl.

"But I do. I need to be independent," declared Grace.

To anyone else that might have sounded a bit ungrateful, but Pearl and Roger knew it was just Grace's direct way of speaking. She was always entirely honest. She had never been known to even tell a white lie. It wasn't surprising that at twenty-two, she wanted her own car, and maybe she might even want to get her own flat in time. Pearl was resigned to that. They had missed her during the last three years, and holiday time was always a time to look forward to. But then she chided herself, because even if Grace did get her own flat, it would not be far away if she was working at Pfizer. It would be close to Sandwich, and she would obviously still visit them.

"There's a pub in the village. We will go there to eat, and then find out if we can stay there," said Roger. "Enjoy your party, and we will come to collect you about ten o'clock tomorrow."

"Thanks Dad," said Grace, then she hugged both of her parents, and watched them walk out to the car which was parked nearby.

After they had gone, she wondered if she had done the right thing. But Belle would like it if she was there, and she had turned out to be a great friend and very supportive and understanding about the times she needed to be alone and have her own space. In fact, the whole group had respected the fact that she was different, and they didn't care. The only person she was a little bit wary of was Toby Ward. He appeared to be really interested in her, but she didn't do boyfriends; all that touching and invading space was not for her. The only times she had any feelings for a boy had been when Jamie had been hanging around with Felicity, but the last time she had visited home he had told her that Felicity was now qualified, and had taken a job in the North of England. She didn't really understand those feelings. Had she been jealous, or just insecure?

She checked whether the shower was free, and it was, so she collected her towel and shampoo, and went in there. It wouldn't be long before other students would appear and want to get in there. She had never liked the idea of sharing, but had learned to tolerate it over the past three years.

After showering and washing her hair, she felt better. So she wrapped the towel around her and headed for her room. She could hear someone walking along the corridor, which was probably Belle, as their rooms were at the end, and then a tap on the door. She changed into her towelling robe and cautiously opened the door, relieved to find it was Belle.

"Hi Belle, I will come tonight for a bit. An hour or so."

"Wonderful. When you see Scott's dance moves, you might be tempted to stay longer," enthused Belle.

"I will be ready at eight o'clock," said Grace.

"Great, I will give you a knock then," smiled Belle. Finally, after three years, Grace had come out of her shell.

Grace checked her wardrobe. Last Christmas Pearl and Roger had given her a blue dress. It had a full skirt with a petticoat underneath it. A very simple style with short sleeves, a round neck, and a nipped in waist, which showed of her willowy figure to perfection. They had hoped it might encourage her to go to parties, but up until now it had just hung in her wardrobe.

Belle had said the girls would be dressing up, and even shown Grace her gypsy-style blouse, and big hooped earrings which would be teamed up with a red floral full length skirt. Grace's dress was calf length, but she felt it would be very suitable.

She had never worn much make-up but decided to experiment tonight. She opened her make-up bag, and found some eye shadow.

163

Apparently, according to beauticians, if you had hazel eyes, and wore a different colour eye shadow, they would stand out more. She applied a small amount of green, and could see it was true, her eyes looked even bigger and in fact blue. After then adding some mascara, and a pink lipstick, she surveyed herself in the mirror. She had made various attempts to straighten the mass of curls in her hair, but every time she washed it they sprang obstinately back. The sun had heightened the strawberry blonde tones in her hair, and as she was not working, she allowed the curls to tumble around her face. Most young women went to this amount of trouble for a man, but Grace was doing it for herself. Going out for a social evening with others was a new experience for her, and she wanted to look her best.

She was ready long before eight o'clock, and so she sat anxiously waiting for Belle to knock on the door. When she did, it was a relief, and she came out to see Belle and locked her door behind her. Belle looked very Spanish in her outfit, and she was wearing a red hairband round her long black hair.

"Wow Grace, you look amazing. I so wish I had your beautiful curls. My hair is so straight."

"Well I would rather have straight hair. It's easier to tame."

"But curls are bubbly and fun. That is my nature, but my hair doesn't match it," laughed Belle.

Grace was silent. Maybe she was right. Curls were bubbly and fun, but she knew she was a serious person. Jamie was fun, and she hadn't realised how much she had missed that fun in her life. But tomorrow she would be going home, and maybe she would see him. Jamie knew just how to make her laugh.

"It's gonna be great tonight. All our exams behind us, so we can truly celebrate," said Belle, excitedly.

Grace was more cautious. She did not want to drink anyone under the table. Getting drunk was not for her, although the others seemed to revel in it. She hoped to enjoy a couple of glasses of wine or punch, whatever was being served. She just wanted to tick another box when she left university, by knowing she had attended an end of year celebration.

They had arrived at the venue now. It was being held at one of the big halls, and students could be seen streaming into it, chattering and laughing along the way. They joined up with a group of students who had been in the same class all year, and over in the corner were tables and chairs, so they all divided into groups of four.

The idea was to seat two women and two men at each table, to make sure everyone mixed. So Belle sorted out a table for them. Scott, whom she had mentioned, was seated opposite her, and Toby, another student, was opposite Grace. Toby was very well mannered and he greeted them both, then went off with Scott to get some drinks.

Belle had told her that the home-made punch was mainly fruit, with very little alcohol, so Grace thought she would try that. When Toby handed the glass to her, she understood what Belle meant. Apart from ice cubes, there were slices of lemon and lime floating on the top, and when she sipped it, the taste was a delightful combination of juice with maybe a hint of wine.

The music was beating out loudly, and then after a few drinks inside them, students were up dancing to Sister Sledge and songs like YMCA, so they could all shout out the words. Grace was happy to watch it all going on, and she agreed to one more drink, which Toby dutifully brought to her. Up until then she had been a bit wary of him, but he appeared to be a perfect gentleman.

"Thank you. Please go off and dance, I am more than happy watching," she told him.

But Toby had other ideas. When he had first known about Grace, he was drawn to her. She wasn't just beautiful; she was unique. She was also a challenge. Nobody had been out with her, let alone got her into bed, and Toby liked to think he would be the one to do it. He had a chequered history with women, and he didn't care whether they were single or not. 'Love 'em and leave 'em' was his motto, and he knew just how to act the perfect gentleman.

He was aware that Grace had only planned to stay for an hour or so, and this was probably her last drink, so before he took it back to the table, he glanced around to check that no one was looking, and then slipped a sachet of powder into her drink.

"I would rather sit here and talk to you," he said softly, as Grace sipped at her drink. But his words troubled her, he was invading her

165

space, and she didn't feel comfortable. She gulped down some more of the drink. It was time to go, but as she did so, an overwhelming tiredness was descending upon her like a thick suffocating curtain. She forced her eyes to stay open, but it was hard.

"I need to go back," she said, rising from the chair, but Toby caught her as she tried to lurch forward.

"Don't worry. Just lean on me, and I will walk you home," said Toby, his eyes gleaming with anticipation.

As they turned to walk away, Grace had no other choice than to let him help her, as her whole body felt limp, and her legs didn't seem to be working properly. Seeing her walking towards the door, Belle came over to make sure all was well.

"What's wrong, Grace? Are you OK?"

Grace tried to move her lips to reply to her. She wanted to say she needed help, but only shouting would be heard above the pulsating rhythm of the music, and she didn't have the energy.

"Don't worry. I am taking Grace back to her room. She's not used to drinking," said Toby in a loud voice.

"Oh, you are kind," said Belle. Toby always had such nice manners, and he seemed to have a soft spot for Grace. How nice it would be if they paired up. Toby's dark and athletic looks were not lost on her.

"She doesn't party much," she said as way of an explanation, but having also had some of the punch herself, she was realising it had more than orange juice and fruit in it. She felt very light-headed, and was soon back on the dance floor, laughing with everyone else at Scott's dance moves.

Toby walked Grace slowly outside. He could see that the sedative had worked well with the punch, and she would be his for the taking. He had desired Grace for a while. She had never said much to him, or even shown any interest, but he could not wait to get her into bed. All that nonsense she had said about not liking to be touched. He was so confident of his sexual prowess that he was convinced that when he started touching her, she would like it very much. Women were drawn to him because of his looks, but this girl was very intriguing. He had listened to her speaking about autism, and he couldn't help wondering if she was frigid, but then she had not been screwed by him; after that he was sure she would be begging him for more.

Grace was vaguely aware of Toby. He had his arms round her and was guiding her back towards her room. Because she felt so dizzy and strange, she could not feel his arms, but she still didn't like the idea that this man, whom she only knew from classes, was touching her. All she wanted to do was go into her room and go to bed, and then, when she woke up, she hoped she would feel normal.

They had reached the door now, and she could hear his voice booming away in the distance.

"Have you got your key?"

She tried to focus on what he was saying. Where was her key? But he hadn't stopped for an answer, instead he had tipped everything out of her clutch bag and found it. She felt like she was an onlooker to what was going on. He was in her bag, and now had her key, and she didn't have the strength to stop him.

Toby unlocked the door, and then pulled Grace inside. She flopped wearily onto the bed. Her legs felt as if they didn't belong to her. She tried to speak, and she managed to pant out:

"Please leave me now. I don't feel well."

The plan had gone well. Toby was delighted; now for some fun.

"Oh no, sweetie, I am not going anywhere. I am going to show you how much you will enjoy being touched."

In spite of the weariness of her body, Grace realised just what was about to happen to her. The red mist that she had managed to control for years was rising inside her, fighting against her lethargic body. In the meantime Toby was tugging at her dress in an effort to remove it, and there was a tearing sound when he lost patience and ripped it from her trembling body.

Grace kicked out at him in an effort to stop his hands. Her body became rigid as he released her breasts from her bra and fondled them.

"I told you it was fun," he said breathlessly. This little lady was really turning him on.

The effects of the sedative were wearing off now. Grace was full of fear, which fuelled her anger even more. This evil man was

167

violating her body, and suddenly without warning, she kicked him in the crotch, causing him to release her breasts and double up with pain.

Without even heeding the fact that she was in her underwear and not wearing any shoes, she ran towards the door and wrenched it open. Then she ran as fast as she could out into the darkness. She had no idea where she was going. Anywhere away from him. Somewhere he couldn't reach her and she could feel safe.

Chapter Twenty-seven

Toby was absolutely livid when he realised Grace had outwitted him and run off. That little bitch had kicked him in the bollocks, and it really did hurt! It was hard to know which was hurt the most, his body or his pride, because no woman had ever turned him down in the past, but she was something else.

He had no idea which way to go to find her, but it didn't look very good for him as she had run off in her underwear, the silly bitch! He was going to have to think up some sort of story to tell Belle when she came knocking at the door, otherwise he might get accused of all sorts. It just didn't bear thinking about. He had just got a degree, but he had no hope of a good job if he got a criminal record.

After some thought, he picked up her torn dress, and left the room. Then he headed back towards his room. That way he would not be there when Belle came to check. He could say he had left her asleep on her bed, and gone home himself. No one could prove otherwise, it was just her word against his, and he hadn't raped her or anything, so nothing could be proved against him. Before he entered his room, he put the dress in a bin. It was a great big industrial bin, piled high with rubbish. Then he went into his room and found as much rubbish as he could from his own waste bin. There were bottles and cans, as well as empty cardboard packets. He then went out and tipped this over the dress. Good luck to anyone sorting through that lot. He then went back inside and went to bed without giving Grace's predicament a second thought.

h

When Belle arrived at Grace's room, she was concerned to find her door unlocked, so she went inside to check that she was all right. When there was no sign of her, she became worried. Her high heeled shoes lay on the floor, and her bed looked ruffled, as if she had been tossing about on it. Surely she wasn't running around outside in her dress and no shoes? Toby was the last person to see her, so she decided to give his door a knock, and see if he knew what was going on. If Grace was in there with him, she would be discreet, but she just wanted to make sure she was all right.

Scott was hanging about having walked back with her, so she said goodnight to him, and pretended to go into her room. When he had gone, she sped quickly along to the area where Toby was. His light was out. He might even be asleep, and get annoyed with her, but she didn't care, she had to be sure that Grace was OK. She tapped lightly on the door, and in a loud whisper she said:

"Toby, wake up. This is important. Is Grace OK?"

At first there was no answer, but she continued to knock. Other students walking by looked at her curiously, but she didn't care, this was important. Inside the room Toby was pretending to be asleep. He didn't want to talk to anyone at this time of night, especially Belle, but after he heard a male voice ask her if she was OK, he reluctantly opened the door.

Belle looked at him. He was all tousled as though she had woken him up, but was he alone?

"Is Grace in here with you?"

"Of course not. Why ever do you think that?"

"Last time I saw her she seemed to be drunk, and you were taking her back."

Toby sighed, and made his voice sound very caring. "Of course I took her back to her room. The poor girl was so dizzy, she could not stand up."

"What happened after that?" demanded Belle.

"I have no idea. I came back myself, and until you started knocking at my door, I was asleep."

"So she was asleep when you left her?"

170

"Well, very soon after. There was nothing more I could do, so I assumed she would sleep it off and then be OK tomorrow."

"But that is just it. She isn't there, and I found the door unlocked. The key was still on the outside."

Toby was fed up with her coming along and poking her nose in. Next she would be asking him to come with her and search for Grace, who could be anywhere, and he had no desire to do that.

When Grace was found, she would of course tell Belle the whole story, but Toby planned to be up early and gone. They didn't know his address, and there was no reason that he would see either of them again. No woman was going to spoil his chances of getting a decent well paid job.

"I think we ought to call the police. She is out there somewhere in the dark. Anything could happen to her."

Suddenly Toby remembered Grace explaining that her parents were staying in the nearby village, and coming to bring her home tomorrow. The lie came so easily to his lips.

"I think she may have gone to join her parents. They are staying at a local hotel. If you call the police, they won't be too happy for you wasting their time."

Belle too remembered the conversation. Maybe the effects of the drink had worn off, and like he said, Grace had gone to be with her parents. The accommodation here was very basic, and right now Belle had her own packing to do for tomorrow, and she was very tired.

"OK, we can check it out in the morning. Thanks Toby and good night."

"Goodnight Belle. Don't worry, Grace will be fine."

He was relieved when she stepped away from the door. If she knew just how much he was sweating. He realised how much trouble he would be in if Grace told people he had tried to rape her. He would be arrested. He came to a quick decision. He had his own car, so could leave whenever he wanted. It seemed like there was no time like the present, so he quickly packed his belongings, then after locking the door, he made his way over to the car which was parked nearby.

There was a special box to put keys in if the office was closed, so he posted his key into it.

171

People were still filtering back from the celebrations. Most of them were the worse for wear, staggering and giggling their way back to their rooms. Nobody really noticed the car that passed them in the dark, and once clear of the campus, he exited through a back gate that was rarely kept padlocked. He had used it before if he wanted to leave campus in the evening. All he had to do was open it, and then close it afterwards. Nobody was around, which was a relief to him as he got back into his car, and then drove off into the darkness.

Grace had no idea where she was going. Anywhere away from that disgusting man who had violated her body. It had upset her so much she felt nauseous. She ran away from the area where the celebrations were going on; she didn't want people. Everything in her life had come crashing down, and she could make no sense of it. Tears were streaming down her face. It felt like her life was coming to an end. The thought of his hands on her body, invading her private parts, was so abhorrent to her.

As she ran, she felt the bile rising in the back of her throat and then she retched, vomiting into a bush. She stopped in her tracks. She didn't even have a tissue. She felt even more vulnerable in her underwear, and all she wanted to do was hide herself away from the world and all the strange intimidating people in it. Instead of being scared of the darkness, it felt far more comforting than people.

She continued on away from the sound of the music and lights, and then she came across a building which was in darkness. It might be a hall or a church, she could not tell in the dark, but when she got nearer she could see a solid wooden door. Some of the buildings were used for storing equipment, but the door was locked, and no way was it going to yield to allow her to go inside. At the side of the building was a ladder, and an urge inside her made her want to climb it and leave this crazy world full of crazy people behind her.

Grace made sure that it was standing up safely, and then she stood on the first rung. As she looked up, the roof of the building appeared to be flat, so it definitely was not a church. Something inside her was telling her to climb it; only then would she be safe.

So she slowly ascended it, and when she got to the top could see the roof was flat. Finally she had found somewhere where he couldn't come after her; nobody could. So she leaned over and hauled the ladder up, then she curled up in a ball in a corner. She buried her head in her hands. It was getting cooler now, and she had no other clothes, so she prayed that it would not rain. Grace retreated into her own safe world, the world that she understood. The panic she had felt when she had run away from him had subsided, as he didn't seem to have come after her. Outside everything was now quiet and still, so the festivities must be over. She could finally breathe easy again.

Pearl and Roger arrived at ten o'clock the next day to take Grace home. Just as Pearl raised her hand to tap on the door, Belle arrived from her room. She was anxious because Grace wasn't there, and worried about how upset her parents would be.

"I am afraid Grace is not there. She went for a walk yesterday evening, and we haven't seen her since."

Pearl gasped with fear, and put her hand to her mouth.

"You mean she's been out all night?"

"We thought she would return. But she left her door unlocked, and I checked this morning, and her room is empty."

"So who upset her, then?" asked Roger, grimly. He knew that would be the only reason, as she had been looking forward to coming home. Someone had upset her for sure.

"Toby was the last person to see her. Maybe we should go and speak to him," suggested Belle.

Pearl and Roger followed her towards Toby's door. After several loud knocks, Belle tried the door, but it was locked. If anything had gone on he obviously wasn't going to tell them, as he had already left.

"Maybe we should call the police," she said, anxiously.

"Not yet. That will frighten her," said Pearl firmly. "We need to do our own search. The grounds here are vast."

Scott appeared beside them. "If you are looking for Grace, she went on quite a walk last night, but she has been spotted about a

173

mile from here by another student out jogging. There is a building where the mowers and gardening equipment are held. It has a flat roof, and she is up there." He refrained from saying 'In her knickers,' which is how it had been described to him, because he didn't think her parents would find that funny.

"Can you take us there? I take it we can't drive there," said Pearl anxiously. She was trying to keep calm, but knowing that Grace was scared of heights made her wonder what on earth was going on.

"Yes, we have to walk there. It's parkland," said Scott.

When they arrived at the building, Roger scanned the top. He could just pick out Grace huddled in the middle, so he called out to her.

"It's OK, Princess, we are here."

Grace did not respond. She continued to hug her knees with her head buried down.

"How did she get up there?" asked Pearl, then she spotted the ladder. "Oh, she must have used that ladder, and then hauled it up."

"Somebody is going to pay for this!" said Roger angrily. He knew Grace would not be up there unless she had been driven to it. "Princess, please throw the ladder down, then I can come up and help you."

"No Roger, that is not a good idea, you know you have blood pressure, and I don't want you fainting and falling off."

"Perhaps we could call the fire brigade. They have ladders," said Scott, trying to be helpful.

Roger had no intention of calling any of the authorities. He knew they had to get Grace down safely, and how she had managed to stay up there all night, he had no idea. "Leave it to me!" he said firmly, and Pearl held her breath, she was finding this all so stressful.

"Princess, you must speak to me. Unless you drop the ladder down, and allow me to climb up, we will have to call the fire brigade."

Grace had been doing her best to close her ears and shut her eyes to all of it, but the fear of falling over the edge was real. However the thought of a strange man, a fireman, climbing up a ladder and carrying her down in her underwear was more than she could bear. Daddy would make it all right, and Mummy. Ever since she was a

174

little girl, whenever everything got too much for her, they were always there. She lifted her head and looked across to him.

"Daddy, I am in my underwear. It's too embarrassing."

Pearl stiffened with surprise. No wonder Grace was huddled up like that. "Whatever has been happening?" she asked in an emotional whisper.

"Most important thing is to get her down. We can ask questions later." Roger reminded her.

Pearl took off her long jacket cardigan, and handed it to him. She knew no matter what she said to him, Roger would be going up there. "She can put that around her."

Roger held the cardigan up and shouted. "I have Mummy's cardigan. If you push the ladder over, I will come up, and you can put it on. It's OK Princess, everything will be OK."

Everybody held their breath, and looked up expectantly, watching Grace. After a short time, she crawled over towards the ladder and pushed it over the edge.

"Step back, everyone!" ordered Roger, as it came tumbling down.

He wasn't going to admit to Pearl just how nervous he was. He suffered with blood pressure which sometimes made him feel dizzy, but such was his determination to get his daughter safely down, he pushed the thought of failure out of his mind; she needed him.

He went slowly up the ladder, with the cardigan hanging from his shoulders and neck leaving both hands free. When he got near to the top he was distressed to see the pathetic figure of Grace, her face streaked with tears, and although it was a warm day she was shivering, and her eyes were full of fear. When he reached the very top, he got up slowly, and threw the cardigan towards her.

"Here you are, Princess, put this on, then I will climb down slowly, and you come after me. Do not look down at any time. If you should slip, I will be there to catch you."

Grace didn't cry very often. A lot of the time her emotions were churning away inside her and she couldn't explain them to anyone, which made her appear to lack emotion. But today she was all cried out, she felt limp and exhausted, and she did so want to be down on

175

the ground again with the parents who had always made her feel safe. So she did not utter a word, but obeyed everything that her father had said.

As he slowly descended the ladder, with Grace following behind him, suddenly the dizziness came over Roger. He gritted his teeth angrily, "Not now, don't let me fall," he said silently to himself, his most precious cargo was following right behind him. He took another step back, and to his relief the dizziness had passed.

He stepped off the bottom onto the ground, and held his arms out to Grace just as she tripped on the last rung of the ladder, and fell backwards into his arms. There was no stopping Pearl now; with a sob of relief she rushed over and put her arms around both of them.

"You are safe now," she sobbed.

Chapter Twenty-eight

"Hello Jamie, how are you?"

"I am fine, and how is Grace? Is she home now? I need to pop round."

"Yes, she is home, but we cannot get a word out of her. She had an experience at university which caused her to climb up on a roof in her underwear, and we can't find out what happened."

Jamie stiffened, surely nobody had tried to attack Grace. He would kill them if they had!

"But Grace is frightened of heights. Something or somebody must have terrified her!"

"I know, and we can't get a word out of her about it. We were so relieved it was her last day at university, because the principal got to hear about it, and we really didn't think she could cope with police being involved."

"Wow, I can imagine that was awkward."

"All she said to them was that nobody had hurt her, and she didn't want to talk about it. Right now she is shut in her bedroom. That is not a good sign."

"I know. Can I pop round and see her, maybe take her to the Hampton Inn? It's such a nice day, and we could sit outside."

"I was so hoping you would say that, Jamie. You are her own age, and she may open up to you."

"I will pop round at midday then. Meanwhile you can mention I am coming."

"I certainly will. We know she doesn't like surprises being sprung on her."

Pearl smiled as she put the phone down. Dear Jamie, whom they had known since he was a new baby; the longest friendship Grace had ever had, and the most loyal of friends. He was like family to Grace, and to them the son they had never had.

Jamie became very thoughtful after he replaced the receiver. Grace had been the centre of his world as far back as he could remember. In his eyes, she was beautiful, talented and unique. He had never been able to hide his feelings for her, ever since the first day when she had allowed him to hold her hand going into school. He had been ridiculed by other boys, as at that age girls were of no interest to boys, and even when he was older, he was considered a sissy to hang around with a girl, but it had not made the slightest difference to Jamie. He simply didn't care what anyone thought. Now she was twenty-two years old, and any man would be proud to be seen with her, but up until now she had shown no interest in anyone, preferring to spend her time learning, and not having a social life.

When he was seventeen Jamie had learned about girls. He had been initiated into sex by Felicity, a voluptuous and sexy girl, whom he had met at college. He had done this to curb his feelings for Grace, because he knew it wasn't going anywhere. So he tried to forget her by hanging around with Felicity. He hoped that Grace might feel jealous, but she had not said anything.

This liaison had lasted for about three months, and then eventually Felicity had got tired of him and moved somewhere up north. It had been a relief to Jamie, as he was not proud of the fact that he had tried to use Felicity to forget his feelings for Grace, and it had not made the slightest difference. Luckily Felicity didn't seem to have been upset by it, and he put it down to life experience.

Now that Grace was home from university, it was quite normal for him to hook up with her, but at the same time he was concerned, and he knew that if he found out that any man had harmed or abused her in any way, although he was not a violent person by nature, they would wish they hadn't.

He decided, as it was a hot summer's day, he would go out in his shorts. It was an unwritten rule if you lived at the coast that during the summer you would wear shorts. It was particularly nice that now that he had finished college, and had passed all his engineering exams, he could relax in his shorts, as he had been wearing trousers all term to classes.

Inside his wardrobe he found some beige coloured cotton shorts, and a blue round necked tee shirt. He could wear light canvas shoes today too. Once dressed, he heard the phone ring again. It was Pearl.

"Just to let you know that Grace knows you're coming."

"Great. Is she OK about it?"

"Well, I guess yes. She is in the shower, and asked if it's OK to wear her shorts."

"Of course, that is exactly what I am wearing." Jamie could not help feeling pleased that they had both had the same thought.

"See you at midday then, and thank you, Jamie."

Jamie smiled as he put the phone down. Pearl had no need to thank him, as he was proud to be taking Grace out, even if it was just for a drink at the local pub. What he was dreading was the day when someone else might come along and snap her up. So he decided that today he was going to unveil his heart to her, so at least she knew that he didn't think of her as a sister, and that he actually loved her with all his heart.

He watched the clock slowly moving towards midday, and with a couple of minutes to spare, he arrived at the front door. Pearl greeted him with a sweet smile, and then she called to Grace to come out.

Grace had always been tall and slim, with beautifully shaped legs. Today she was wearing white shorts and a peach coloured blouse, which accentuated the red gold hue of her hair. She only had very light make-up on; her eyes were so big, she didn't really need it. Her gold hooped earrings swung every time she moved her head, and her face lit up when she saw him, which made his heart glow.

"Hi Jamie, it's good to see you," she said, and to his absolute delight, she put her arms around him, and briefly kissed him on the cheek. It was something she had done for all of their lives. Nothing unusual, but to him it was special, because she did not hug anyone outside the family.

179

"You are looking lovely as always," he murmured, allowing his arms to hold her for as long as she wanted.

Grace had never minded Jamie touching her. They had always hugged after being apart for a while, and today she particularly found his hug comforting. He was wearing a very pleasant aftershave, and he looked so handsome, she felt proud to be with him. She could feel sensations going through her like electric currents, which were not unpleasant, and after the way Toby had bullied and groped her, this was an entirely different experience. She decided that if they could find a quiet spot she would tell him about it, as she needed to offload the distress Toby had caused her.

They had reached the pub now, and because it was such a nice day, all the outside seats were taken. There was a direct view of the sea, which was glistening in the sunlight, so there would be no privacy with people around them.

"Do you mind if we sit inside?" she asked him.

"No, of course not." Jamie was on her wavelength. "What would you like to drink?"

"I am thirsty in this heat. How about a shandy, with two thirds lemonade and one third lager."

"Yes, that sounds good. I might have one too."

Jamie went up to get the drinks, and she saw a table by the window which was unoccupied. This afforded a view of the sea and the beach where the car park was. Because the Hampton Inn stood on a corner, the sea could be seen from both sides. Jamie brought the drinks over.

"Oh, this might be reserved. I didn't realise," said Grace, noting the other tables were laid up. Further over was a long table, where a row of men sat sipping their beers.

"It's fine," smiled the landlady. "You can sit at that one. This lot are so noisy!"

They both sipped their drinks, and then Jamie said casually, "How was university, and are you glad you are home?"

Grace often found it hard to let things out, but this time she needed to share her experience with Jamie, as she was still shocked at Toby's behaviour.

"I have something to tell you, but I don't want my parents to know. I have never discussed intimate things with them."

180

Jamie touched her arm gently. "It's OK. In your own time."

"I have never liked parties, as you know, but after I got my results I decided I would go to the party, maybe have a couple of drinks, and then go back to my room."

"Go on."

"Everyone was having punch, and a boy called Toby went to get some for me." She then went on to explain how strange she had felt. Then Toby helping her home, and the terrifying ordeal he had put her through, until she had no choice but to run out of the room, away from him, in just her underwear.

Jamie could feel extreme anger towards Toby for what he had done to her. It made him want to go and find the bastard, and teach him a lesson, but that would not help Grace. He was aware that where parties were concerned, because she had not frequented them, she would be unaware that some men preyed on women, and drugged or got them drunk for their own evil ends.

"If you don't mind telling me, where did he touch you?"

Without hesitating, she put his hand on her breast. "Here, but inside my bra. It was vile."

"But you don't mind me touching you."

"When you touch me it's different. You make me feel safe."

His spirit soared at her words. Maybe there was a chance for him in the future.

"But he did not rape you?"

"Not for want of trying. He ripped my dress off, but I kneed him in a sensitive place."

Jamie roared with laughter, and Grace smiled too. "Well done. And so that is why you were up on a roof in your underwear."

"Yes, but I can't explain to my mum and dad; it's too embarrassing. We have never discussed things like that. When I started my periods I thought I was bleeding to death, then my mum said it was a normal thing for women. I think she had trouble discussing such things with me."

"Yet you have just told me?"

"I don't know why, but I can tell you anything."

"How would you feel if I explained all this to your parents, as they are worried about you."

181

Grace did not reply immediately. It had been a relief to tell Jamie. She felt so much better now, but she was home, away from evil Toby, and due to go for a job interview next week. She did not want anything to spoil it.

"You can tell them, as long as they let it go after that. If they report it to the police, I won't tell them anything; I can't."

This was very much what he had expected her to say. It was amazing just how well he understood her. "I will make sure they do let it go," he reassured her.

Grace took another sip of her shandy. It was cool and refreshing, and the safe feeling she got when she was with Jamie was balm to her after the experience that she wanted to forget.

Jamie touched her hand gently, and the words he spoke came right from his heart.

"Grace, when I am with you, it feels so right. All I want to do is keep you safe. As from next week I am going to be a humble car mechanic, but you will be a scientist at Pfizer. In spite of that, will you be my girlfriend, rather than my sister?"

He had wanted to completely bare his heart to her, and tell her how much he loved her, but if he was too intense he might lose her, and that just couldn't happen.

Grace felt so happy now that he was back in her life. It was a completely different feeling when his hand touched hers. It was warm and tingly, making her want more from him. She realised that this must be what people meant when they mentioned the word attraction. Maybe she was a late starter at twenty-two, but she now felt ready to explore what love was all about.

"Jamie, I wouldn't care what job you did. Nobody understands me like you do. I would love to be your girlfriend."

Chapter Twenty-nine

Ellen 2002

Life became easier for Ellen after she had told Charlie about his sister Grace. Every year, on Grace's birthday in November, as a family they remembered her, and drank a toast to her. Charlie had very much wanted to try and find her, but Jeremy had explained it was not possible, unless she wanted to be found, and they had to accept that Grace considered her adoptive family as her real parents.

Ellen still felt drawn to Herne Bay. It was comforting and distressing for her in equal measure. They took day trips there, and she even took them to Bentley Avenue at Studd Hill, but in recent years many of the old bungalows had been pulled down and replaced with new ones. Betty Lomax's bungalow was no more, nor was the one she had stayed in with Edna and Sam. The shed she had sought shelter in with Grace was no longer there either.

She could see quite a difference in Herne Bay, as since the nineties, a lot of the spare land had been used to build modern houses, and the sleepy town that was Herne Bay now buzzed with people of all ages relocating to the coast to live a healthier life.

The end of the pier had broken away during a turbulent storm, so it had been rebuilt. It was much shorter, but now housed fairground rides for children, and some interesting food places from foreign cultures. There were also small huts along one side of the pier where local people sold their home-made wares. It had become a thriving and interesting town, with many ice cream parlours and cafes along the front. The bandstand remained, but inside it housed a coffee shop where all the locals met up to chat, and during the summer live music played. The rough ground along the front had now changed into beautiful gardens with seats aplenty, and palm trees, and beautifully tended flower beds which were a riot of colour.

Ellen expressed how much she liked Herne Bay, and Jeremy agreed. He was due to retire in a couple of years, so maybe they could think about retiring there. But first there was Vera to consider. She was now seventy-six, and her memory was failing. Eddy had taken care of her until he died of a heart attack. They had enjoyed a happy marriage until then. Ellen and Jeremy had moved her into their house, and Ellen had looked after her with support from a live-in nurse.

Charlie had married Abigail in 1998. He was then twenty-seven, and Ellen and Jeremy very much liked their new daughter-in-law. He had met her when he was training to be a teacher. He had kept up his swimming until he was sixteen, but then his life took a different path. He had an accident whilst playing football at school and broke his leg. It meant he could not continue swimming any more at that time, but during his competitive years he had amassed a lot of medals and trophies, which his parents were very proud of.

So after completing his education he had trained to be a teacher, and now taught at Archbishop Tenison's Grammar school at South Croydon. His leg had now healed, and he taught games, and swimming, but also maths and science. He made it his mission to encourage all pupils to learn to swim, not just to be competitive, but to maybe save their life if they ever fell into deep water.

In the year 2000, Charlie and Abigail welcomed their daughter Chloe into the world. When Ellen held her granddaughter in her arms it took her right back to when Grace was born, and the tears she shed were a mixture of happiness and emotional pain, which she had learned to accept would never completely leave her.

During the last months of Vera's life, it had been distressing for Ellen to see how badly she had deteriorated. She no longer recognised anyone from her family, and she just sat in a chair with a vacant look in her eyes. Tom too, came frequently to see his mother, but she was not eating, and slowly they watched her slip

184

away before their eyes. The nurse had explained that such deterioration was normal for anyone suffering from dementia, and all they could really do was keep her warm and comfortable. The family did their grieving for her at this time, and when she passed away in her sleep in 2002, they could feel nothing but relief.

Jeremy knew what a toll it had taken on Ellen. She had never forgotten how her mother and brother had given her a reason to keep living way back in 1962, when they had come to Herne Bay and found her, so she had spent a lot of her time sitting with her mother, and holding her hand when she became distressed and upset. Together with Tom they had tried to take her out for trips in the car, thinking a ride into the countryside would brighten up her day, but Vera was never out for long before she was asking to go back. It seemed she only felt safe when she was in her room.

Jeremy decided what Ellen needed was a holiday. So after the funeral had taken place, he booked a cruise which would last about two weeks. Just before they left, Charlie told them that he was going for the job of deputy headmaster at Herne Bay High School in Herne Bay, and if he got it, they would be moving into one of the new modern estates, which looked very inviting. The one he had been looking at had a play park running along parallel to the other houses, which would be perfect for Chloe, and any other children they might have in the future.

"Well, this seems the perfect time for us to move too. What do you think?" remarked Jeremy.

"Yes, when we come back from our holiday, we must put the house on the market, and we can start hunting for one down there," said Ellen. The thought of that made her feel much brighter. She wanted to put the tragic events to the back of her mind, and try to remember her dear mother as she had been before she became ill.

Charlie had kept his sense of humour right into his adult years. He had inherited it from Jeremy, and the two of them had made Ellen laugh over the years when she had been at a low point. As a schoolteacher it was a definite advantage to have a sense of humour because sometimes pupils could do and say the most unexpected things, and Charlie had found himself very popular with the students. When he went for his interview, his references spoke about

185

his dedication to getting the very best out of his students, his wit, his sense of humour and ability to deal with a crisis. He seemed perfect to assist the head at Herne Bay High, so was offered the job immediately.

Ellen and Jeremy came back from the holiday feeling really refreshed, and Jeremy decided that now, at the age of sixty, and Ellen being fifty-nine, it was a good time to retire. They were both very fit for their age. He still played golf and there were golf clubs everywhere in that area of Kent. He could think of nothing nicer than playing a round of golf on the green, with the blue sea shimmering in the background.

Ellen also played golf sometimes, and she loved swimming as well. She knew there were plenty of swimming pools in the area, as she had been a spectator at many of them when Charlie had been competing for his club. She might even venture into the sea during the warmer weather. She had also heard that there was a badminton club, and they were looking for players, so maybe she could work on Jeremy to come there with her. In the past, people had moved to the coast to retire, but they were looking forward to going there to enjoy life. Seeing her mother fading away had made her realise that life was for living, and they needed to make the most of it.

She was also looking forward to helping out with Chloe, who was now two years old. Abigail was thinking of going back to work for a couple of days a week, and Ellen was more than happy to take care of her granddaughter. She wondered if Grace would have looked like Chloe at that age. She would never know, but being a part of Chloe's life helped her to cope. She had not wanted to miss out on any of Chloe's milestones. She had even been there when she took her first steps, which was a bit of solace because she had missed all of Grace's.

She would miss Tom, of course, her brother who had steadfastly supported her through her breakdown, but Tom and Linda had pointed out that now the new motorway had been built, and they didn't have to travel through the endless traffic in Sittingbourne, it was only just over an hour away, and they would be visiting very frequently, especially in the summer.

The house was put up for sale, and it sold immediately. The part of Shirley Hills where they lived was very sought after, and the estate agent had been very positive about selling it quickly, mainly because he had clients on his books who especially wanted to live in that area.

In the meantime, they had gone down to Herne Bay armed with brochures from the local estate agents. They wanted somewhere smaller now, as Jeremy would not be needing a surgery and a waiting room, and the idea of a bungalow appealed to them both.

They found a large bungalow with a mature garden including shrubs and fruit trees. It would need redecorating. The estate agent had told them about a local man who was reliable, and his prices were fair. So Jeremy booked another holiday, this time in America where he hired a car, and they toured for six weeks whilst the bungalow was transformed to their liking.

The bungalow dated back to the 1970s. It had large rooms, and the kitchen was also very spacious. A conservatory ran along the back of the house, which faced a wooded glen, and various paths that led down to the beach could be viewed in the distance from the conservatory. The four bedrooms all had their own en suites, and there was also a family bathroom, so there was plenty of room if the family came to stay with them.

It was situated at the end of a road, and up the end of a drive, and had housed the man who built it and his family for many years. At the end of the road was a sign which had Bishopstone written on it. This was a little hamlet situated on a hill between Herne Bay and Reculver, and not many people had even heard of the place. It had its own bay, which mostly only the locals knew about. Jeremy and Ellen felt it was the perfect place for them.

Just before they moved, Tom, who had always hoped that Ellen would one day meet Grace again, found out that a new law had been passed which allowed mothers who had given their babies up for adoption to be given access to information about who had adopted them. Seeing as Ellen was moving very close to where she had given birth to Grace some forty-one years ago, she should know this. He came round to see her and shared his news.

Ellen looked a little troubled. "Tom, I would love to, but so many years have gone by, she would be forty-one years old now."

"So are you moving to the area because you hope to bump into her one day?" he asked.

"I don't know, I really don't. I just love the area, even though it also has some bad memories. Something inside me has always driven me on, but until now I didn't really have the opportunity."

"Well sis, after you get settled, we will pay a visit, and there is no pressure here, but if you want me to come to the office in Margate with you to check the records, we could at least find out what her new surname was. But, of course, she may well be married now."

"OK Tom, let's do it!" she exclaimed, and he hugged her excitedly.

"I would love to see you have peace of mind," he said, kissing her goodbye.

After he had gone, Ellen had time to reflect. It had always been there, and always would be no matter how many years had passed; the image of that tiny baby, all dressed in pink, clutching at her little finger. She had learned to live with the pain and regret, and had frequently told herself how lucky she was to be married to the love of her life, and to have an amazing caring son as well. But, unlike others, her family could never be complete.

She couldn't help wondering if Grace looked anything like her, or was it Jeremy? Was she married, and did she have children? If she did get the surnames of the parents who had adopted Grace, would she be able to track her down, and if she did track her down, would Grace have anything to say to her? So many questions without answers.

A couple of weeks later, Tom and Linda came to stay. The girls were off somewhere doing their own thing. Tom decided to broach the subject again.

"How do you feel about going over to the office at Margate?" he asked.

"I have been thinking about it, and it wouldn't do any harm to find out the surname of the couple who adopted her," said Ellen. She had thought about it constantly, and whether they still lived in the area.

Jeremy looked concerned. He knew it was a big step for Ellen. "I can cancel my game of golf and come too."

"No darling, you don't need to do that. Tom is happy to come with me."

"As long as you are sure."

"Very sure." She went up to him and put her arms around him. "I don't want you worrying. It's OK."

When they were in the car, she explained to Tom just how supportive Jeremy had been for all of their married life. "You and Mother were too; you helped me pick up the pieces and live my life again after you found me living rough."

It flashed through Tom's mind, that if she had waited for just one day, Ellen would not have needed to leave home. But how could any one of them know that her father was going to be killed in a car accident? It was a chance in a million that the one person who would have reacted badly to her pregnancy was suddenly taken out of the equation. His mother had told him that she would have helped Ellen to care for the baby, no matter what the neighbours thought. But it was all such a long time ago. He shook himself back into the present.

"We are family, Ellen, of course we did. And now let's head off and see what we can find out."

When they arrived at the office, they were greeted by a lady wearing glasses, her hair drawn severely back into a bun. Ellen had brought her birth certificate to prove who she was, and it was carefully scrutinised.

"I have to go into the archives. This was forty-one years ago," she explained.

Every minute seemed like an hour whilst they were waiting, but when she eventually came back, she was clutching an old and dusty folder. They watched whilst she opened it and read through the papers. When she had finished, she put it down.

"You gave birth to a daughter, whom you named Grace on 16th November 1961. You signed adoption papers on 30th November, and your daughter was adopted by Pearl and Roger Hart."

Ellen and Tom exchanged glances. "Did they live round here?" asked Ellen.

"The papers gave an address here in Margate, which was rented, and they were shortly going to move, but it doesn't state where."

"Can you give us the address?"

"Yes, it's 20a Victoria Road, which is literally just around the corner."

Tom could see that this was going to be difficult, and he did not want Ellen to be disappointed, but they would pay a visit to Victoria Road. They both thanked the clerk and left the office. As she had stated, it was just a couple of roads away, but difficult to park with yellow lines everywhere.

They parked the car in a less busy area, and walked back to the road. It had rows of terraced Victorian houses with very dark basements, and the flats were divided off by 'a' 'b' 'c', and 20a was on ground level.

"I don't know how helpful this will be after forty-one years, but we have to try," urged Tom.

As they walked towards the door, an elderly lady surveyed them with curiosity from next door. She was probably in her seventies, and this gave Tom an idea. He smiled at her.

"Good afternoon. Have you lived round here for long?"

"I certainly have. Over fifty years. I was twenty-one when Sid and I moved in here, but of course he's gone now, and it's just me."

"Do you remember Roger and Pearl Hart? They rented here in 1961."

The old lady furrowed her wrinkled brow, searching her memory, and Ellen held her breath.

"They adopted a baby," added Tom.

Then realisation came to her. "Oh, that couple. I do remember, they were so happy when they got their little baby. The day they brought her back I saw her; cute little baby all dressed in pink."

That all too familiar pain was like a dagger in Ellen's heart, but she had to know more.

"Do you know where they moved to?"

"I am sorry, they never said."

They both thanked her, and then walked back to the car. For a while Tom drove in silence, but then he spoke. "Well at least we know their name now: Hart."

"We do, but Tom, we have no idea where they moved to, and if they are still alive they will be elderly. I really don't want to turn up and cause any upset."

190

Tom considered her words. Ellen always thought about other people's feelings and forgot about herself, but he realised it could never work if she had any doubts. Family ties bound them together, and it would be the same with Grace and the parents who had adopted her. If Ellen didn't want to go through with it, it was best to acknowledge that now.

"I understand what you are saying, sis. You are the most unselfish person that I know, so if you want to leave it, then so be it."

"I do," said Ellen, but deep down inside herself she really wished she had the courage to see it through. "Now let's go home."

Chapter Thirty

Grace 2002

Grace and Jamie got married in 1985. It was no great surprise to either of their families. They had been inseparable for years, so it was a natural progression. Although Grace had never really had another boyfriend, she knew instinctively when their relationship became closer that he was the one. He made her feel safe and secure, and more importantly, he understood her.

On the wedding day, Pearl watched with misty eyes as Grace walked down the aisle on her proud father's arm. If she had to choose a husband for Grace, nobody could possibly have been better than dear Jamie.

Grace still enjoyed learning very much, and was totally obsessed in her work as a scientist. Sometimes she needed to be on her own, and Jamie made sure she was always allowed to be her own person. He accepted her exactly as she was. To him she was unique, beautiful and as he laughingly said, "The brains of the family."

Jamie himself had done well. He had started off as a junior car mechanic, but now owned three garages. They had a comfortable lifestyle, and money was never a problem, although they both worked very hard to earn it.

They had bought a house close to Pearl and Roger. It was in Grand Drive, which was just up the hill past the Hampton Inn, no more than a ten minute walk away from them.

In 1990 the twins were born. Julian arrived first, then his sister

Verity shortly after. Grace had immersed herself into her job, but when they heard the news that she was carrying twins, Grace and Jamie were over the moon. After they were born, she stated quite candidly:

"That is good. One of each, that means no more pregnancies, and I can get back to work."

Jamie roared with laughter; straight to the point, as she always was, but he heartily agreed; one boy, one girl, both healthy, and now their family was complete.

Grace took advantage of the new rule that allowed mothers to take a year's maternity leave from work. She was anxious to breastfeed them both, knowing it would give them the best start in life. It was comforting to know that her job would still be there when she wanted to return to work.

Grace had decided that she would only work three days a week until the children started school. Her children took precedence over everything.

Pearl and Roger, both now in their sixties, were only too happy to help with their grandchildren. Both Grace and Jamie made sure that this was only for a few hours by having a nanny to give support. If her parents wanted to take the children out for a couple of hours, then the nanny would use her spare time to do their washing and ironing. It was nice for her parents to be included, but not for a whole day. They were lively children, and Grace and Jamie both knew how shattered they felt after the little ones had gone to bed.

In 1995 the twins started school. After a family discussion, Grace went back to work full time. Pearl and Roger adored their grandchildren. Julian was quiet and studious, whereas Verity was a tomboy, full of mischief and energy. They would have been happy to meet them from school every day, but Grace felt her parents deserved to have their own life now. She knew she had not been an easy child, and although it was never mentioned, she wanted them to have a bit of their own time together. As parents, she felt they had been the best, but she just couldn't express that. So Jamie, who could come and go between his three garages as and when he pleased, finished work early three days a week to collect them from school, and Pearl and Roger did it for the other two days.

193

j

When Grace went back to work she became immersed in a new project. It was trying to find a cure for cancer, and also helping to prolong the lives of patients who had it. She continued to study and go on courses, and then she was made a head of department with a team of people working to support her.

In 2002, the twins were now twelve years old and ready to go to Grammar School, having passed the entrance exam. The Kings School Canterbury dated back to medieval times, and they were excited about the prospect of going there. When they went for their interview, it was made clear to them that they would not be in the same class, because the school believed that they must make friends with other students and not rely on each other all the time.

When they thought about it, Grace and Jamie agreed with that as well, and after making sure the twins were going to be happy with that arrangement, they accepted the places that had been offered to them. Their parents had agreed they could travel to school on public transport. So many other parents gave their children a lift, but the twins wanted to be independent, and Grace and Jamie were absolutely in favour of that.

They coped with being separated, and found their own friends at school. Verity, being attracted to all sports, made friends with like-minded girls, whereas Julian, who like his mother always seemed to have his head buried in a book, found friends like himself who enjoyed studying and taking exams.

Jamie and the twins were all very proud of Grace. She worked tirelessly with her team to understand how to cure cancer. It was a long road, but some cancers were now curable, and many drugs were developed to prolong the lives of patients who had the disease. In that same year, Grace became a Professor, and Julian particularly looked up to his mother and hoped he could be like her one day. He was also interested in medicine and was hoping to be a doctor.

Grace saw a lot of herself in Julian. Verity was more like Jamie. Julian had always been the quiet and serious one, whereas Verity had always been full of fun. They had always assumed that when they were tiny, and Verity had spoken for him sometimes, it was because Julian couldn't get a word in edgeways. But as he was getting older, Grace wondered if Julian was also autistic. If he was, it was not affecting him the way it had with her at school, but in recent years, society was learning to be more tolerant of anyone who did not exactly fit into the mould. She mentioned it to Jamie as they were going to bed one night, in her usual direct way. Grace never did beat around the bush.

"Jamie, do you think that Julian is autistic?

Jamie gave her a startled look. He had never even thought about it. Certainly there was no problem at school. Children did not pick on him, but Julian never had a lot to say, and he let Verity be the spokesperson for them both.

"Why do you ask, honey?"

"Because he is so like me, and he wants to learn. He shuts himself away at times, but being a twin means it's not so noticeable."

"Well, I suppose it might be true, but it certainly isn't holding him back. His school report is excellent. They call it being on the spectrum now, don't they?"

"Yes people are learning about autism all the time, and nobody judges. I think he is only mildly affected, and he probably doesn't want to be given a label."

"Well, it's never held you back, Professor Grace Parker."

"Being different makes you work harder to prove to yourself that you can do the same as others."

Jamie laughed and put his arms tightly around her. He loved her with all his heart. Always had, and always would, she was totally unique. At forty-one she was still extraordinarily beautiful, with her red gold hair and curls she couldn't tame. Julian had those same curls, but darker, and Verity's hair was also dark, but straighter, more like his was. Although, he thought ruefully, now when he looked in the mirror he could see touches of grey.

"You know how proud of you I am, producing our two beautiful twins."

Grace smiled, it was impossible being serious with Jamie for long.

"We produced them together."

"Certainly we did, and I am the luckiest man alive to have such a great family, and a wife like you."

His words touched Grace's heart. Deep inside her she felt the glow, but as always she was unable to express her feelings back. It was locked away inside her, as it had been all her life. Because she couldn't say the words, she had to show Jamie with her actions just how much he meant to her.

"If you look in the hall cupboard, you will find something," she said mysteriously.

When Jamie found a new set of golf clubs, he was so happy. "I do so love you," he said kissing her.

Chapter Thirty-one

Ellen 2012

The year 2012 was not a good one for Ellen. She was now sixty-eight, with Jeremy a year older, and the life at Herne Bay had suited them well. They were both able to remain active and enjoy all the benefits of living at the coast.

But one evening, as she was getting ready for bed, she noticed a lump on her breast. It was only a tiny one, the size of a pea, and her first instinct was to ignore it and then maybe it might go away. She mentioned it casually to Jeremy when he came into the bedroom.

He felt it gently, his hand touching the hard little lump. Inside he was thinking, oh no, please, let it be benign! He saw her worried face and kissed her cheek gently.

"It's probably nothing, sweetheart, but it's best to get it checked out."

"I will do it tomorrow," promised Ellen.

"Would you like me to come with you?"

"There's no need. I will be fine."

So the next day Ellen booked a doctor's appointment. Then she had a biopsy. When she was called back again, she felt very nervous. The doctor told her she had breast cancer, and Jeremy, who had feared the worst but kept quiet about it, was with her when the doctor gently broke the news. He was glad he was because Ellen was devastated.

But the good news was that it had been detected early. The doctor was confident that an operation followed by a course of radio therapy would stop it from spreading, and she would not have to lose her breast. Ellen felt very depressed, and inside she wondered if she was being punished because she had abandoned her baby. All through her life she had continued to be hard on herself because she had too much guilt.

She knew that if she told Jeremy he would tell her to stop being silly. People became ill all the time, it was not a punishment. But she could not understand how someone as fit and active as she was would have developed cancer. She didn't smoke or drink, and ate all the right foods. She was not overweight, either. To her it didn't make sense.

Jeremy was the eternal optimist. He knew that curing cancer had come on quite a bit since he had been practising as a doctor, and it was significant that Ellen only needed radio therapy, if she had needed chemotherapy it would have been a lot more serious.

He wanted to make sure that her mental health would not be affected, so he provided the support that she needed all the way through. He took her to all her treatments, and was by her side as often as the hospital would allow him to be.

Charlie and Abigail were also supportive. Charlie adored his mother, and was aware of how much she had suffered when she had to have Grace adopted. So this illness was quite a blow. They now had a son, Henry, who had been born in 2003, a brother for Chloe, and Ellen had taken great delight in being a part of her grandchildren's lives.

Ellen didn't feel great whilst she was having radio therapy. It left her feeling nauseous, and also very tired. But once the course had finished, gradually her strength picked up again, and she found herself able to do tasks that before had been too much. Jeremy laughed and joked with her to stop her being depressed. She found herself wanting to pick up her life again. She told herself what an amazing life she had; a great son and daughter-in-law, wonderful grandchildren, and the best husband in the world. She was only sixty-eight, with many more years ahead of her.

The day that she was told the cancer was in remission was a very happy one. As a precaution, she had to go back and be checked regularly, and carry on living a healthy lifestyle as before. Jeremy felt like shedding tears of relief. Ellen was his whole life, the love of his life, and the thought of being without her was something he had not wanted to contemplate.

"When you feel up to it, my darling, I thought a nice cruise would be good for both of us."

Ellen had not wanted to go anywhere other than be at home whilst she was ill, especially when she had an off day. She had worried that if she was on holiday she might collapse somewhere, but each day she felt an improvement and her confidence was returning, and the thought of a nice holiday really lifted her spirits.

"Oh Jeremy, you always think of me. I really think that is a nice idea," she said, smiling happily.

"You can get yourself some nice new clothes, too," he said, knowing how much Ellen loved going clothes shopping.

"Great. I will ask Abigail to come with me," she said.

The one thing she missed was having a daughter to share shopping trips and visits to hairdressers or nail bars with, but she tried to think of Abigail as a substitute daughter. It had even crossed her mind, not previously knowing if she would survive this illness, to ask Jeremy if they could try and trace Grace, so she could just meet her once and explain why she had to give her up.

But now she was feeling better, she could think more clearly. Ten years previously she had been close to trying to make contact, but had decided it might upset Grace's adoptive parents. If they were still around, they would be very elderly, so no, she could not do it. Her biggest hope was that one day Grace might find her, and then she could finally have peace of mind.

Chapter Thirty-two

Grace 2012

Grace had her most challenging year in 2012. She was now aged fifty-one, and still working full time. But with Pearl and Roger well into their eighties, they were beginning to need more help to enable them to stay in their home. So she made the decision to drop to three days a week. As Professor Parker, with a team of scientists to assist her, she could more or less do as she wanted. There was huge respect for Grace and all she had achieved through the years, and she wasn't ready to retire yet. It had never been about the money she earned, it was about the challenge of finding ways to overcome and treat deadly diseases.

Jamie, whose parents were no longer alive, had always been a tower of support. Roger was going to stop driving, because his eyesight was fading, so Jamie had assured them both that he was there to ferry them around to wherever they needed to go. Grace and Jamie shared the daily visit between them without the need for carers, as they were going to make sure her parents could remain in the home they both loved so much for as long as possible.

But in spite of all this, one particular day Pearl had an appointment at the Queen Victoria Memorial Hospital in Herne Bay. It was no more than a couple of miles from their home at Hampton, so Roger didn't think they would need Jamie's help. When they set off it was a fine day, but when they came out it was raining.

Roger managed to safely negotiate his car out of the car park, but when he pulled out onto the road, he did not see another car approaching from his right. When he did see it, he tried to brake to avoid it, but the car skidded, he lost control, and it ploughed straight into a tree on the other side of the road.

The man in the car he had almost hit, jumped out of his car, incensed with rage. But as he approached the car he realised that the occupants were not moving. An ambulance was very soon at the scene, but it was too late for Pearl and Roger, as they had died instantly, although could not be pronounced dead until the ambulance reached the hospital.

Jamie was the first to hear the news, as he was at home that day. When they telephoned, his first thought was for Grace. However would she cope with this devastating news. So he went over to Pfizer. He knew he had to move quickly before it was announced on the regional news.

Grace welcomed him into her office, where she was working on her computer, and as soon as she saw him she knew something terrible had happened.

"Is it our twins?" she asked, shaking with fear.

Jamie took her in his arms and held her tightly, wishing he could take all her pain away.

"No darling, the twins are fine. I am afraid it's Pearl and Roger."

"What's happened to them?"

"They were in the car, and had an accident. I am afraid they didn't make it."

Grace drew her breath in. It had always been hard for her to show her emotions, and no matter how upset she was, she rarely cried. But this did not mean she didn't care. Inside she was crying, because the only parents she had ever known, who had loved, cared and supported her through so much, were now gone in the blink of an eyelid. It would be easy to say why had her dad driven after what had been decided, but that would not bring them back.

She drew away from Jamie, desperately trying to compose herself.

"I need to go home right now," she said.

"That is why I am here, sweetheart," he said gently, knowing that inside she would be devastated. Not being able to shed tears made it even harder for her, but he knew her parents had been everything to her, and this was a huge shock.

When they got home he knew she would want her own space to process this news, so he took on the task of telling the twins. They were both married now, and living and working in London, but were ready and willing to come down to support their mother. Jamie suggested they waited a day or so to allow Grace to come to terms with the events, and Julian also thought that a good idea. So they were going to travel down together at the weekend, leaving their partners in London. They would then return with them for the funeral.

Grace put all of her energy into organising a funeral that she felt was fitting for her much loved parents. She invited anyone who had been connected to her parents. They had lived in the same house since 1961, so were well known and liked in the area. The only time she did shed any tears was when their two coffins, marked Mum and Dad with white flowers, were carried into the church. The realisation that they had gone forever, their bodies inside those coffins, hit her, but as always Jamie was there to put his loving arms around her, and give her a tissue to wipe her eyes.

It was business as usual for Grace afterwards, when she greeted everyone who had come to the funeral as they came out of the church, with Jamie beside her. The wake was being held at the Hampton Inn, the place where Roger had drunk his pint of beer regularly since 1961, and everyone knew him. Pearl had been known to accompany him for the odd glass of wine occasionally; usually on her birthday or at Christmas. Grace knew how much her dad had loved his local, and there was a huge gathering to support the passing of two very well loved characters.

Although Grace had never been a chatty person, she wanted to speak about her parents and honour them in any way possible. She had prepared a speech which was direct and to the point, praising them for the unconditional love and support she had always received from them.

"I am autistic, and not an easy person to live with, but my parents coped with everything that was thrown at them!" she declared, which was greeted with a round of applause. She had no fears about

202

speaking about her autism, it was not an excuse for any of her past behaviour, but an explanation. People admired her courage and frankness. Autism was now fully recognised as a condition that caused difficulties, and this woman who was so gifted and had become a professor could only be admired.

After the funeral, Grace took a month off work, and spent it quietly at home. Her parents had been cremated, and their ashes were scattered at Barham Cemetery. Jamie had been with her when she did it, always quietly supportive. She silently squeezed his arm, which spoke volumes, and he knew how much she cared.

"We make a great team," she said simply.

With her month at home now over, she decided to go back to work full time again, as there was no reason not to. She absolutely threw herself into working hard and for long hours, as without her parents there was a gaping hole inside her. She tried to comfort herself with the thought that they had reached a good age, and their death had been so quick it was unlikely that they could have suffered, but it didn't stop her from missing them.

She had given her birth mother very little thought during her life because the parents who brought her up were the only ones she knew. She had never felt the need to trace her, especially as it might upset Pearl and Roger. But she had felt great empathy for her mother when she heard how much she had wanted to keep her. The place for her father's name on her birth certificate was blank, so she started to wonder about him, too.

But then, even if her mother was still alive, she would be quite elderly. To suddenly turn up out of the blue might be a huge shock. As much as Grace was interested to find out more about her blood relatives, the grief she was still suffering felt too new to allow her to cope with any more trauma. So she decided to throw herself back into her work.

Chapter Thirty-three

Ellen and Grace 2024

"I am so sorry, Ellen. I am afraid the cancer is back, but this time it's in your womb."

"It can't be. She's been clear for twelve years!" said Jeremy desperately, whilst Ellen crumpled into tears. Her worst nightmare had returned. She had even stopped going for check-ups, because they had said there was no need. Then she had passed blood, so guessed that there was something sinister going on.

Dr Taylor looked at them both. Jeremy, now eighty-two years old, but still walking upright and definitely not ready to give up yet. Ellen, aged eighty-one, and only an operation plus chemotherapy could save her. But at the age she was now, it would be a risk. He spoke gently.

"We can offer you a hysterectomy, and then after that a course of chemotherapy, and hopefully with the courage you have shown before, you will see it off."

Ellen wiped her face, Crying wasn't going to make her better, but she really wasn't sure if she wanted to fight any more.

"The radiotherapy made me feel ill, and I was twelve years younger. I am not sure I could face it again," she said tearfully, her lip trembling.

Jeremy felt desperate. He didn't want to lose her, because she was everything to him, but neither did he want her to suffer. After the operation she would be in pain. It was a lot to inflict on a woman of her age. He knew that right now, whatever path she chose, he must support her. He put his arm around her shoulder gently.

"My darling, you must do what is best for you. I will be right beside you, and support whatever decision you make."

Ellen gulped. She felt so scared, and not ready to die yet.

"Can I have the operation and then decide about the chemo after?"

"Of course you may. We just have to take one step at a time," said Dr Taylor gently. Looking at this white-haired little lady, who looked frail as she had lost weight, he realised she might not even come through the operation, and he wondered if he should warn her of that.

Even though he had been retired as a doctor for some years, Jeremy realised there was a possibility that Ellen might not survive the operation. Her age was against her. But she was a fighter, for all her life she had to be, as it had not been an easy path for her. Even though his heart was breaking inside him at the thought of it, it was better that she accepted the treatment, while there was still a grain of hope, because if she did not, she would probably only last a few months.

"There are risks with this operation. . ." Dr Taylor started to say.

". . .I know," Ellen interrupted him, "but I am a coward, you see, and I think I would rather not wake up from my operation than sit at home declining every day."

"You are no coward. You are a very brave woman," said Dr Taylor, looking over his glasses at her. He was a man in his fifties with grey hair, neatly styled, and a pleasant face. It was always very distressing telling patients news like this, and he could see how devastated Jeremy was. Ellen now seemed a little calmer, and resigned to having the operation.

"I will book you in a soon as I can, Mrs Scott. We have some wonderful new medicines now to help with the pain after the operation. I promise we will take care of your wife," he said kindly to Jeremy.

"Thank you, and now we need to go home. She looks exhausted. Darling, you need a rest," he said anxiously.

Dr Taylor watched the elderly couple as they left his room.

205

Jeremy had his arm around his wife, and they walked slowly out together. It was touching to watch them, now in the twilight of their life, but still very much together. It was clear that Jeremy adored Ellen, so he really hoped they could have a few more years together, and the operation would go well.

When they got home, Ellen didn't want to go to bed. She just wanted to rest on the sofa, so Jeremy tucked a rug around her, and then put the kettle on to make some tea. But by the time he had made it, and taken the cup into her, she was asleep. Her face looked a little pale as she lay there, with her white hair framing the pillow he had slipped under her head. He took himself out of the room and went into the study, where he sat down and sobbed. All the pent up emotion he had done his best to conceal before now bubbled over. In his eyes Ellen was still the beautiful seventeen year old girl he had fallen in love with all those years ago. Being selfish he had always hoped he would go first, because he didn't know how he would cope without her.

When he had finished weeping, he chided himself for being so weak. Ellen needed strength, not a wimp like himself! He went into the cloakroom and washed his face with cold water, and then returned to the lounge where she was still sleeping. He sat watching her whilst he drank his tea, and eventually he started to feel a bit better.

She slept for about an hour, so he then made her another cup of tea. She looked a bit better when she awoke, and she had more colour in her face. "Drink this sweetheart," he said gently, handing her the tea. She sleepily took it from him. The warm tea was comforting.

Jeremy looked at the calendar hanging on the wall, marked with various things that were going on. They both needed that now, so nothing got forgotten.

"Tom and Linda are due to come for a visit, but if you don't feel like it honey, we can postpone it."

"I do feel like it. Let them come," she said firmly.

Tom was now eighty-four years old, but nobody would have known it. He still played golf, and went for long walks. After all his years in the police force, retirement had been a chance to catch up on many things he had not had time for. He had even run as a

206

councillor in Croydon last year, but after just missing out on being elected, had spoken about maybe coming down to the coast and living nearer to them. He very much favoured the idea of living in Canterbury. It was a short car ride from Herne Bay, and he had visions of getting involved with the local council there.

Ellen and Tom had remained close for all of their lives, and she liked the idea of Tom and Linda being a short journey away. When they came down they would be viewing suitable houses, as they had just sold theirs in Shirley. It was a long time since Ellen had been up that way, but she knew that although Shirley and South Croydon had remained the same, apparently Croydon was no longer the little town she remembered where you could park outside East Croydon Station, and walk down to Surrey Street and the Market. It was now a fast and busy area with a red route flowing right through it, a big underpass, and roundabouts with fast flowing traffic everywhere.

She had no desire to go up there now, preferring the easy access of the A299, which was not challenging to drive, and had local towns like Herne Bay and Whitstable close by, and was easy to negotiate around. She was sure from what she had heard, if they still lived near Croydon, she would have given up driving by now.

"I am going to tell Tom about my operation. We don't need secrets at our age." she said thoughtfully.

"What about Charlie? You know he worries about you."

"Of course, Charlie, but we must sound positive," she said, eyeing Jeremy, and also knowing his medical experience on this occasion might be best ignored.

"Of course we are positive!" said Jeremy, putting his arms around her. "You are not going anywhere!"

Two weeks later Tom and Linda arrived for their visit, and by then Ellen knew her operation would take place whilst they stayed with her. She waved away any talk of them not coming, as although she didn't say it, she was sure having them around would be support for both her and Jeremy. Charlie and Abigail would also be around some of the time, as it ran into school holidays, and Ellen was never happier than when she had her family around her.

When Ellen woke up after her operation, the first thing she saw was her beloved Jeremy. He was leaning over the bed holding her hand, and urging her to take a sip of water. Jeremy felt so relieved that she had survived the operation, although he had been warned she might feel weak for a while.

"You're OK now, honey. Let me know if the pain is bad and I will get someone."

Ellen couldn't really feel any pain, only this sensation of floating. It was weird. His face was in a mist, and she wanted to put her hand out and touch it, but she couldn't seem to move her limbs. It was all too much, so she closed her eyes and went back to sleep.

The next time she became aware of what was going on around her, she heard them talking.

"How is she doing? Is she in pain?" that was Jeremy, and then another voice said.

"Give her time. She's just had her womb taken out."

In her bleary state she wanted to shriek at them that it wasn't right. She was carrying a baby and they shouldn't have taken her womb out, it would die! She cried out with anguish, and then she felt a cool flannel on her face.

"It's OK, honey. You are just having a bad dream."

She opened her eyes to see Jeremy. His eyes looked full of anxiety. His hand was holding the flannel, as he bent over the bed. She held out her hand to him, and he nestled his face next to hers.

"You're doing well, honey," he said, encouragingly.

"Have they done it?" she asked in a whisper.

"Yes, it's all done, and everyone sends their love. The whole family are at home."

"That's nice. When can I come home?"

"As soon as you feel up to it, but whilst you are here you must rest."

Ellen leaned back on her pillow. She liked the idea of the family being at home. Family was everything, but there was just one person missing, and she would always be missing. All these years had passed, but she still missed her.

*   *   *   *

The surgeon had suggested that convalescence might help Ellen to get stronger, and Jeremy was prepared to do anything to make her well again. However, Ellen was adamant, she wanted to go home to her family. So her wish was granted, as there was always someone waiting for a bed. Tom and Linda were still at home, and so were Charlie and Abigail. All of them hoping she would be able to get back to a normal life soon, but in the meantime they were all there to give her any help she needed.

Jeremy brought her home in the car, and she felt totally exhausted just walking into the house. He put her to bed, and then they all came in to see her. This brought a smile to her face, because she had her loved ones around her.

Another week went by and there didn't seem any more signs of improvement. Ellen was not eating much and was now very thin. Jeremy and Tom were extremely worried. It seemed like Ellen was giving up, as she needed to be much stronger than this to have chemotherapy. One evening, in despair, Jeremy voiced his fear; "She seems to have given up, Tom. What are we going to do?"

Tom felt the same. "We have to face it, she doesn't seem to be improving. "He still carried a vision in his mind of the day they had come to Herne Bay and found his sister mentally out of her mind, and he knew there was only one thing that might help her want to live, and even if that didn't work, at least she would die with peace of mind.

"We have to find Grace, and this time we must do it properly. No going to Margate. It's a lot easier to trace relatives now, and we can hire a private investigator. It has changed so much in recent years. There are DNA data bases, but we can leave that to the investigator."

Jeremy knew he was right, and it might be the last thing they could do for Ellen. He felt the tears form in his eyes. "OK, Tom, let's put the wheels in motion. I, too, want to meet my daughter."

Grace had not wanted to stay in Hampton after the death of her parents in 2012. There were too many painful memories. She kept the pain inside her, never expressing it to Jamie. She had used working in Sandwich as an excuse to suggest a move. If Jamie had guessed the reason, he never voiced it. He didn't mind where he lived as long as he had Grace. So they found themselves a period cottage set in the quaint back streets of Sandwich, and close to the beautiful St Peter's Church.

They had lived there until 2022 when she had decided to retire. During her long and illustrious career, she had attained the title of Professor, and with her team had made advances in the prevention and treatment of cancer. When Covid had struck, it had been necessary to work quickly to find a vaccine, test it, and then make it available to the public. Pfizer had been one of the first companies to achieve this, and she was excited to have been able to contribute towards this. The icing on the cake was receiving an MBE from Queen Elizabeth in 2021.

Now aged sixty-three, but looking much younger, Grace still had her head of curls, but they were now just below her ear, and she kept her reddish gold colour by putting a rinse on her hair every time the tiniest bit of grey showed through. Keeping herself smart had always felt important to her. Just because she worked in a white coat in a laboratory all day, didn't mean she couldn't look nice when she came out. Jamie had always been very appreciative of her efforts. He was incredibly proud of her; she was not only a high achiever, but also a beautiful wife.

But after she had retired, Jamie had wondered if it might be good to go back to the coast. Not necessarily Hampton, but there was a little village just outside Herne Bay, and on the way to Reculver, it was called Beltinge. Grace was now happy to leave Sandwich and Pfizer behind her, so they found themselves a very nice and spacious chalet bungalow. It overlooked the beach, with rugged cliffs around them, and it had a balcony where they could sit and even have a barbecue whilst enjoying watching the tide come in and out.

They were private people. Grace had never been into joining the neighbours WhatsApp groups, or even telling anyone that she was a professor and had an MBE. Their house had electric gates which were left open when visitors were expected, whom were mainly family.

When she received the letter from Tom and Jeremy, which had been sent by a private detective, explaining how ill her mother was, she was immediately concerned. She had frequently wished that she had found her mother, and even asked who her father was, but now it seemed there was a heartbreaking situation. Inside the letter was a photograph of her mother when she had been eighteen. She could immediately see that she looked like her. Another photograph showed her mother as she was now; a little white haired lady with a kind looking face.

She held the photograph to her face. It was unusual for Grace to feel such emotion, and it even took her by surprise. She showed the letter and the photographs to Jamie.

"I am going to find her!" she said determinedly.

"Absolutely, my love, and I am right with you," he agreed.

"The amazing thing is that they only live a couple of miles away in Bishopstone, and we never knew."

The meeting was arranged for the next day. Ellen was not strong enough to leave the house, but that didn't worry Grace, she would go to the house and Jamie would be outside in the car. She was finally going to meet her mother after sixty-three years. She could feel a pang inside that she didn't quite understand.

Now that they knew that Grace was coming, Tom and Jeremy broke the news to Ellen. Her face took on a look of fear. "She might be angry with me. I let her down."

"You most certainly didn't. You did what was best for her, and it took a great deal of courage!" said Jeremy. His heart felt like it was breaking, seeing the frail little figure of his wife sitting in an armchair with a blanket covering her.

"I must get dressed. She can't find me like this tomorrow!"

So the next day, Ellen got out of bed, ignoring the feelings of dizziness, and Jeremy helped her to dress. She put on a loose floral dress which was calf length. It hid her swollen stomach, which was still sore from the operation. Jeremy had helped her to bath and wash her hair. She had styled it neatly and clipped the sides back, and a bit of rouge gave her some colour. She finished it off with a pink lipstick and a touch of eye make-up.

"You look lovely, darling. Now stop worrying," said Jeremy, giving her a kiss on her cheek. He made her comfortable on the sofa, with a cushion on either side of her, but she had totally refused to have her legs covered by a blanket.

Jeremy was also very nervous yet excited about meeting his daughter, although helping Ellen had kept him busy. When he had found out how talented she was, and had met the Queen and been awarded an MBE, he felt so proud. Fancy that, his daughter was a Professor!

When Grace arrived, she got out of the car quickly. Usually she didn't like meeting new people, but there was an inner force driving her on. The front door had been left open, and she made her way to the lounge, which was where she was told her mother would be. As she opened the door, and saw Ellen sitting on the sofa, to her surprise she could immediately feel a connection.

Ellen stood up when Grace entered the room. She had been told her daughter was autistic, so might not hug her. Nevertheless, She stood up out of respect to greet her at the same level. Then, to her surprise, Grace came straight over to her and, before she knew it, she was being hugged by her daughter. Tears of relief and happiness streamed down her face. Her beautiful baby, all dressed in pink, had grown into this lovely looking woman. They stayed like this for a few minutes, both trying to capture the moment and keep it forever.

Then they sat down, and Ellen asked the all important question:

"I wish I could have kept you. Did you have a good adoption?"

Grace, never one to mince her words, replied, "I had the best parents ever. I had a difficult time at school because I was autistic, but they were so patient with me. I have so much to be grateful for."

"I am so glad you have had a happy life. I have never forgotten you, or been able to move on from my guilt."

"You don't need to feel guilty. I always understood why you gave me up."

"I also deprived you of Charlie, your brother."

"I have a brother; that is amazing! Well, maybe I could get to know him now. I just want to ask one question: Who is my father?"

Jeremy, who was standing outside the room, tapped gently on the door. As he entered, Ellen pointed to him. "This is your father. My much loved husband Jeremy, who, of course, is Charlie's father too."

Grace found herself hugging Jeremy too. They didn't feel like strangers. They were her blood parents, and she could feel a warm feeling inside that she had finally been able to meet them.

Ellen and Jeremy then explained how they had come to be separated for seven years, and as she listened, she could see how close they were. They were soulmates, and her parents truly loved each other, so she had been born out of love, and inside she felt a warm glow.

When they had finished chatting, Grace realised she had a complete new family, and it felt wonderful. She brought Jamie in from the car, and then they met Tom and Linda, and Charlie and Abigail. Everybody was talking at once; all of them excited and happy to be united.

A couple of hours later, Ellen was looking tired, so everyone left her with Grace so that Grace could say goodbye. In spite of her tiredness, Ellen felt truly happy. Suddenly the years had slipped away, and she had her little girl back. And she now knew Grace had never been angry with her.

When Grace said goodbye to her, she promised to return with her twins, so they could also meet their grandmother. "But in the meantime, you must rest and get strong," she said to Ellen.

As Grace was leaving, Tom came to say a few private words to her.

"It's so lovely to finally meet you, Grace. I just wanted to say that when your mother gave birth to you, she didn't murder anyone, or rob a bank, or rape anyone, yet she was considered an outcast of society and treated like a criminal. Nowadays nobody cares if a girl is an unmarried mother, but it wasn't like that then. It nearly killed her, and it took a long time for her to recover. It is very sad."

"It really is," said Grace. "I hope she can get stronger now, as I want her to meet my twins."

Grace kept her promise, and returned a week later with Julian and Verity and their partners. Ellen was so happy. Her dearest wish had come true, and that night, after they had returned home, she slipped peacefully away in her sleep, knowing that she was surrounded by people who loved her.

Chapter Thirty-four

The Funeral

Grace had only met her mother twice before she died, and she felt very sad to know this. She wished that back in 2012, after her parents had died, she had made the decision to find her real mother. But it was too late now. She had been surprised at how easy it had been to meet her parents, and how close she had felt to them immediately.

Now, after all these years, she had a brother. After seeing how quickly Ellen had faded away, it made her realise how precious life was, and not to waste a moment of it. Now she was retired, and Jamie was too, they were going to have some nice holidays and spend more time together.

She could see how devastated Jeremy was, and Charlie too. Ellen had been very precious to them, and they had hoped she would recover from her operation and be able to fight off the cancer. When it came to organising the funeral, they both seemed to be in bits. However, it was only right to give Ellen a good send off, so she asked Tom if she could be of any help.

Tom really liked Grace. She was direct and honest, and she didn't beat about the bush with anything. What a tragedy that he had only got to know his niece now, and not sixty-three years ago. She had said she also regretted waiting so long. He spoke his thoughts aloud to her.

"It would be great if you could help, Grace. Your father and

Charlie are full of grief at the moment, and I feel as if I am on auto pilot too."

"I knew her less than any of you, of course, but if we can find out her favourite songs and find a nice poem to be read, then maybe get everyone together, it can be organised."

So after consulting Jeremy and Charlie as to what they wanted for the service, and asking them to choose the flowers, Grace and Tom managed to organise the funeral for a couple of weeks ahead.

There were going to be a lot of guests because Ellen had been very popular. Jeremy had asked everyone not to wear black, but to be in bright colours, as Ellen had never liked black, and he wanted to feel that everyone was celebrating her life.

Grace dressed smartly that day. She had a pale blue suit with a pencil skirt, and she teamed it with a white blouse and grey stiletto heels. Everyone was meeting at Thanet Crematorium where the hearse would be.

When they got out of the car, she saw the family all gathered waiting to enter the chapel, and inside the hearse were the flowers laid around the coffin. They were all doing their best to remain in control, so without even thinking about it, Grace hugged all of them, and Jamie followed suit.

The music started, and Charlie and Tom took their places with Julian and Jamie as pall-bearers. Grace put her arm through Jeremy's, smiling gently at him.

"Come on, Daddy, let's put dear Mummy to rest."